the House in the Tuscan Hills

BOOKS BY ANITA CHAPMAN

The Florence Letter

The Tuscan Diary

The Italian Vineyard

The Venice Secret

ANITA CHAPMAN

The House in the Tuscan Hills

bookouture

Published by Bookouture in 2026

An imprint of Storyfire Ltd.
Carmelite House
50 Victoria Embankment
London EC4Y 0DZ

www.bookouture.com

The authorised representative in the EEA is Hachette Ireland
8 Castlecourt Centre
Dublin 15 D15 XTP3
Ireland
(email: info@hbgi.ie)

ISBN: 978-1-80550-699-7
eBook ISBN: 978-1-80550-698-0

For all the recipes passed down through generations

CHAPTER 1

JEN

CAMBRIDGE, AUGUST 2019

Saturday nights at Da Nonna were always especially busy, and tonight was no exception. The restaurant was heaving – with locals, tourists, students who'd decided to stay in Cambridge over the summer – and, being in the midst of a heatwave, the air was hot and thick. All of the sash windows facing King's Parade were pushed up as far as they would go, bringing some respite but not quite enough.

I paused for a moment to mop my brow with the tea towel from the back pocket of my jeans. How I needed this shift to be over. I went into the kitchen, picked up two steaming bowls of spaghetti carbonara, and took them over to the couple who'd ordered them. He held her hand across the table, his eyes fixed on hers as he spoke. I couldn't make out what he was saying above the din of surrounding chatter mixed with music coming from the speakers. But she had a huge grin on her face, and was hanging on his every word. This wasn't a first date – more likely a few dates in, but not so many that they'd begun to clock each other's flaws. They were immersed in that first few weeks of glorious, intense longing for each other. Messaging and calling and FaceTiming all day, every day. Making arrangements to meet as much as possible, despite their busy schedules – time could always be made. Yes, there was no doubt that they were immersed in those joyful early stages of a beautiful love affair. She twirled a strand of her blonde hair around a forefinger, in full flirtation mode, her head tipped to one side, big blue mascaraed eyes wide open, lips pressed together, and he was clearly utterly mesmerised.

A pang of envy tugged at my stomach, and I tried to push memories of endless candlelit dinners with Harvey out of my mind. Those days were well and truly over, and my 'best friend', of all people, Amanda Peters, had taken my place. I approached the couple, announcing myself with a cheery, 'Here we are!' He reluctantly let go of her hand, and she carefully unfolded the white linen napkin and put it on her lap while I placed the bowls of spaghetti in front of them. I went to the dresser and returned to grate fresh Parmesan over their pasta. I picked up the giant pepper mill and offered them a twist or two, and they mumbled their thanks, before he took her hand once again. I hoped they'd eat the spaghetti before it got cold, otherwise what a waste of the best pasta they'd find in the city. Stopping to take a breath, I scanned the room, and noted a table that needed to be cleared. I approached my younger brother, Giuseppe, and delegated this task to him.

And then I spotted a man standing by the front desk, all alone. He was scratching his head and looked a little awkward, as if he wasn't sure he should be there. Maybe he was on a date and had turned up early? As I walked over towards him, his face broke out into a smile. He was tall, and rather nice-looking, and I had a hunch that he was Italian, with his thick dark hair and brown eyes. He did seem to have a certain presence about him, as if he was *someone* – we often had celebrities coming in, especially since a hugely influential food critic, Miles Anderson, had written a gushing piece about us in the culture section of *The Sunday Times*. Shortly after that, we'd won our first coveted Authentic and Tasty Award. We'd been ever so grateful – for every restaurateur in the country dreamt of having an ATA. In the autumn, we'd finally be able to afford to install air conditioning. I couldn't help inhaling the aftershave this man was wearing – it had notes of citrus, possibly bergamot. He'd no doubt doused himself in it for his date's benefit. She was probably a model or some kind of influencer.

'Buonasera. Can I help you?' I said.

He fixed his eyes on the name badge attached to my navy-blue polo shirt, above the words Da Nonna in maroon letters.

'Buonasera, Jen,' he said in an Italian accent.

So, he was from Italy rather than descended from Italian grandparents, like myself. When I studied him properly, it was actually easy to tell by what he was wearing – pale-blue jeans cut slightly above the ankle, and tan-brown loafers with no socks. And then there was his olive skin, tanned from the summer sun. A crisp white shirt, open a few buttons to show a tuft of chest hair, and sleeves rolled up. A grey cashmere jumper around the shoulders, tied neatly at the front. But the real giveaway was his fine head of hair – dark and lots of it, with a little wax running through those strands at the front to keep them out of his face – not too much, just enough. And *those* eyes – large and chocolate brown, and looking directly into mine, his matching thick brows slightly raised. Yes, he was Italian, all right.

He swallowed, and looked down at the floor, and shuffled from side to side. Did he want a table or not? Had he made a reservation?

'Have you booked?' I asked.

He shook his head. 'No, I haven't... and I'm wondering, actually, whether I should come back another day.' His English was good. 'You seem to be quite busy, and I...' he continued.

So, he wasn't on a date. I would see if there was a table available. It was unlikely on a Saturday night, but I would do him the courtesy of looking in case we'd had a no-show, at least – especially as I quite liked the idea of him dining with us. Something about his undemanding, nonchalant manner made me want to find him one.

'Okay, hold on.'

I checked the computer, clicking the mouse, and he stood there, and I could sense that he was studying me – as if he found me intriguing. I couldn't help enjoying his attention, even though I was strictly off men since Harvey had left me for Amanda a week before our wedding day, only three months ago. There was a no-show for a table booked for half an hour earlier – he could have that one. It was a nice table too, in the corner, with a view out of the window of the chapel at King's College – an iconic building. It was still light outside, and he could watch life go by on King's Parade – a lovely way to pass the time when eating out alone.

'You're in luck, we have a table for you over there, by the window.'

'Well, I don't want to be any trouble.'

'Really, it's fine. The people who booked it haven't turned up. So actually, you're doing us a favour.'

He shrugged.

'Well, okay, I guess I am quite hungry. I haven't eaten since this morning.'

I tipped my head to one side. He was talking as if he hadn't been intending to dine with us. Why else would he be here? I gestured for him to follow me over to table six, and handed him a menu.

'Can I get you an aperitivo?' I said.

'I'll take a Peroni, and what do you recommend to eat?'

'Well, everything is good, but then I would say that.'

He smiled, displaying a set of perfect white teeth.

'All of the pasta is freshly made by my brother, Alfonso,' I went on. 'And the Tuscan dishes are my grandmother Liliana's recipes. She came here after the war.'

'What would you have?'

I thought for a moment.

'My favourite.'

He leant forward and put his elbows on the table, resting his chin on his hands.

'Which is?'

'Spaghetti cacio e pepe.'

'From Rome – it's one of my favourites too,' he said.

'I like its simplicity – who would think that butter, peppercorns and pecorino could create such a delicious dish? Will you be ordering that then?'

He nodded. 'Yes please, followed by the sea bass.'

'Va bene.'

'And a glass of Gavi.'

He handed me the menus, and I thanked him. We exchanged a smile, and I went to get his Peroni and place his order in the kitchen. Giuseppe would usually take care of him for the rest of his meal, but I made a snap decision to serve him personally, just because I was enjoying our interactions. They were totally harmless, but also giving me a lift for the first time in weeks. I'd been living under a dark cloud, working all hours at the restaurant to take my mind off what Harvey and Amanda had done to me – but this man, whoever he was, had brought a glimmer of light into my world, and I would savour every moment while I had the chance.

At the end of the evening, there were only a few diners left, settling bills. Some were still drinking coffee and sipping Italian liqueurs. The noise had died down, and now there was only the faint hum of voices and a clinking sound as Giuseppe polished cutlery in the corner with a tea towel and dropped it into a tray.

The Italian man was still at the table facing King's College Chapel, and he had an espresso cup in front of him, along with a shot glass filled with grappa. He knocked the grappa back, and looked out of the window, and I couldn't help being curious about what thoughts were running through his mind. It was now dark outside, but King's Parade was lit by old-fashioned streetlamps. Passers-by ambled – couples holding hands, and groups of youths out on the town on a Saturday night. As acting manager, it was my job to get rid of the Italian man, politely of course, and so I made my way over.

'How was your meal?' I said.

He looked up at me with earnest eyes. 'It was really good, thank you. As you said, authentic Italian food. You have a wonderful restaurant here.'

'Well, it's actually my mum and dad's place. I'm just helping out, temporarily.'

'Oh, I see.' He nodded, and our eyes met, and then he looked away.

Although I should be gently coaxing him to leave, I found myself not wanting him to go. I wanted to get a glass of grappa and join him at the table, and just sit there, opposite, and get to know him a little – maybe practise my Italian. Something was pulling me to him. Perhaps it was just that he seemed like a nice person to talk to. And I wanted to know where in Italy he was from, and what his life was like there. What did he do for a living? But I needed to put him in a position where he asked for the bill. At Da Nonna, we didn't like to just bring it over, because then that was openly saying, 'We need you to go now'. And that wasn't our style.

He opened his mouth to speak. Ah, he was saving me the trouble.

'I have a confession to make.'

Caught off guard, I blinked.

'Oh?'

'I didn't intend to eat here this evening. I actually came here to see you and your grandmother, Liliana. But I've been travelling so much lately, I lost track of the days, and had forgotten it was Saturday – your busiest night of the week.'

I knew it. Something about the way he'd been standing there when I first saw him had told me he wasn't our usual diner.

'What? But... why would you want to see us?'

'Is your grandmother here tonight? I haven't seen her, but...'

'Yes, as a matter of fact, she is – well, my nonna lives in the flat upstairs. I can go and get her, but may I ask what this is all about?'

'I'm sorry. I'd rather wait until she is here.'

I nodded, understanding, while at the same time clueless about what he wanted and suddenly feeling protective of my nonna. What did he want from us? Should I trust him?

'All will become clear... I hope that's all right?' he added.

From what I could tell, he seemed to be a genuine person – my first impressions were usually spot on. I had got it wrong with Harvey, but I put that down to being blinded by his charm.

'Okay, I'll go and get her.'

I went through the kitchen, down the hall, and up the stairs. On the landing, I unlocked the door to Nonna's flat.

'Nonna, it's me, Jen.'

'Jen, cara... vieni.'

She was on the sofa in the living room, an espresso cup on the coffee table. The television was switched on, but muted, and she had a pair of knitting needles and a ball of maroon wool resting in her lap.

'Busy night?' she asked.

'Yes, very... but also, there's a man downstairs who wants to talk to us.'

'What do you mean? Who is us?'

'You and me.'

She put her knitting needles down. 'Well, I'm curious – let's go and see who this man is shall we, dear.'

I helped her up, and she threaded her arm through mine, and we made our way down the stairs and into the restaurant. All of the other diners had gone now, leaving just the Italian man. He saw us approaching, and stood up.

'Buonasera, Signora Farina. Mi chiamo Matteo Bianchi.'

He proffered a hand, and Nonna, with a confused look on her face, shook it.

'Matteo Bianchi...' She thought for a moment. Then she spoke in Italian. 'You have come from Italy?'

He nodded.

'But who are you, young man?'

'It's a long story. I'm hoping that you and your granddaughter might listen to what I have to say.'

She shrugged, and sat down opposite him, and I pulled up another chair and placed it between them.

'Allora?' she said.

He took a deep breath. 'I have some sad news, I'm afraid, Signora Farina. I have come here from a village called Cintaldo, just outside of San Gimignano, in the Tuscan hills. My family were your neighbours during the war – you might remember Paolo and Nicoletta from Casa Luna? Paolo was my grandfather. His papa was good friends with your papa, I understand, and our families helped each other to survive by sharing food and provisions.'

'I remember your great-aunt, Nicoletta, very well – she was a good friend of mine. We spent all our childhood summers together.' Her eyes glazed over and her hand started to shake. 'It's Francesca, isn't it?'

Francesca was Nonna's sister, and all I knew was they'd fallen out a long time ago, at the end of the war. Nonna had never told me what happened. I wasn't sure if any of my family knew the truth.

He swallowed, his face serious.

'She died recently,' he said. 'The funeral was a few days ago.'

Nonna closed her eyes. 'Riposa in pace, cara sorella,' she said, softly.

'I offer you my deepest condolences, Signora Farina,' he said, gently.

Even though Nonna and her sister had been estranged, this must be an immensely sad moment for her.

I put a hand on hers and gave it a squeeze. 'I'm really sorry, Nonna.'

'So, is that why you came all this way, Matteo, to deliver this news?'

It did seem strange that he'd come here to tell Nonna in person when he could have written or made a telephone call.

'I got to know Francesca a little during her final years,' Matteo said, his eyes filled with sadness. Clearly, by the way the pitch of his voice changed, they'd known each other well. 'I spent some time at Casa Luna – my family's home – next door to Casa Stella, where she lived. I helped with the garden, and lifting heavy things, if she ever needed me to. And then, sadly,' he said, with a sigh, 'her health deteriorated, and she had to go into a care home.'

'My poor sister,' Nonna said. 'Did she lose her memory?'

'No, not at all,' he said, brightly. It was clear that he'd been fond of my great-aunt. 'It was just that, physically, Francesca couldn't manage on her own. She would fall over sometimes – I drove her to the hospital when she sprained her ankle. And with the arthritis in her hands, she couldn't open any jars or tins or bottles. Cooking became difficult for her, and she burned herself a couple of times.'

Nonna swallowed and looked down at the table. 'Ah, I see,' she said.

'And so,' Matteo continued. 'She asked me to make arrangements to rent out Casa Stella so she could pay the fees for a care home. I sensed she was a little lonely too, and craved company with her peers. She settled in quickly, making friends. I visited her every week, and—'

'That was very kind of you to help her with the house, and to stay in touch,' Nonna interrupted him, her voice cracking. Hearing about her sister's final weeks must have been heart-wrenching for her.

'It was nothing, really,' he said. 'Our families – the Bianchis and the Magginis – had known each other for many years. They helped each other get through the war. My great-grandfather and your papa, as you'll know, both lost their lives because they chose to help someone try to reach a place of safety.'

Nonna nodded, ruefully. 'So many Italian civilians lost their lives that way, trying to do the right thing. They will never be forgotten for their bravery.'

'When I went to see Francesca shortly before she died, she gave me an heirloom that she wanted Jen to have. And she wanted you to inherit Casa Stella, Liliana, seeing as your papa originally bought the property at Corte Paradiso along with my great-grandfather. They divided it into two houses together. But when I pointed out that you perhaps wouldn't be able to travel to Italy, she decided to leave Casa Stella to Jen as well.'

'Oh well, the circumstances could be better, but I am glad that dear house with so many treasured memories is coming back to my side of the family,' Nonna said, pressing her hands together, and looking across at me with a slight smile.

'Francesca was adamant that the heirloom and the house should both be passed down the female line,' Matteo said. 'So, Jen, you are a very lucky woman.'

While worrying about whether Nonna was all right, I'd

somehow not registered that I'd actually inherited a house in Tuscany. And an heirloom too, whatever that might be. This was all such a surprise, out of the blue on a Saturday night when I was too tired out from a busy shift to appreciate it.

'Wow, I don't know what to say,' I said. 'Are you sure this is right?'

'Yes, and the house will be yours to do whatever you wish with,' Matteo replied. 'You can use it yourself, or rent it out like Francesca did. I recommend you come and see it before making any rash decisions.'

'Yes, you must do that, Jen,' Nonna said.

I'd got so used to my daily routine lately, with nothing unexpected to deal with, that this was all quite overwhelming. I was grateful for the sudden windfall, but it would mean stepping out of my comfort zone, travelling to Italy alone. Owning a house in a country where I only spoke enough of the language to get by seemed like a huge responsibility – could I handle it? Did I *want* to handle it?

I fiddled with the gold stud in my ear – a habit when feeling under pressure. I appreciated their encouragement but needed a minute.

'Goodness, thank you, Matteo for coming here, and... I must admit that I'm struggling to get my head round all this,' I said.

'Well, I guess you just need a chance to take it all in,' he said.

'Do you have this heirloom with you?' Nonna asked, her voice shaking. 'I'm interested to know what it might be, although I do have an inkling... but surely not... no, it couldn't be,' she said, looking away and talking to herself.

What on earth was this heirloom – small enough to carry on his person? I was curious to see what it was. And why was Nonna so on edge?

Matteo nodded. 'Yes, of course!'

He reached into the pocket of his jeans, and brought out a

small, cube-shaped box, and then he placed it on the table in front of me. What was this, a ring of some kind? I shuddered. Seeing the box made me feel a little sick, as it brought back the memory of when Harvey had proposed to me in Paris, just over a year ago. Matteo lifted the lid and removed a gold ring with a milky-white stone from the velvet cushion.

'Oh Madonna,' Nonna cried, putting a hand over her mouth and shaking her head. 'I was right. Let me see it.' He handed the ring to her, and she held it between her fingers, and gulped, but then she accidentally dropped it onto the table. The ring made a tapping sound as it hit the wooden surface, and then it spun around and rolled to the edge before dropping onto the floor. Almost as if it had a life of its own.

I pushed back my chair and crouched down to look for the ring. The lighting was so dim in the restaurant that I had to put on my phone torch. And then I spotted the milky-white stone catching the light. I reached out and picked up the ring, and passed it back to Nonna. By now her eyes were welling with tears. This all seemed to be too much for her – the ring was clearly evoking memories from a distant past.

'I never thought I would see this again, Jen,' she said, quietly, as she looked up at me, her forehead all scrunched up, and then back at the ring. She ran a wrinkled finger over the stone, as if she were searching for some kind of connection with her estranged sister, and with whatever the story was that came with this piece of jewellery. 'After all these years, I don't understand why...' Her voice trailed off.

'Francesca wanted Jen to have it, even though they haven't met,' Matteo said. 'I'm sorry if this is upsetting for you, Liliana – I understand that you haven't seen your sister for many years?'

'No, I haven't,' Nonna said, and then she looked up at us both. 'And it's all because of this opal ring.'

CHAPTER 2

LILIANA

THE TUSCAN HILLS, 14 JULY 1944

Salvatore took my hand in his as we ran across the field of sunflowers, their beautiful big yellow and brown heads pointing in the same direction – I always marvelled at how clever they were, knowing where the sun was. San Gimignano had been liberated the day before by Allied troops – the French and the Americans. It had been a long, hard war for both of us, and our families and friends. We'd lost many loved ones between us, sometimes under horrifying circumstances. But today every part of my entire being was filled with joy because my amore was here with me. And this was a special day for us and our families. The war was still ongoing in other parts of Tuscany and in the north, but we would do our best to gather together all the food and wine we could find and celebrate – *a tavola*, at the table, with our families.

Salvatore was only back in our small village, Cintaldo, just outside of San Gimignano, a medieval town in the Tuscan hills, for a short time, because other parts of Italy still needed to be liberated. Soon our beloved home city of Florence would be free, my family hoped, and he wouldn't rest until that day came. But I was savouring every precious minute of our time together. How I'd missed him during these long months while he was away fighting with the partisans – the Italian freedom fighters. Now here he was, staying with his family on their olive farm, Oliviera Santa Chiara, at the other side of the village from where I was living at Casa Stella, the house my family normally used during the hotter summer months. Our main home was Residenza Cinzia, our pensione or boarding house in Florence. But since the armistice in September the previous year, when the Tedeschi, the Germans, had become our enemy and the war had taken a significant turn for the worse, we'd moved to the Tuscan hills permanently – our house here had been our refuge. Here we could support ourselves by growing our own food and by keeping chickens, rabbits, and even a goat too. And all around, in the countryside, we could forage for mushrooms and wild asparagus and rosemary and snails amongst other things. And Salvatore's family kept us supplied with olive oil, which we would struggle to get our hands on in Florence.

Salvatore stopped running and lifted me into his arms, swinging me around, the breeze lifting my hair. Our eyes met, and we laughed together.

'Cara Liliana, you must come with me,' he said, putting me back down.

'Where are we going?' I said.

He let go of my hand and opened the gate leading to the ancient olive grove. We passed through to the other side, and then he took my hand once again, and led me to a familiar spot next to one of the olive trees.

'I bring you here to the oldest tree on the farm – our tree,' he said, his lips upturned at the corners.

I looked up at him – he was so handsome, and he had chosen me out of all the girls in the village. Was it time for him to ask the question I'd been waiting for?

'For this tree holds special memories for us,' he continued. This was true – it was where we'd shared our first exquisite kiss. 'As you know, this ancient tree is over a thousand years old, and I have brought you here to ask you something, cara Liliana.'

He reached into the pocket of his trousers, and then he knelt down on the grass, and gestured for me to hold out my hand. Oh my goodness, it really was time. I could hardly contain my excitement. I quietly inhaled, doing my best to hide that I'd worked out what he was going to say.

'Liliana, cara, we have known each other for many years now, and we've talked about spending our lives together. When I was away fighting, thinking of you, and picturing this face' – He ran a hand over my cheek as he looked into my eyes, my gut fizzing with excitement – 'got me through every day and night. I love you, Liliana. Will you marry me?'

At last – this was the moment I'd been waiting for. Salvatore, my amore, the most handsome man in Tuscany, and heir to the largest olive farm in the area, was asking me to be his wife. I had been planning our wedding for years, for we were childhood sweethearts, and the union of our families had been on the cards for as long as I could remember. I had a scrapbook filled with drawings of my bridal gown and the flowers in my bouquet – different versions depending on the season. There were also menu ideas for the reception and a list of hymns, psalms and readings for the service at Chiesa Santa Maria – along with pages of notes describing our wedding day from beginning to end. I kept this scrapbook under my bed at Casa Stella – I had brought it from Florence especially because I liked to look at it every night before sleeping and visualise our wedding day as my head touched the pillow. And I had done this ever since Salvatore had handed me a sprig of mimosa from his garden one day when I was walking back from the pasticceria next to the oliviera. Salvatore had been sitting on the gate, waiting for me to go by, as I did every morning. He called me over and held out the mimosa. I took the sprig, its clusters of tiny fluffy flowers a bright cheery yellow, from him with delight. He then asked if he could kiss me and I said no, not yet, because it was too soon. I placed that sprig of mimosa in a jar of water in my bedroom, on the dressing table. And then I cut off a piece and pressed it in between the pages of my scrapbook. When it was dry, I could lift it to my nose and treasure the memory of that special day when our romance began, whenever I wished – its scent sweet and woody, with a hint of almond. A few months later, we kissed on the lips for the first time, beside the ancient olive tree, where he was now kneeling and asking me to be his wife.

'You know how much I love you, Salvatore. Yes, of course I will marry you!'

'Bellissima Liliana, you make me the happiest man in the whole world.' He looked up at me, gesturing for me to hold out my hand, and then slid a ring onto my finger. 'This ring belonged to my grandmother, Nonna Claudia. Before she died, she said that I should give it to the girl I loved, and who I wanted to spend the rest of my life with.'

I looked down at the ring, a gold band with a milky-white stone. It was a beautiful ring, and I would be proud to wear it – proud to be engaged to the man who was heir to Oliviera Santa Chiara. I would now be able to call him my fiancé.

I moved my hand around, admiring the ring, and imagining the reactions of everyone I saw as I showed it to them with pride. They would congratulate me on my engagement and ask when the wedding was. I noticed how the stone caught the light, and how pretty it was.

'I am honoured that you are giving this special heirloom to me, Salvatore.'

'The stone is opal – isn't it beautiful?'

It was, and highly unusual.

'So beautiful,' I said.

He stood up and kissed me on the lips, and a jolt of electricity passed right through me.

'And now we must go and show my family,' I said. 'You did ask my mamma for permission, did you not?'

'Sì, certo, of course, and she was so thrilled that we will be getting married – uniting our two families.'

My dear papa had been killed during the war, and so Salvatore had needed to ask Mamma for her approval instead. Of course she would be delighted, for her eldest daughter to be marrying Salvatore Ricci, a man with such good prospects. His family would never be short of money, or olive oil, and all Mamma wanted was for me to be financially secure. When Salvatore's father, Giorgio, retired – and that day would come before long, for the war had aged him – Salvatore would take over Oliviera Santa Chiara. And I, as his wife, would run the olive farm with him.

'All right, andiamo,' he said.

Salvatore took my hand, and we threaded our way in between the olive trees until we reached the farmhouse. Then we took the path leading down the side to the front gate.

'We'll come back and tell my family after,' he said. When we reached the gate we entered the village of Cintaldo, and walked along Via del Bacio, the road leading to San Gimignano. The views from here were majestic – Tuscan hills for miles and miles with rows of vines, luscious thick forests, and grand buildings on hilltops surrounded by cypress trees. I could make out the turrets of Castello dell'Uva, the castle on the edge of some chestnut woods, where I worked for an English couple. We kept our hands entwined and, every now and again, Salvatore would stop and lean in to kiss me on the lips, and look me in the eyes oh so intently as he brushed my cheek with a finger. I couldn't have been any more on cloud nine during that walk from one end of the village to the other.

We passed the pasticceria, and after reaching Chiesa Santa

Maria, where our wedding ceremony would take place, we reached Casa Stella. We passed through the gate, which announced us with its familiar creak, and then we took the path down the side of the house to the back garden. And there were Mamma and my younger sister, Francesca, and my maternal grandmother, Nonna Paola – a veritable matriarch. She ruled the roost, especially since Papa's passing. They were all sitting at a table on the terrazza, under the shade of the awning, shelling peas from their pods, dropping them into a large bowl in the centre as they talked and laughed together.

Mamma looked up as we approached.

'Ciao, cara, and you have brought Salvatore with you.'

'Buonasera, Signore Maggini,' he said, addressing the three of them.

'Salvatore and I have something to tell you all,' I said, hiding the hand with the ring behind my back. I didn't want to spoil our surprise. I just knew Mamma and Nonna would be thrilled with the news, even though they'd apparently had prior warning. I couldn't wait to see the expressions on their faces. Mamma had been hoping he would propose as soon as there were signs the war was coming to an end. And now she'd get her wish.

Salvatore mopped his brow with a handkerchief, for it was a balmy August day, and we'd been running, and the sun was shining directly down on us.

'Come, sit with us in the shade, both of you,' Mamma said, batting away a fly with her hand.

We sat down at the table. I picked up a pod, and joined them in shelling the peas, being careful to hide the ring on my finger. I'd always enjoyed sitting with the other women in my family and sharing this task.

'So, what do you have to tell us?' Mamma said, casting a glance at Nonna Paola. The corners of her mouth were slightly upturned, as if she were suppressing a smile.

Salvatore and I exchanged a glance.

'You tell them,' I said with a giggle.

'Signora Maggini...'

'Gina, prego, Salvatore. Call me Gina.'

'Gina, I have asked your daughter, Liliana, to marry me, and—'

'I said yes!' I couldn't help interrupting.

Mamma clapped her hands together.

'Ah well, how wonderful. I am delighted that you have proposed to our Liliana. You know I already see you as part of our family.'

Salvatore blinked, and his handsome face was filled with an enormous smile.

'Grazie, Signora Maggini— Gina.'

'Bravo, Salvatore,' Nonna Paola said.

'Auguri,' Francesca said.

'Liliana's papa, Alessio, would have been so happy and proud of his daughter,' Mamma said, making the sign of the cross. A lump formed in my throat. Papa had only been gone for a matter of months, and we were all still grieving heavily, for he'd only been fifty-five years old. The Tedeschi had caught him and Signor Bianchi from next door helping a stranded British fighter pilot, whose plane had been shot down, to reach the Swiss border. They'd been taken away and shot by firing squad in the village square, along with other civilians who had helped the Allies. Reprisals like these were carried out by the Tedeschi in an attempt to deter partisans and civilians from doing what Papa had done. But this vile act didn't stop partisans like Salvatore from wanting to fight for our freedom. It only made them want to fight harder. Our family, and the Bianchis, who had been family friends for many years, would never recover from the horrific tragedy. Papa would have been over the moon to know that I was marrying into the Ricci family – something he'd wanted for me since he'd first bought the house in Cintaldo. It was common knowledge in the village that Salvatore would inherit the olive farm one day, and so our relationship had been encouraged at every opportunity.

My dear sister, Francesca, got up and kissed me on the cheek.

'I am so happy for you, cara sorella.'

Nonna Paola rested her elbows on the table, and interlocked her fingers. There was a heavy pause while we all waited for her to speak. 'We must celebrate! Let us make a delicious cena, and eat here together tonight – *a tavola*. During these tumultuous times, it won't be as grand a celebration as it should be, but between our families we should be able to gather enough food and wine to make it an enjoyable evening.'

'That sounds like a splendid idea,' Salvatore said. 'Grazie mille, Signora Maggini.'

'Not only has our small corner of Tuscany been recently liberated, but now our two families are joining together – the Magginis and the Riccis – in this wonderful union,' Mamma said. 'Go and fetch your parents and brothers, Salvatore. We shall prepare the most delicious dinner stasera, here on the terrazza, outside, under the stars.'

'Andiamo, Liliana – let's go and tell my famiglia the happy news,' Salvatore said.

'Yes, let's!' I said, unable to wipe the huge beam from my face.

'Oh, but aspetta, where is the ring. Did you give her a ring?' Nonna Paola asked.

I proudly held out my hand to show her the beautiful engagement ring that had belonged to Salvatore's grandmother. Nonna Paola took hold of my hand, and studied the ring carefully. Mamma leant in to take a look too.

And then the smile swiftly dropped from Nonna Paola's face. This was not the reaction I'd been expecting.

'What is it, Nonna Paola?'

She looked over at Mamma, who was no longer smiling either. Then she slowly shook her head. 'Mamma mia, cara Liliana.'

'Tell me, what is the matter?' I said.

Nonna Paola lifted her arms in the air, and shook her head. 'Mah... you tell her, Gina.'

Mamma inhaled. 'Salvatore, do you realise what you have done by giving this ring to my daughter?'

He knotted his eyebrows together.

'What could I possibly have done wrong? This ring belonged to my grandmother, Nonna Claudia. She gave it to me when I was ten years old, shortly before she died, and told me to put it on the finger of the woman I want to spend my life with.'

'But the stone is an opal. If you'd spoken to your mamma before proposing, she would have told you the same thing.'

'What would she have told me?'

'It is unlucky to wear an engagement ring with an opal stone, unless you are born in October.'

My heart plummeted. I would turn nineteen at the end of August. What did this mean for Salvatore and me? I knew how superstitious Nonna Paola could be. This revelation about the opal stone changed everything. What would we do now?

'But I love your daughter. Is the ring really so important?' Salvatore said.

Nonna Paola shrugged.

'It is your decision. But let me ask you this: do you want to live your whole lives looking over your shoulders, waiting for bad luck to find you?'

Her words sent a shiver down my spine. Salvatore and I exchanged a glance, and he pressed his lips together. The wind had completely been taken out of his sails, and also mine. Surely this wouldn't impact our plan to get married?

'Well...' He paused, and looked into the distance, as if gathering his thoughts. 'My love for Liliana is stronger than this silly superstition you speak of.' He got up and pushed his chair under the table. 'We are getting married and this is the ring that my fiancée will be wearing. Let us have this celebratory dinner you promised us this evening. Liliana and I shall go and tell my family the good news now.'

'Very well,' Mamma said. 'But Salvatore... will you at least consider giving my daughter a different engagement ring to wear on her finger?'

'But I promised Nonna Claudia that I would give this ring to the woman I loved.'

'Did she not tell you about this superstition?'

He scratched his head and sighed.

'It was so long ago... I was only ten years old. Maybe she did and I wasn't listening, or perhaps I thought nothing of it. What does it matter anyway?'

'If only you had realised that Liliana's sister, Francesca, is born in October. You have chosen the wrong sister,' Nonna Paola said with a laugh.

I did not find this comment funny at all, and when I looked over at Francesca she rolled her eyes and pulled a face. Clearly, she was as horrified by Nonna Paola's thoughtless suggestion as I was. My mouth suddenly felt very dry, and I was lost for words.

'Nonna Paola, what a terrible thing to say. Take it back,' Francesca said.

'Mamma! You shouldn't have said that,' Mamma said.

'But it's the truth,' Nonna Paola said.

Salvatore looked over at my sister for a moment, and their eyes met, but then she started to shell the peas from their pods again, concentrating on her task, her face reddening. Francesca had turned eighteen the previous October, while Salvatore was away fighting with the partisans. Over the past few months, my sister had transformed from a pretty girl into an attractive young woman. Francesca was more beautiful than me – she had Papa's dark looks, and her face was oval-shaped with a button nose and lips shaped like a bow. I, on the other hand had light-brown curls like Mamma, and my face was more of a pointed shape with a Roman nose and thin lips. This had never bothered me much, especially as I was a more skilled cook, and I had always performed better than Francesca at school. Her beauty was just something I'd come to accept. But it hadn't impacted me until now. How could Nonna Paola say such a thing, and put that idea into Salvatore's head like that? I doubted he would listen to her, but still, I didn't like it. Fury rose up inside of me, my heart racing, and I had to pause to catch my breath.

'Nonna Paola, you have just spoiled such a special moment for me,' I said, instantly regretting my tone of voice as well as my words. Nonna Paola commanded a great deal of respect in our household, and no one should speak to her like that. But she really shouldn't have uttered such hurtful words – this was my future, not hers.

My grandmother rested her head in her hands as if she were dealing with a huge crisis. She had always allowed superstitions to run her life. God forbid anyone should leave a hat on a bed or see a black cat in her presence or bring anything with the number seventeen into her home. Her whole life always seemed to revolve around them. Italian superstitions were different from British ones, with a black cat bringing bad luck instead of good luck, and the number seventeen being unlucky rather than the number thirteen. She was entitled to have her beliefs and ways of doing things, but I didn't see why this should influence my life.

I got up from the table in a huff, my chair making a scraping sound on the stone floor, and then I went to stand beside Salvatore – my fidanzato.

He took my hand in his, and we faced my family together, united as one.

'Vieni, Liliana, let's go and tell my famiglia the happy news, and then we shall come back here to celebrate,' he said. 'And I don't want to hear another word about this ring – such nonsense.' He shook his head, as if he'd expected more from my family. I felt ashamed by the way Nonna Paola and Mamma had treated him.

Mamma sat up in her chair. 'Va bene,' she said, brightly, as if it had suddenly struck her that she and Nonna Paola were fighting a losing battle. 'I shall go down to the cellar and see what wine we have. I'm sure there are a few bottles of Montepulciano d'Abruzzo that we've been saving for such an occasion.

'Grazie, Mamma,' I said, softly.

I looked over at Nonna Paola, but she couldn't bring herself to meet my gaze. She was in a difficult position – torn between her beliefs and the future happiness of her granddaughter. But still, I felt as though she had ruined what was supposed to be one of the happiest moments of my life.

Salvatore must have registered the look of disappointment on my face as he squeezed my hand tightly, and ran his thumb over the ring as if to say, 'Don't worry, amore mio, everything will be all right.'

I looked down at the opal stone, and considered whether we ought to listen to what Nonna Paola was saying. But should a mere superstition influence such an important, life-changing decision?

Absolutely not, I could not allow my grandmother's meddling to come between me and my fidanzato. This would be my engagement ring, and that was that – and it would remain on my finger forever.

CHAPTER 3

JEN

Nonna let out a deep sigh and placed the ring carefully back into its box, but she didn't close the lid. She slid the box across the table to me.

'Well, this is yours now, Jen, to do what you wish with.'

I had no idea what to say. Seeing this ring was clearly upsetting for Nonna. I wasn't quite sure why she'd left Italy in the first place – although I did know that she'd fallen out with her sister, Francesca, at the end of the war. Was that the reason she'd come to England? And then why had she chosen Cambridge? What could have happened that meant two sisters never spoke to each other again?

'Go and fetch the grappa and two more glasses, will you, cara,' Nonna said to me.

I got up and grabbed the bottle and two shot glasses from the old wooden dresser standing in the far corner. I poured out shots for all of us. Nonna raised hers in the air, and then we all clinked our glasses together.

'Cin cin,' Nonna said, and Matteo and I said the same, meeting each other's eyes, as was customary, across the candle that flickered in the centre of the table.

Nonna took a big glug. 'Ah, that's better. Grazie, Jen. Va bene...' She took a handkerchief out of the pocket of her pale-green house dress, and dabbed her eyes. 'You must excuse me, Matteo, for this ring has brought all of my emotions to the surface.'

'I'm sorry,' he said.

'Mah.' She raised her arms in the air. 'It is not your fault. Your visit has brought back memories for me from many years ago. But I am most grateful that you have brought this ring to my dear granddaughter, Jen. Cambridge is so far out of your way.'

'Well, actually, I have been in London on business, so it is no problem at all. Cambridge is only a short train journey from there, and I've never visited this beautiful city before.'

'Ah, well that is wonderful to hear. And of course, dinner is on us. How long will you be here for?' she said.

'I'm staying in a hotel round the corner tonight. And then I leave early tomorrow to fly back to Florence,' he said.

'That's a pity. We could have offered you breakfast in our coffee shop next door,' she said.

Matteo shrugged. 'It's too bad. Never mind... So, Jen, when will you come to see Casa Stella?'

What a beautiful name the house had – *stella* meant star. I was still getting my head around this news. To inherit a ring and a house out of the blue, from a great-aunt who I'd never met, was more than a bit of a shock, and I wasn't sure how to answer his question. I needed the chance to finish my shift and to go back to my flat and get a good night's sleep in order to process it all.

'I'm not really sure,' I said, tightening my ponytail. My hair needed a wash, as well as straightening, hence why I was wearing it up today. I had inherited Nonna's light-brown curls, but I rarely wore my hair naturally. I wished Matteo could have met me when I'd had a chance to spend more time on my appearance.

'Well, you don't inherit a beautiful house in the Tuscan hills every day,' Nonna said. 'You should arrange a date to go.'

Nodding, I said, 'It's wonderful, and I feel very lucky indeed and so grateful – but Nonna, I just need a day or two to work everything out, that's all.'

'Let me tell you that this particular house is one to treasure,' Matteo said, his eyes lighting up.

I was curious to go and see the house where my grandmother had spent so much of her childhood.

'You must go before the summer is over,' Nonna said, matter-of-factly.

'But I can't leave the restaurant,' I protested.

'Your brothers, Giuseppe and Alfonso, are more than capable of looking after the place until your parents get back from Italy,' she said.

My mum and dad were on their annual trip to the east coast of Italy, where Mum's family were originally from – a small town called Riccione, south of Rimini.

Matteo yawned, and put a hand over his mouth, then glanced at his watch.

'I am sorry, it has been a very long day. I must go to bed.'

'Yes, of course,' I said.

'Thank you for coming here, and for bringing the ring,' Nonna said.

'Prego, it is nothing,' he said.

'Why don't you see the young man out, Jen,' Nonna said.

We got up and headed for the front desk.

'So, as I was saying, about Casa Stella...' Matteo said.

'Yes?' I said, looking up at him.

'When your great-aunt said she wanted to leave Casa Stella to you, I offered to ask my cousin, Fabrizio, who is a solicitor, to organise the paperwork. Seeing as our families have been so close over the years, he said that he would do everything gratis.'

'Really? Is he sure?'

Matteo nodded. 'It's already done, ready for you to sign.'

'How kind of him. Please pass on my thanks.'

'I will. So, you can come to Casa Stella whenever you like – I would visit before the end of the summer when it's at its best. And I have a pool, which you are welcome to use, if you like.'

The thought of lazing by a pool was tempting.

'Oh, well, that's very kind, thank you.'

'Let me give you my details.' He took a business card out of his wallet and handed it to me. 'Just send me a message and let me know when you're coming. I have some time off during the last two weeks of August, after Ferragosto – the public holiday. So, I can let you into the house, and drive you to Florence to get the paperwork signed.'

'I would appreciate that very much.'

'It's my pleasure.' He looked down at me, and smiled, and said, 'I shall be going now. Thanks for the delicious dinner.'

Well, it is the best cacio e pepe in Cambridge,' I said with a laugh.

He smiled, and turned round, and went to open the door. As he passed through it, he looked over his shoulder at me, and gave me a wave. I waved back, and then I watched him walk away until he disappeared from view.

What had just happened? I'd inherited a ring with a mystery attached to it, and a house from a great-aunt I'd never met. What would I even do with a house in Italy?

I went back over to Nonna, who was still at the table.

'I must say I was surprised to see that ring,' she said.

'What's the story behind it all?'

'It's a very sad story, I'm afraid. I...' Her eyes glazed over, and she stared into space, and it seemed that this evening was all getting a bit much for her.

'Is it time for you to go back upstairs now, Nonna?'

'Yes, in a minute, cara. I will tell you the story about this ring, but another time. This has all been quite a surprise. I did always wonder who might go first out of me and Francesca. But you must promise me you'll visit Casa Stella. During the war when food was scarce in Florence, it became our refuge. We were almost self-sufficient when we lived there with everything that we grew in the garden, and with the chickens, and so on. A trip to Italy could be just what you need after all you've been through lately. You haven't been yourself, Jen, and I keep meaning to ask if you're eating properly, as you seem to be getting rather thin.' She reached forward and pinched my cheek as if I were a young child. 'The house could now be your refuge in your time of need.'

I smiled weakly. Nonna was right. I had lost some weight, not intentionally as I loved my food, but because I'd been living on sandwiches at home and snatched meals during my breaks at Da Nonna. But I had lost my appetite for the hearty dishes I usually liked to make – I hadn't felt like cooking anything substantial recently.

'I'm not sure I can go and stay in a house in Italy all on my own, and I do have a lot going on right now.'

'Like what?' Nonna said.

'You know how I've been through so much, what with Harvey running off with my best friend. I've lost two people who were a huge part of my life, and to top it all, I lost my beloved cupcake business too.'

I had come up with the idea for Jen's Bakes one day when I'd noticed that cupcakes were suddenly 'in' – and I liked to make unusual flavours like limoncello and tiramisù. I'd assumed this would be an easy way to make money, with the odd Instagram post here and there, and by delivering them around Cambridge on my bicycle with a basket – building up a local clientele who would order them in batches for birthdays and special occasions. But I'd been mistaken. There was a lot more to sales and marketing than I'd expected.

'There is nothing wrong with failing at something – you need to use the experience to make you stronger.'

'How would I do that?'

'Reach inside yourself and show them what you're capable of.'

'Who is "them"?'

'Harvey and that awful girl who called herself your friend. What was her name again?'

'Amanda Peters.'

'Amanda Peters.' Nonna spat out her name and shook her head. 'How dare she run off with my granddaughter's fiancé.'

Perhaps Nonna was right. If I could just make a success of *something*, that would make me feel better. While preparing for the wedding – and there had been so much to do – I'd become distracted from running my business, and its failure was mostly down to me not dedicating enough time to it. I should have promoted it more on social media and put more energy into attracting new clients locally, but instead I'd been wedding dress shopping and working out the table plan and choosing readings for the service. Not only had I lost my fiancé and my best friend, but also I'd lost my business too. Although sometimes I had wondered whether perhaps the business wasn't my future because my heart hadn't been fully in it. I'd been jumping on a bandwagon rather than considering what I actually wanted to do.

'Cara, I've watched you feel sorry for yourself all summer, and now it's time, as autumn approaches, to pull yourself together. A man I used to know, a classics lecturer at the university, used to say carpe diem, a phrase worth remembering as you go through life. It means seize the day, and that's what you need to do now, instead of dwelling on the past.'

These words were difficult to hear, but I knew Nonna was right. Then it came back to me – my goal for so many years had been to get a cookbook published. I'd created one when I was a child, just like one Nonna had brought over from Tuscany, with drawings and cut-out pictures and scribbled recipes, passed down the family. Nonna used to say that making those recipes was a way of staying connected to previous generations. After completing my university degree in food science, I'd worked as a nutritionist for a while. But I hadn't found my job very fulfilling – it offered limited opportunities to nourish my creative side, a need I seemed to have. And so, I waitressed at Da Nonna while writing a food blog called *Jen's Italian Bites*, thinking it could lead to getting a cookbook published. The blog had done quite well, and often people would comment and use my recipes and send me their photos. I sent a few chapters of a cookbook idea – based on recipes Nonna had taught me – to literary agents, optimistic that I might get a book deal. But the agents sent rejection after rejection. Sometimes they just ghosted me. The whole process had been so dispiriting, and in the end I decided to stop submitting to save my sanity. Instead, I set up the cupcake business to try to make some money. The cookbook idea had gone on the back burner. Perhaps I would be inspired to cook again if I spent some time in Italy.

'Okay, Nonna, I'll look into it.'

'You can start by booking yourself a flight to Florence – and then go and have a look at Casa Stella. You've never been to Tuscany, have you? I'd like you to visit my home city of Florence, as well as see the beautiful countryside nearby.'

I had been to Italy, but we'd always spent summers with Mum's family in Riccione. It would be interesting to see Tuscany with my own eyes after all I'd heard and seen in films. *Under the Tuscan Sun* was one of my favourites, along with *A Room with a View* and *Letters to Juliet*.

'Are you sure you don't need me at the restaurant until Mum and Dad get back later in the month?'

'As I said before, your brothers have Da Nonna covered. Your parents only gave you the work because they wanted to keep you busy after everything that happened. It isn't difficult to find waiting staff in Cambridge, dear.'

'All right, I'll mull it over when I get home.'

'You do that. I can't wait to see you go on an adventure that will no doubt bring you out of this slump. Italy cannot fail to lift you up, and it's time you stopped moping around now.'

Goodness, by the way Nonna was speaking I must have been such miserable company lately. Besides, the thought of going on an adventure was exciting. Was it time to start submitting my cookbook again – and work on some new recipes in Italy? I wasn't sure if I could go back to all that rejection – it had really brought me down. But maybe I should try to be more optimistic, keep persevering.

'And if for some reason you don't like Casa Stella – which I couldn't imagine because, Jen, it is in the most glorious location with panoramic views of the beautiful Tuscan hills – you can always rent it out or sell it. Although that would be such a pity.'

'That's an idea, I suppose,' I said, thinking about the money I could make from doing that. Maybe this was my moment – and not having to worry about money for a while would be a nice break. My credit cards were maxed out, and I still had to pay back some of the loan I'd taken out for the cupcake business. All of it had been keeping me awake at night for some time.

'But...' she said. 'You'd be a fool to let go of Casa Stella, Jen, because it could be just what you need. This has all happened for a reason, I'm sure of it.'

Perhaps Nonna was right.

'And that Matteo... Who wouldn't want to live next door to him?' she said with a laugh.

He was rather handsome, but bound to be taken already. Besides, I was taking a break from men. I stood up and leant down to kiss Nonna on the cheek.

'It's getting late, and I'm going to cycle back. Okay?'

'Come and see me in the morning during your break. We can have pastries and talk some more.'

'Goodnight, Nonna. Thank you.'

'Buonanotte, cara.' She put a hand on my arm. 'Aspetta, don't forget to take the ring.' She tipped her head in the direction of the table. It was still sitting there in its box with the lid open.

'Shall I take it, or I could leave it here instead?'

'Take it, please. It only ever brought me bad luck.'

'Won't it bring me bad luck?'

She shook her head. 'Oh no, of course not. You don't need to worry about any of that. The bad luck is related to a superstition. Sometimes I wonder whether I should have listened to Nonna Paola.'

'What do you mean?'

'I'll explain another time – it's a long story. Just get yourself home for now.'

I closed the lid on the box, and dropped it into my handbag. 'But will you be all right getting upstairs?'

'Giuseppe will help me.'

'Okay, goodnight, Nonna.'

I went outside, the night air still warm, and unlocked my bike, attached to railings nearby. I thought about the ring and the house and Matteo. Then I remembered – I'd put his business card in the back pocket of my jeans. I took it out and read: *Matteo Bianchi, TV Producer* with an address in Florence, and a phone number and email address. Wow, he was an actual TV producer. Impressive. I climbed onto my bike and bumped over the cobblestones of King's Parade, and then made my way up Trumpington Street, in the direction of my flat on Cherry

Hinton Road. I wondered what kind of programmes Matteo worked on. He could be an intriguing person to get to know. I would have to google him to find out more.

CHAPTER 4

LILIANA

That night we celebrated as though there was no tomorrow, as though my amore would not be going off to fight again. But Florence still needed to be liberated, and Salvatore wanted to play his part in making that happen. I struggled to understand why he felt the need to continue risking his life now that Cintaldo was free. Despite this, I felt a duty to support my fiancé. Jeeps passing through our village now contained Allied soldiers rather than the Tedeschi. We were no longer living in fear for every minute of every day and night. And we no longer had to bury our hams and salamis and valuables in our gardens to hide them from the Tedeschi. Salvatore had more than played his part during this war. He had fought briefly as an Italian soldier in Tunisia, and now, as a partisan, he'd already spent some time living like a contadino, a peasant, in the Tuscan hills. There he foraged for food, and lived in rags, and with holes in his boots. He spent his days working with other partisans and the Allies to attack German and fascist targets. But I hated to think about the risks he was taking, and how he would be killed if discovered.

Salvatore's family had been delighted by our news when we

told them. His mamma, papa, and three younger brothers brought over a salami, tomatoes, courgettes – and a few bottles of coveted Chianti that they'd stored in a hidden part of their cellar. Our neighbours, the Bianchis, who lived at Casa Luna, joined us – for they were family friends. Poor Valentina, like Mamma, had been widowed by the war. Signor Bianchi had been a plumber who kept everything running at our pensione in Florence. He and Papa had become firm friends, and they'd bought Corte Paradiso together and divided the grand old pink house into Casa Stella and Casa Luna so we could escape the heat of the city during the summer months. They'd spent a year refurbishing the houses with the help of a couple of builders until they were ready for us to enjoy. Francesca and I had played outside with their daughter, Nicoletta, and son, Paolo, ever since we could remember.

Paolo carried over a table from Casa Luna next door and put it with ours outside to make one long table for our celebration. Nicoletta brought over tablecloths and decorated the centre with jars of marigolds picked from their garden. She added candles that we would light at dusk.

In the kitchen, I helped Mamma prepare a veritable feast: gnocchi made from flour and potatoes from our garden, served with a butter and sage sauce. We drizzled sliced tomatoes with olive oil, then we scattered them with fresh basil leaves from the terracotta pot kept by the back door. Signora Bianchi brought a loaf of bread, baked that morning, and we sliced and arranged it into baskets. For dessert we feasted on peaches taken from the tree in the garden at Casa Stella, baked and stuffed with ground almonds. They were quite delectable.

We all sat at the long table with Salvatore and me at the centre. That night, I felt like a princess. I wore my favourite dress, left behind by a guest at the pensione as she hadn't wanted to take it on the long journey back to England. It was made from emerald-green silk with a scoop neck and it rustled when I moved. Salvatore wore a suit with a white shirt and a royal-blue tie. He looked so handsome. All eyes were on us and I relished the attention. To become part of such a prestigious family was what every girl dreamt of growing up. I couldn't have been more fortunate.

The mood was dampened a little though by Salvatore's mamma, when she reacted in the same way as Nonna Paola to the opal ring.

'How could you have forgotten what Nonna Claudia told you, Toto,' his mamma said, shaking her head. His family would call him Toto, short for Salvatore.

His papa, Giorgio, didn't seem to think it mattered, for he was not superstitious.

'Non è vero, ma ci credo,' he said. Meaning, 'It's not true, but I believe it' – something we Italians would sometimes say when we also needed to be practical about matters and couldn't allow superstition to override our decisions. 'During these times of war, if you love each other and want to be together, that is the most important thing,' he went on.

Everyone listened to Giorgio, who was the master of his house, naturally. I missed my papa, who would probably have agreed with him. I did worry about who would walk me down the aisle on my wedding day. But that was something to think about when the time came.

And so Salvatore and I decided to keep the opal ring on my finger. I did not care, for I was going to marry the man I loved more than anything in the world, and that was all that mattered. I was not as superstitious as my nonna and mamma. What had it done for them? Mamma had lost her husband during the war, and Nonna had lost my grandfather during the Great War. Their superstitions had done nothing to save them from losing their husbands. Whether I was superstitious or not, I doubted it would make any difference to whether I got to keep the man I loved.

On that wonderful night, we sat on the terrazza, with bougainvillea trailing over the veranda above us. The sky was so clear that we could see all of the stars twinkling above. As we ate and drank like kings and queens, we forgot the horror of the war and became immersed in celebrating the joy of our families uniting.

The next morning, when I woke up, the first thought that came into my head was that my amore would be leaving me once again.

Salvatore came to see me at Casa Stella, and I took a break from kneading dough in the kitchen to sit with him in the garden. We drank espressos and talked under the shade of the veranda, facing the hills, so luscious and vividly green – always at the height of their beauty during the summer months.

'I am so sad that you are leaving me, once again, Salvatore. What will I do if you don't come back this time?'

'Do not worry about me, Liliana, for I shall return to you before long. And then we shall get married in the Chiesa Santa Maria, and afterwards we shall have the most wonderful festa to celebrate our love for each other. I cannot wait.'

'I will pray for you every single day, dear Salvatore, in the morning when I wake up and before I go to sleep at night. And I shall attend Mass at the Chiesa Santa Maria,' I said. 'But I shall miss you so much.'

He leant forwards and kissed me on the lips, and, as always, butterflies fluttered in my gut. For I would never love any man more than I loved Salvatore right now at this very moment. He was so courageous putting himself forward to continue to fight for our country's freedom, and I was proud of him.

Standing up, he ran a hand through his hair and inhaled.

'When you look out at those Tuscan hills, think of me, hiding somewhere, and send me your love.'

'I will,' I said.

He took hold of my hands, and gently pulled me up out of the chair, and into his arms. Then he squeezed me tightly, and I tucked my head into the crook of his neck, inhaling his scent – the musky cologne he wore combined with tobacco and coffee. He let go of me before I was ready, and stepped back, his eyes filled with sadness.

'Arrivederci, Liliana.'

'Arrivederci, Salvatore.'

Arrivederci doesn't just mean goodbye, it also means until we meet again, and how I hoped we would. And then, he gave me a nod and slowly walked away, up the garden path, towards the gate. I sat back down in the chair, for I could not watch him go. My heart was breaking. I heard the creak of the gate as he opened and closed it again, almost announcing his departure. And then he was gone. How I wanted to go and wave him off from the front of the house. But I just couldn't. Instead, I looked out at the beautiful scenery before me and I thought about Salvatore on his way to Florence to oust the Tedeschi. Only then could we return to the lives we'd lived before the war began, just over four years ago in June 1940. My world had changed a great deal since then. I had only been fourteen years old when it started, almost fifteen, and now I was almost nineteen. I had become a young woman during those turbulent years. Many people who I had been close to had tragically lost their lives – I'd lost my dear papa. Somehow, so far, the rest of my family had survived against all odds. Our house in the Tuscan hills had played an important part. Now the Allies had taken control of the land that I could see before me, but Florence remained occupied. And Salvatore would not come back to me until my home city had been liberated. How I hoped it wouldn't take too long – I was desperate for my amore to return to me and finally make me his wife.

CHAPTER 5

JEN

After cycling back to my flat, I opened a couple of windows because it was still baking hot, and then went into the kitchen and put on the kettle. Working two shifts back to back at the restaurant always left me feeling exhausted, especially on Saturdays when it was fully booked all day and night. And Matteo's surprise visit had been particularly eventful too. I went into my bedroom and plugged in my phone to charge, and let out a long, deep sigh. The blue numbers on my alarm clock showed it was eleven thirty. I made a cup of tea and snapped a piece of chocolate off the bar I was keeping in the fridge. I'd had dinner at the restaurant mid-shift – that was the upside of working there as I rarely needed to buy food, which saved me a small fortune. I showered, and removed my make-up, and then put on my cotton dressing gown, instantly feeling better.

Remembering the ring, I sat on the bed and reached into my handbag to take out the cube-shaped box. I opened it, and slid the ring onto each of my fingers, but it only fitted on my wedding finger – and was perhaps even a little snug. Then I shuddered as I remembered the engagement ring that had been on that very same finger only months before. It had been a simple diamond stone, princess cut, set on a platinum band, and we'd bought a platinum wedding ring to match. We hadn't got round to collecting our wedding bands from the jeweller, so the refund had been the one upside of the wedding being called off. I'd left the engagement ring at Harvey's cottage along with the Xbox console he'd been keeping at mine – I certainly wouldn't be missing *that*, and all the time he'd spent gaming instead of talking to me. I'd then dropped my copy of his key through the letterbox and swiftly cycled away, my eyes brimming with tears.

I thought back to what Nonna had told me about her sister, my great-aunt, Francesca. What was the story there, exactly? I'd known of her existence, but we hadn't been allowed to bring up her name because they'd had some big fall-out at the end of the war. No one in our family seemed to have any idea what it was about, as Nonna always kept her cards close to her chest. Sometimes I wondered if Dad might know more than he let on, though. He was fiercely protective of his mother. Nonna had once shared with us – when rather drunk at our fish supper one Christmas Eve – lovely memories from being at their house nestled in the Tuscan hills with her sister, at the height of summer. She'd talked about running through fields of sunflowers, podding home-grown peas at a table on the terrazza under a veranda covered with hot-pink bougainvillea that trailed down the sides – all with her mother, sister and grandmother. It had sounded so idyllic. Then anger seemed to rise up inside her as she talked about the German occupation of Italy, and how the Nazis had commandeered her family's boarding house in Florence. And how her father lost his life because he chose to help someone reach a place of safety. We'd pressed further for more stories about her family and the war... but suddenly, she shut down, as she always did whenever her former life in Italy came up. I was sure that I spotted a tear in her eye, as she got up and made an excuse to leave the room.

But now, here I was being given a ring that Nonna said had

brought her bad luck at around that time. Did I even want to own something that had clearly made her life miserable? Nonna did appear to be happier about me inheriting the house than the ring, which seemed to stir up a lot of emotions for her. But then I remembered her saying the ring couldn't bring me bad luck because the superstition didn't apply to me. What superstition though? I would have to try to find out what she'd meant.

After Harvey had called off the wedding, I'd spent a few weeks lazing around the flat, feeling sorry for myself, watching Netflix boxsets from the comfort of the sofa, snuggled under a throw and using a cushion as a pillow – working my way through one boxset after another – *Virgin River*, *Gilmore Girls*, any comforting series I could find. And the more seasons it had the better. But I'd wasted those precious few months of the year that I always loved so much – from May to September when the weather was mostly good. The trees bloomed with spring blossom, and daffodils, crocuses and snowdrops were popping up everywhere. Cambridge was such a lovely place to be at that time of year, with endless warm, sunny days, and longer, light evenings. Usually, I'd walk or punt with friends along the River Cam to Grantchester, and we'd buy a bottle of beer and a bag of crisps in the pub, and then sit on the riverbank. Sometimes we'd take a picnic, if we were organised enough. This year though I hadn't had a proper spring or summer at all. After my period of lazing on the sofa, I'd worked all hours at Da Nonna and turned down invitations to do lovely things with friends – I just couldn't face talking about the whole Harvey and Amanda situation. It was so embarrassing, having not only the man you loved, but also your best friend, letting you down like that. Now it was almost mid-August, and there were only a couple of weeks left before the arrival of autumn would mark the end of summer for another year.

With the ring still on my finger, I opened my laptop. I took out the business card Matteo had given me, and googled him. A website came up for Produzioni Tivu Bianchi. I clicked on it, and there was a biography and a photo. And what a photo it was. He was absolutely gorgeous. But a man like him had to be taken. I typed 'Matteo Bianchi TV producer girlfriend' into the search bar, giggling to myself. And then there she was – a glamorous woman called Natalia Valentini. She was a presenter on the show he produced. But hold on, there was an article about their recent break-up, and it was dated June. Perhaps he was single then... But I really shouldn't be interested in whether he was or not. Because I was off men. I wasn't sure if I could trust another man again, however charming he might be. Harvey had been charming initially, then I'd discovered that he could be quite moody and also manipulative at times. Being someone who always saw the best in people, I'd kind of accepted this. Mum had pressured me to ask him if he wanted to get married though and, after he proposed in Paris, I just got swept up in it all. Before I knew it, I was planning our wedding at Healey Manor, a swish country house between Cambridge and Ely.

I checked my phone calendar and, apart from Da Nonna's eightieth-anniversary lunch the Sunday after next, there was nothing in the diary for the rest of August. Or at any time in the near future, as most of my friends were away. I hadn't arranged anything with those who were around – because I'd been avoiding everyone. It struck me that this had been a silly thing to do – my friends were thoughtful and kind, and perhaps their moral support might have been helpful. But also, I had needed some time to myself to process everything.

The sound of drumming came through the ceiling from the flat underneath me – it was almost half past midnight now. The tenants below were having an impromptu jam session once again. This happened most evenings and they tended to go on much later on Saturday nights. Talking to them had made no difference. They would always say, 'Sure, okay, we'll try to keep it down,' but then carry on as they were. And it seemed so unfair that they got to have access to the garden just because their flat was on the ground floor. The lawn hadn't been mown in months, and the flowerbeds were filled with weeds and overgrown shrubs and flowers that needed deadheading. If it was my garden, I would plant pots of flowers and herbs on the patio, and get a nice table and chairs so I could enjoy the evenings outside with a glass of wine.

Yes, I really should experience at least a taste of summer this year... How easy was it to book a flight to Florence? Would there be any availability? The house was in the Tuscan hills, in a village called Cintaldo, just outside a medieval town called San Gimignano, around a forty-minute drive from Florence. I looked up flights and, before I could change my mind, booked to go next Saturday, returning on the following Friday. That way I'd be back in good time to help out with the anniversary lunch. I would get the National Express coach to Stansted airport. Perfect. I would tell Nonna in the morning when we met for coffee and pastries. She'd be so thrilled.

I took out Matteo's business card and tapped his number into my phone.

Hi, it's Jen. Thanks for coming to the restaurant earlier. I've booked a flight! I'll be arriving next Saturday afternoon at Casa Stella. Will you be in so I can get the key?

The three dots danced and I bit my lip in anticipation as I waited for his reply.

Ciao, Jen. Brava! I am filming that day in Siena, but will be back at around 7 p.m. I'll leave the key under the terracotta pot of basil outside the door

I thanked him. How exciting. The ring was beginning to feel uncomfortably tight on my finger, and I took it off and put it back into the box. The milky-white stone caught the light from my bedside lamp. What was the superstition all about? I didn't want to bother Nonna by asking her a lot of questions that were going to make her even more sad and upset. She did seem pleased that the house had come back to her side of the family, and that I now had possession of the ring – even though it hadn't brought her any luck. I could get it resized, I supposed... but did I even want to wear it? I typed 'opal rings superstition' into the search bar. And then a blog post came up about birthstones. I clicked into it and scrolled down to what it said under the heading 'Opal'.

> It's bad luck to wear an opal engagement ring unless it's your birthstone i.e., you are born in October.

Hold on. What did this mean? Nonna was born in August. Had this been her engagement ring? But then what had happened to the man Nonna had been engaged to? Had he died during the war? That must have been it. He died and she left the ring at Casa Stella when she came to Cambridge. I still didn't understand why she'd come to Cambridge in the first place. And then why had she stayed? Perhaps she'd been too heartbroken to go back to Tuscany if her fiancé had died there. And then she'd met Nonno and married him. But none of this explained why she had fallen out with Francesca. It was all certainly food for thought and perhaps I'd find more clues at the house in Tuscany. Or Matteo might know more.

I yawned. I was so very tired. Barely able to keep my eyes open, I closed my laptop and put it on my desk, then I got into bed and clicked off my bedside lamp. The band downstairs seemed to be getting louder, somehow... but there was no point in talking to them. Next weekend I wouldn't be here – I'd be at my new house in the Tuscan hills. Closing my eyes, I tried to picture what the house might look like, with beautiful countryside all around me. I so hoped it would be a peaceful, calm place to be. I could take Matteo up on his offer to use his pool and sunbathe in the garden. And I'd explore the surrounding area, and hopefully return to Cambridge feeling recharged. If for any reason I didn't like the house, I could still rent it out – Matteo would surely help me do that as he'd done for Francesca. And then there was Matteo himself. What would it be like having him as my neighbour? I pictured us driving to Florence to see his solicitor cousin, as he'd suggested. I quite liked the idea of spending some time with him. And I'd be very lucky to have someone local showing me around too.

CHAPTER 6

LILIANA

JULY 1944

That morning, after I'd said goodbye to Salvatore, I walked to Castello dell'Uva, where I worked as a housekeeper for an English couple, Professor Jeremy and Lady Enid Beaumont. He was in his mid-forties, and she was younger, in her early thirties. They'd come to Tuscany from Cambridge a year or so before war broke out in England, in the summer of 1938. He was a classics lecturer who was in Italy on sabbatical to research and write a book about the Etruscans. The Etruscan stronghold of Volterra was only twenty miles down the road from the castello. Lady Enid was a poet and she liked to paint, but she wasn't actually a real lady. Apparently, her mother, an actress in the West End, had taken an elderly baron as her third husband, and inherited his estate when he died. This made Enid the daughter of a baroness, and so she adopted the formal title of Lady, even though the baron was not her father. She and Jeremy were friends with many of the expats who had adopted Tuscany as their home. It was Mrs Gwendolene Sparks, a resident at our pensione in Florence, who had recommended me to this couple, for the role of cook. I'd helped out in the kitchen at our pensione since I was a child, obsessed with preparing delicious things to eat ever since I could remember. Sometimes, I'd use Nonna Paola's *libro di ricette*, recipes passed down through generations of my family. This book taught me how to prepare many Italian dishes.

After the armistice in September 1943 when Italy 'changed sides', our allies, the Tedeschi suddenly became our enemies. My parents took the decision to go and live at our summer house, Casa Stella, until the war was (hopefully) over. At Casa Stella we had a vast garden where we could grow vegetables, and there were apple, plum, peach and fig trees. And we kept chickens and rabbits and a goat. Papa soon became acquainted with Signor Conti who owned the local fattoria, a farm between Cintaldo and San Gimignano. This farmer provided us with hams, salamis, and mozzarella on occasion. Food had been harder to come by as the war progressed, and the signing of the armistice meant that the country was suddenly thrown into chaos: British and American, and other Allied soldiers, were released from prisoner-of-war camps, and, if they actually managed to evade being captured by the Tedeschi, they had to then try to find their way to safety. Often, they joined the partisans, and many Italian civilians risked their lives in order to help these Allies reach a place behind enemy lines. At the same time, after the invasion of Sicily, Allied soldiers were also trying to make their way up the boot to push the Tedeschi out of our country. On top of all this, we had to endure Allied planes dropping bombs on us from above. This inevitably led to the death of civilians who happened to be in the wrong place at the wrong time. It was a difficult choice for Italians – did we want the Tedeschi and the fascisti to continue to run our country? To be free of them once and for all meant helping Allied soldiers by giving them shelter and food and clothes and showing them the way to places of safety. Many Italian civilians risked their lives for the Allies, who were also bombing their country. And they were putting themselves in grave danger – because if the Tedeschi discovered what they were doing they would be killed. Like Papa and Signor Bianchi. Either way, there would be a great deal of bloodshed, and all we could do was continue to pray for the survival of ourselves and our loved ones.

'We will have a better life in the Tuscan hills where we can grow our own food and stand a chance of surviving this terrible war,' Mamma had said the previous September, shaking her head. We packed our belongings into Papa's car, and made the hour-long journey – the four of us – into the Tuscan hills. In the meantime, our neighbour and friend in Florence, Signor Fumi, had reassured us that he would keep an eye on the pensione – and inform Papa if he needed to return for any reason.

The professor and Lady Enid were typical creative types, and they were always sitting around talking about books and writing, exchanging ideas about their work or listening to opera on the gramophone. Sometimes Lady Enid would sit on the terrazza with an easel, mixing watercolours in her palette. She loved to paint the Tuscan hills with a glass of brandy by her side, and a cigarette hanging from her lips. She wasn't a particularly gifted artist, but the activity seemed to bring her a great deal of joy. I had learnt some English words from the two of them. Lady Enid was more fluent in Italian than the professor. As a classics lecturer, he would sometimes speak to me in Latin while puffing away on his pipe. There was a chance a particular Latin word was similar to the Italian equivalent, or I might be familiar with it from Mass. I would usually smile, and say, 'Bravo, Professore,' and he would stroke his thick grey beard with pride. I liked them both, and they had been kind to me, and generous too. The professor certainly had an appetite, and the paunch to go with it. Lady Enid, on the other hand, was as thin as a stick, and she was quite happy with a plate of salad leaves. The professor told me that I was the best cook in the whole of Italy, and I think Lady Enid was grateful that she didn't have to spend her time preparing food for him. They were the best employers one could hope for, and I considered myself to be fortunate indeed to have had Mrs Gwendoline Sparks recommend me to them.

When their housemaid had to leave to help out her family when her mother was taken ill, they asked if I would like to be promoted to housekeeper. This would involve some cleaning as well as cooking and generally making sure that everything at the castello ran smoothly. They offered to double my salary, for they weren't short of money, and so how could I say no? Every lira I earned went towards helping my family survive. Without the pensione, they were living on meagre savings and whatever food we could produce from the garden and from foraging to get by. Before Papa had died, my family did all they could to help the partisans and prisoners of war hide from the Tedeschi. Mamma and Nonna had knitted jumpers and repaired and donated clothes and boots that Papa could manage without. For a short time, we'd provided shelter in the shed in our garden. After dark, I had taken out plates of food to these fugitives. We were all risking our lives doing these things, but at the same time playing our small part in winning the war.

That morning when I arrived at the castello, Lady Enid was sitting in her drawing room, a notebook and pen on her lap, and a cigarette in her hand. There was a glass of brandy on the trestle table beside her. This was her usual tipple, and she would drink it from after breakfast until she went to bed each night. The war didn't seem to impact her and the professor as much as it had us in terms of what they could get hold of. Money being no object was bound to help. I expected they bought a lot of provisions on the black market through their expat contacts.

'Buongiorno, Lady Enid,' I said.

'Buongiorno, Liliana,' she said. 'How are you today?'

'I am well. In fact, I have news... the man I love, Salvatore, proposed to me last night.'

She sat up in her chair. 'What? Oh, well that's wonderful news, Liliana.' She stubbed out her cigarette in the ashtray beside her, really pressing it down and twisting it around. 'Many congratulations. I had thought – well, *hoped*, actually, that you might come back to England with us.'

This proposition was coming from nowhere, and I didn't know what to say. What was Lady Enid thinking?

'Oh... really?'

She fixed her eyes on me and nodded. I stood with my hands clasped behind my back. I was wearing my work uniform – a black dress with white apron tied around my waist.

'Yes... it was rather silly of me really to presume such a thing.' She placed another cigarette in her mouth, and struck a match to light it. 'We – well especially the professor as he so enjoys your food – were really hoping you'd come with us. I doubt very much we'd be able to find anyone who can cook like you in Cambridge.'

'Oh, well, thank you for the compliment. That's very kind of you, Lady Enid, but well, I'm engaged now, and when my fiancé returns from fighting with the partisans we shall get married at the Chiesa Santa Maria in Cintaldo.'

She nodded. 'Well, all right, I can't argue with that, I suppose.'

It then occurred to me that when they left for England I would be without a job. Hopefully they wouldn't leave until Salvatore and I were married, as then I would live on the olive farm as his wife.

'When will you go back? After the war is over?'

'Yes, Liliana, presuming that we can find a way of getting back. I imagine the transport links aren't what they were with bridges having been blown up everywhere, and the railway network more or less obliterated. The roads won't have been repaired for some time and there will be potholes all over the shop. But the military will assist us, no doubt, especially as the professor is firm friends with Hugo Edwards who works at the Foreign Office.' She lowered her voice. 'They are well acquainted, school chums from Harrow, which comes in rather handy. The old boys' network is a real wonder sometimes.'

'Well, I had better get on with my tasks, signora.'

She dragged on her cigarette, turned her head to the side and exhaled a cloud of smoke.

'Yes, I suppose you should do that. Thank you, Liliana, and congratulations on your engagement – very well done. What does he do for a living?'

'He's going to inherit an olive farm.'

'Well, isn't that marvellous – to be the wife of someone as prestigious as that, and as much olive oil as one wishes too.'

I smiled. Lady Enid always knew what to say.

'Grazie, signora.'

'Very good, well you had better get on, and I had better produce some good words this morning.'

I gave her a nod, and made my way to the kitchen to prepare lunch. There was a new bag of flour, and eggs from the chickens in the garden, and I would make orecchiette – pasta shaped like little ears – with sugo di pomodoro. I tipped flour out of the bag onto the table, and swirled my fingers around to make a well in the centre. Then I broke and dropped in the eggs followed by a dash of water and mixed everything together with my fingers, producing a dough. I kneaded the dough until, when I pressed it with a finger, it bounced back. And then it was ready to roll into a sausage shape and cut off small pieces to make into orecchiette by rolling a knife along them, before turning the pasta shape inside out on my finger. I enjoyed this task as I could take a moment to breathe and mull things over.

I thought about Lady Enid asking me to go back to Cambridge with her and the professor to be their cook. What an absurd idea! And so unexpected. They were both rather eccentric though, and so more open-minded than most, never hesitating to ask for what they wanted. The idea of living in another country seemed strange to me – I hadn't even been south of Tuscany. There were Italians living in England, especially those from the poorer regions of southern Italy – they tended to emigrate more than the rest of the population to seek out a better life. But to be so far away from my family didn't make any sense, even if I wasn't engaged to Salvatore. How could I leave Mamma, Francesca and Nonna Paola? It was good of Lady Enid to make me such an offer, but I would be staying in the Tuscan hills for the foreseeable future – there was no doubt about that whatsoever.

CHAPTER 7

JEN

It was impossible not to be engulfed by the sticky heat as I walked down the steps off the plane at Florence airport. But damn it felt good to be in Italy. The bus took me to customs to have my passport checked. I'd brought a carry-on suitcase, so I didn't have to hang around at baggage reclaim. I took a taxi from the rank, asking the driver to take me to Casa Stella at Corte Paradiso in Cintaldo. My stomach churned and it dawned on me that I was inexplicably nervous. What did I have to be nervous about? Maybe it was because the driver seemed to be approaching the exit barrier quite speedily. This was an exciting new adventure for me, but perhaps deep down I was fearing the unknown. What if I didn't like the house? And what if I found it difficult to sleep in a strange place, all alone? I had found Casa Stella on Airbnb while waiting to board the plane, and in the photos the house was rather grand and lovely. It was pink and couldn't have looked more Italian. Matteo had sent me a message to say I wouldn't need to worry about towels or bedding because everything at Casa Stella had been provided for renters. Now all of those things belonged to me.

When I'd met Nonna for coffee and pastries the morning

after Matteo turned up, I told her I'd booked my flights. She'd been so delighted, but I hadn't stayed for long because she'd come down with a sore throat overnight and it hurt to talk. When I left she'd made me promise to look for her nonna Paola's recipe book, and to send her a postcard. After that, she'd taken to her bed for the rest of the week. I'd been hoping to ask her more about the ring, since googling the superstition. And I'd wanted to ask questions about Casa Stella, but it would all become clear in time, I was sure. There was no rush. For now, I just wanted to see the house and make the most of the Tuscan sun.

At first, the driver took us on busy dual carriageways with cars and lorries teeming all around us, and we dashed in and out of tunnels – it was headache-inducing and I put on my sunglasses. There wasn't much scenery to see at first, apart from the odd glimpse of a hill with a house with a terracotta roof. But then we reached the countryside, and there before me were the beautiful luscious, green Tuscan hills. We passed fields of vines and sunflowers and olive groves, and went through the occasional village, with rows of pretty houses in lemon and terracotta and pink all huddled together. And then the road began to twist and wind uphill, and the driver slowed down to negotiate the hairpin bends. I looked out of the window and took in the view – it was truly breathtaking. If I was an artist, I would want to paint. If I was a writer, I would want to write. This scenery made me want to be creative. I was struck with the sudden urge to draw upon what I was now seeing and turn it into something beautiful – although I wasn't sure what. The car slowed as the road narrowed and steepened, and we passed more pretty houses – many of them with olive-green shutters and washing hanging from lines beneath the windows.

Inspiration continued to take hold of me as we progressed, and I found myself wanting to cook something really delicious for the first time in quite a while. As Nonna had mentioned, I did need to start thinking about finding ways to enjoy food again – both preparing and eating it.

Despite being blessed with such breathtaking views, I found myself replaying the scene in my head – almost like a cinema trailer – when Harvey had come back from work, exactly one week before our wedding day. He sat me down on the sofa, saying that we needed to talk. Distracted by all the wedding arrangements, I'd been totally caught off guard. 'I'm sorry, Jen,' he'd said. 'I just couldn't help falling in love with her – I've never met anyone like her.' My best friend, Amanda and I had grown up together. We'd attended the same schools, and stayed in touch through university. I'd asked her to be my maid of honour, excited that she would help me plan the wedding to the man of my dreams.

Harvey Mills and I had first met when he came into Da Nonna one lunchtime with a client. He was an architect, and he'd got some big new deal with a company that wanted to build new offices on the outskirts of Cambridge. He and another man in a suit were celebrating with a bottle of champagne, and an extravagant lunch, with no expense spared. Harvey wasn't your traditional man of dreams – he was quite nerdy really, and wore glasses, and his hairline was receding faster than most men of his age – but he was tall and broad and, when he made eyes at me while paying the bill, I couldn't help being drawn to him. When he asked for my number, I wrote it on the back of his receipt. He messaged me the next day, suggesting we go punting. One thing led to another – a series of romantic dates, picnics by the River Cam, on 'The Backs', under a willow tree. And we spent time in the garden at his charming cottage in Grantchester. He was older than me, in his late thirties, and he'd saved some money over the years. Admittedly, I was as much in love with the cottage as I was with him, and couldn't wait to live there permanently.

We'd had the most wonderful summer, last summer. When

autumn came, and the leaves on the trees began to turn on Jesus Green, I found myself dropping hints about whether we might get married. We were spending every spare moment together, and I stayed at his most of the time. But also, Mum kept saying that we should get married now I was approaching thirty – it was time to settle down, she'd tell me over and over again. After a few discussions, he took me to Paris and proposed in front of the Louvre. Mum and Dad had been saving some money to put towards my wedding, and, with a generous contribution from Harvey, we booked Healey Manor as our venue. Mum wanted to invite all of our family and friends, which already made the numbers quite big even before we added any of Harvey's family and friends. We chose Lake Como as the location for our honeymoon, and I'd been swept up into the excitement of becoming a bride.

A few months later, during that week between Christmas and New Year, Amanda came up from London with her boyfriend, Jeff, to stay with us in Grantchester for a couple of days. She'd always been the kind of woman who attracted admiring glances wherever she went – with long blonde hair and piercing blue eyes. She was a big flirt too. But I never thought she'd make a move on any man of mine. Amanda and Jeff stayed for a couple of nights before going on to her parents for the rest of the Christmas period. Although she and Harvey seemed to get on well, I hadn't noticed the beginnings of something forming between them. She'd recently set up a handmade jewellery business that she referred to as her side hustle. When she complained about having hardly any followers for her new Instagram account, Harvey had got out his phone and followed her instantly while they were chatting at the kitchen island. 'Just to be supportive,' he'd said. On reflection, I guessed that was the start of them communicating with each other in private – over direct message. Harvey often travelled to London on business, and, as Amanda lived alone, they no doubt began to have secret meet-ups in the new year. I noticed he liked every single one of her Instagram posts, without fail, including the ones of herself posing with pouty lips. The first time I'd seen his name under one of her posts, I let out a jealous groan. But I'd brushed it off as my fiancé being nice to my best friend. In hindsight I should have listened to my intuition – it had been a huge red flag staring me right in the face.

So, when he told me that he was in love with her, a week before our wedding day, I found myself thinking back to when she'd first visited the cottage in Grantchester. The glances they exchanged, her giggling at his funny stories and giving his arm an affectionate squeeze. The two of them going off to the petrol station together to get supplies when we ran out of wine. She just *had* to pay, and he insisted on driving her there. I didn't think anything of them going on a short car journey together, but they were gone a long time. They came back saying, 'Oh we had to try a few petrol stations as none of them had that rosé you like, Jen.' As if it was all my fault that they'd fancied each other. Who knew what conversations they had on that car journey? What a fool I'd been.

Nonna had never been a fan of Amanda.

'Keep that girl away from any man you're in love with, cara,' she'd told me once.

I replied, 'Nonna, don't be so ridiculous. She's my best friend. She'd never betray me like that.'

Nonna wagged a finger at me.

'Mah, as you wish, but don't say I didn't warn you. Nonnas know these things.'

I hadn't given this another thought until recently. After Amanda went on to betray me, Nonna didn't say, 'I told you so.' She'd never do that. Instead, she said, 'We have to make mistakes to find our way.'

At the time, those words had washed over me. But as the weeks passed, they began to resonate. If I had kept Amanda away from Harvey, he probably would have cheated on me after we were married anyway. We'd lost the deposit for Healey Manor, and he ended up taking Amanda to Lake Como instead of me. She'd actually gone on *my* honeymoon. And had the nerve to post photos of the pair of them on Instagram. I should have blocked her so the photos didn't show up in my feed, but I felt some ridiculous urge to see them. How could I not take a peek? Even though seeing them made me feel physically sick.

And how did she deliver the news that she'd run off with my fiancé? Silence. Not one text or phone call. She didn't feel the need to apologise for stealing my future husband. How dare she! But now a few months had passed, my anger had turned into sadness. I'd spent enough time wallowing in self-pity. Nonna was right – it was time to move on. Being in Italy would give me a chance to re-evaluate my life before my milestone birthday arrived in November.

We passed through the village of Cintaldo – with a bakery, butcher and all the usual shops; a bar called Bar Tosca with people sitting outside with coffees and glasses of beer, vaping and smoking cigarettes. And there was a pizzeria tucked down a side street – Pizzeria Spera. I loved Italian pizza, stone baked with a thin, crispy crust. We went up a narrow and bumpy lane with cypress trees on either side, and beyond, through the gaps, I could see fields – of sunflowers on my right and vines on the left. And then a grand pink house came into view, just like in the photo. A sign said Corte Paradiso, and underneath, Casa Stella and Casa Luna, meaning star and moon. The driver took us round the back of the house – and there were two generously sized gardens with a white picket fence running in between them. On one side, a pool, crystal blue, glistened in the sun. It looked so inviting, and I couldn't wait to take Matteo up on his offer of using it. I hadn't done much exercise recently, apart from cycling to and from Da Nonna and waitressing. The last time I'd been swimming was in the sea at my grandparents' house in Riccione the previous summer.

The driver pulled up, and I paid him in euros. He lifted my suitcase out of the boot and placed it down on the gravel drive. I thanked him, and he got back into the car and whizzed off, bumping up and down on the narrow lane. I looked around me and breathed a happy sigh. Here I was, in the middle of the Tuscan countryside. A sense of calm swept over me. Was this house really mine? It didn't seem believable. I approached the door with the sign CASA STELLA and saw the small terracotta pot that Matteo had mentioned in his message. I bent down and breathed in the sweet scent of basil leaves – this herb was Italy to me. All of a sudden, I felt the urge to make pesto. Perhaps I would do that while I was here.

I lifted up the terracotta pot and there were the keys to Casa Stella. I unlocked the door, and wheeled my case inside and left it there in the hall. I took off my sandals. The terracotta tiles were refreshingly cool beneath my bare feet. The house had a slightly musty smell – understandable as it hadn't been occupied for a few weeks. Matteo had told me the previous tenants had left at the end of July. Out of respect for Francesca, he'd cancelled any subsequent bookings. Through the door from the hallway there was a vast living room with views of the back garden and French doors, leading to a terrace with table and chairs, and a veranda covered in hot-pink bougainvillea. The thought of sitting there in the evening with a glass of wine and a board of antipasti made me smile. Next door, at Casa Luna, there was a similar terrace, and a barbecue made from bricks. Both terraces were filled with terracotta pots bursting with bright flowers, and it was all so pretty, especially with the undulating hills below, dotted with cypress trees and vineyards and grand-looking houses in the distance. I had certainly landed on my feet!

I went through the door to a kitchen, where part of the wall was cut out, bringing in light from the vast windows in the living room. The kitchen, from what I could see, had all the usual pots and pans and utensils hanging from hooks on the wall, adding to the rustic feel. An old wooden table and four chairs took up the centre of the room. I went to explore upstairs. The walls were white, and filled with paintings of Tuscan scenes and portraits. The master bedroom had cherubs painted on the ceiling and a big glass chandelier. On the dressing table were a few black-and-white photos in frames. I studied them briefly – a couple on their wedding day, two young girls, three women. I imagined that this was Nonna's family, and that she was one of the girls. Through the tall windows, I could see the garden, and beyond were yet more jaw-dropping views of the countryside. I stopped to breathe and take it all in, smiling to myself, before exploring the rest of the floor. There were three other bedrooms, and I thought of the friends I could invite to stay – what fun we would have! The bathroom had a roll-top bath that I could picture myself soaking in. At the top of the stairs was a cupboard, and, curious, I went to open it. But it was locked. Oh, I wondered what was inside. And where was the key? I would ask Matteo. The recipe book could be in there, and possibly clues about why Nonna had fallen out with Francesca. I was determined to find something before returning to Cambridge, in order to solve the mystery connected to the ring.

I opened the master bedroom window to bring in some fresh air, and went back downstairs. It struck me that there wouldn't be any food or drink in the house. I'd have to go into the village and get supplies before the shops closed. But when I went into the kitchen and opened the fridge, there was a carton of milk, bottles of water, a punnet of strawberries, a block of cheese, a small salami, a pot of olives. On the worktop was a basket filled with a loaf of bread, olive oil, balsamic vinegar, and beside it a bottle of Chianti. And then a fruit bowl, filled with giant peaches, tomatoes, still on the vine, a cantaloupe melon and a few figs. Wow, Matteo had thought of everything!

When he returned from filming in Siena that evening, I hoped we might have a glass of wine together on one of our terraces. In the meantime, I would shower and change out of the jeans and top I'd been travelling in. I carried my case upstairs, and then, as promised, I took out my phone and called Nonna. There was no answer. I left her a voicemail to say I'd arrived, and that the house was just wonderful! I would look for the recipe book, and remember to send her that postcard too.

When I'd showered and changed into a pale-blue summer dress with spaghetti straps, I went downstairs and opened the bottle of Chianti. I half-filled a glass and put together a few items from the fridge on a plate with a slice of the bread on the side. I opened the French doors, took everything outside to the table, and sat myself down. It was time to just breathe and take in the view. There were so many photo opportunities, I had to snap some for my Instagram story. I smiled to myself, glad to have some interesting content to share at last. It did feel a little like showing off, but everyone else posted photos of their holidays all the time. If Harvey saw the photos, he might be curious to know what I was doing in such a grand house in Tuscany. 'I still care about you a great deal, Jen – I'm still interested in your life,' he'd said when I messaged him to ask why he was still viewing my Instagram stories, and even going as far as liking them by pressing the little heart. I hadn't blocked him because a small part of me wanted him to know what I was up to. Perhaps he'd grown tired of Amanda flirting with every man in sight already, and realised he would have been better off with me. Well, too late, Harvey.

I sat there on the terrace, savouring each sip of the Chianti, which was warm and rich, feeling pretty content. Casa Stella had a calming effect on me and my mind began to wander. My thoughts were interrupted by the crunching of tyres on the gravel drive. I looked sideways and there he was at the wheel of the approaching car. Matteo Bianchi, a pair of sunglasses on his nose. He was exactly as I remembered him, but cooler. He lifted a hand and waved. I raised my glass and grinned in return.

He switched off the ignition and got out, pushing the sunglasses up onto his head.

'Ciao, Jen,' he said, cheerily, as if we were old friends. He went to the boot and lifted out a large brown paper bag, filled to the brim, a bottle of wine sticking out of the top. 'You like steak?'

I nodded and smiled. 'Yes.'

'Good because I picked up the best bistecca you will ever have in your life.'

I liked his enthusiasm – what a cheerful demeanour he had. He approached, put the bag on the table and leant down to double-kiss me. Ah yes, the Italian double kiss, always an icebreaker when you barely knew someone. There it was again, that cologne... oh yes, citrus, possibly bergamot, like when we'd first met – whatever it was, he smelt good.

'Tutto bene?' he said.

'Yes, thank you so much for leaving the food and wine in the kitchen. I have made myself at home, as you can see.'

'Brava. Right, I must go and shower, and then you help me cook?'

Cooking with Matteo might be fun. And afterwards, I'd have someone to eat with too. I actually relished the thought of sitting at a table with him. Here I was, at the beginning of a new era in my life, with all these wonderful, fresh ingredients around me and a stunning setting too. How could I not be inspired?

I nodded. 'Of course.'

He unlocked his door, said, 'Great. See you soon, Jen,' and then he disappeared inside.

A warm feeling enveloped me. I picked up my glass of wine, and raised it to my Tuscan adventure before taking a sip. I mustn't forget to quiz Matteo about Francesca, to see if he knew any more about why she and Nonna had fallen out. Could he tell me anything else about the opal ring? With any luck, he might know something. And I needed to ask if he had a key to the locked cupboard too. But also, I wanted to enjoy my first evening in Tuscany... and spend it talking and getting to know each other with good food and wine.

CHAPTER 8

LILIANA

4 AUGUST 1944

Life went on without Salvatore once again, and oh how I missed him. A few weeks passed, and one evening, after cycling back from Castello dell'Uva, I entered Casa Stella to find Mamma and Nonna at the kitchen table, drinking coffee, made in the silver moka pot on the stove. Before them on the table was a plate of bruschetta – slices of chargrilled bread rubbed with a clove of garlic that was then sliced and chopped up with tomatoes and added as a topping. This was all drizzled with olive oil, and a basil leaf added as a garnish, finished off with a pinch of salt and a twist of pepper. I did like to eat bruschetta – a simple and frugal snack.

I joined them at the table, and poured myself an espresso.

'We have good news,' Mamma said.

'Oh, what is it?' I said.

'Florence has been liberated today.'

'What? Oh, that's wonderful!' I said, registering what this meant for me. Salvatore would return soon, and we could get married at last.

'Tonight, we celebrate,' Nonna said. 'We shall drink the grappa I have been saving for such an occasion. And we have a couple of bottles of Montepulciano d'Abruzzo. Salvatore's mamma told me he will return tomorrow. We shall have a big celebration together – the two families once again united.'

After Salvatore and I were married and living at Oliviera Santa Chiara, would Mamma, Nonna and Francesca return to the pensione and host boarders once again? Our neighbour there, Signor Fumi, had written to say our pensione had been commandeered by the Tedeschi – we dreaded to think what state the place would be in. Mamma couldn't bear the thought of her beloved home being taken over by Nazis. The thought of them living in our home – and what might have occurred there during those late wartime years – was unsettling. If Papa had still been alive, he would have gone to Florence to do a recce. If any work needed to be done to repair our beloved pensione that had been hosting boarders since 1850, he would have made the necessary arrangements. After some discussion, we decided it would be wise to allow the dust to settle before going back to check on our home. In the meantime, Mamma would ask Signor Fumi to take a look at the pensione on our behalf. There was no hurry because who would want to visit Florence as a tourist while it was in such a state of disrepair? It would take time to rebuild our beloved city – and still it would never be the city it had once been. The Tedeschi had destroyed bridges crossing the River Arno as they retreated, although I was relieved to hear they'd spared the Ponte Vecchio. I expected tourists would be scarce for some time yet. Which begged the question, should we keep the pensione, or sell it so Mamma, Nonna and Francesca could live off the proceeds? But would anyone actually want to buy it?

'Surely, Salvatore will come back for good now?' Mamma said. 'And then at long last you can get married.'

I hoped she was right.

The following day, Salvatore came back to Cintaldo. He walked to Casa Stella from Oliviera Santa Chiara, for he'd been there first to see his mamma, and to wash and change his clothes. They would be filthy from being worn for weeks on end in caves and in the woods while fighting. His face was clean-shaven and he smelt of cologne. Presumably, he'd just removed a thick beard, grown while he was away. There had been a storm that afternoon, bringing out the woody scent of the cypress trees nearby, and the pungency of the earth. I was sitting on the terrazza, shelling cannellini beans. During the war, we would get a lot of our nutrients from these white kidney beans as they were full of fibre, protein and carbohydrates, giving us energy. That afternoon, Mamma would stew them in a big pot on the stove with onion, garlic, oregano, olive oil and tomatoes. Some of the beans would be dried and stored throughout the winter. Usually, we would keep supplies in the larder – salami, Parma ham, preserves and so on. During the war, though, we had got into the habit of hiding items we didn't want the Tedeschi to take from us. Now and again, soldiers would knock on the door and make demands. We would have to give them something to make them go away. One time they took our chickens and we lived without eggs for weeks until Signor Conti from the fattoria was kind enough to give us two of his chicks.

When I heard the creak of the gate, I dropped the pod I was holding into the bowl on the table. I raced to the path that ran down the side of the house, and leapt into my fiancé's arms. He lifted me up and carried me to the terrazza, where he swung me around, and then he lowered me so that I was standing on the paved stones in my bare feet and leant in and kissed me on the lips. It was a kiss so very sublime that butterflies danced in the pit of my stomach. My amore was finally home, and now we could be together once and for all. I had a wedding to plan!

'Is Florence free at last, amore mio?' I said.

His face split into a huge smile, his eyes twinkling.

'Yes, my darling, it is.'

He removed his flat cap and put it on the table, before sitting down.

'Can I get you an aperitivo? We saved some grappa from last night.'

'Certo, grazie, carina.'

I went into the house and brought back two small glasses of grappa, and we clinked and said, 'Cin cin.' Mamma, Nonna and Francesca were in the kitchen, preparing dinner and chatting away. They were being considerate leaving me to have a little time alone with my amore.

'Well done, my hero,' I said. 'I am so glad to have you back.'

'I am happy to see you,' he said, downing the grappa. He took a packet of cigarettes out of the pocket of his waistcoat, placed one in his mouth and struck it with a match. He proffered the packet across the table, but I shook my head. He leant back in his chair, and drew on his cigarette, and exhaled a cloud of smoke along with a big sigh. 'But I am tired, so very tired.'

'Well, tonight you must get plenty of rest at the oliviera, and then, tomorrow, we celebrate your return! Mamma and Nonna will be so glad that you are back safely – they have been worrying about what might happen to you, hiding in woods and caves, and doing such brave things.'

Salvatore continued to puff on his cigarette, his eyes glazing over as if he were deep in thought, or was he just falling asleep because he was so very exhausted? It must be strange for him to be home after having to survive out there for so long, and in such dangerous circumstances, with the risk of being shot if the

Tedeschi found out he was helping Allied soldiers to reach safety. He didn't respond to what I'd said – he seemed like a different person, so affected by what he'd lived through, no doubt. I told myself he would be all right after some rest, a hearty meal and a night in his own bed.

'So now you're home, I'll ask Mamma to speak to Padre Luca at Chiesa Santa Maria. I shall wear her white lace bridal gown – the one she married Papa in all those years ago.' I was rambling, but I couldn't help it. He continued to puff on his cigarette while studying his fingernails. I noticed that they were dirty underneath. 'We can plan a traditional menu of several courses – we'll do our best to get the ingredients we need. And we must compile a guest list. All of this is so exciting!' I added, clapping my hands together.

Salvatore looked across the table at me, but his eyes did not reflect my excitement about our impending nuptials. Instead, they displayed no emotion whatsoever. He sucked air through his teeth. Did he no longer wish to get married? Leaning forward, he stubbed out his cigarette in the ashtray on the table, squashing it until the butt no longer glowed.

'What is it, caro? Tell me,' I said.

He pulled his chair closer, rested his elbows on the table and scratched his nose.

'Florence has been liberated, Liliana, but the Tedeschi are still holding on to northern Italy. The war isn't over yet.'

'Yes, but it is for us, isn't it?'

He shook his head.

'I have to carry on, until all of Italy is free. I cannot rest until the war is officially over in the whole country.'

'But... I was so glad to have you home safe and sound. What, now you're saying you want to go back out there and risk losing your life again? Haven't you done enough?'

'No, Liliana, I haven't. Not yet. I must carry on.'

'You can be so proud of what you've achieved already – helping to liberate parts of Tuscany, and now our dear city of Florence. What does your mamma think?'

'She thinks I am pazzo, of course.'

Of course she would think her son was mad, when he had already managed to survive for all this time. What was he thinking, carrying on when he no longer needed to? He had played his part in liberating the areas of Tuscany that mattered to us.

'But still, not even she can stop you?'

'Like you, Mamma was delighted to see me when I came to the oliviera early this morning. She wanted to have a big celebration tonight, to prepare a veritable feast and invite our neighbours – to sit out on the terrazza under the stars. She has been putting things aside for such a long time, for this day when I return. Her face dropped when I told her that I will go back and continue to fight until we are completely done.'

'I don't know what to say,' I said, quietly, looking down at the table. For I couldn't meet his gaze. He had lifted me up, and now he was bringing down again. At least before he'd returned, I had been living with the hope that he would come back to me soon. I'd rather he had stayed away until he was completely done with it all. 'And so you leave me once again...' I eventually said, my voice trailing off.

His only response was to drum his fingers on the table while staring into space. Although I was trying to understand his need to finish saving his country, our country, I had sensed that he was being less affectionate, perhaps a little more distant. I put this down to all the time we'd spent apart from each other. It was difficult to remain close to someone when you barely saw them. I hadn't even been able to write him letters because there was nowhere to send them. I blamed his changed demeanour on everything he'd been through, and nothing more. I twisted the opal ring on my finger, a symbol of our love and commitment to each other. I had long forgotten Nonna's superstition – it didn't make a difference to anything. He had survived the war so far, hadn't he? Longer than Papa, and Mamma had never worn a supposedly unlucky engagement ring.

I broke the silence. 'You do still want to marry me don't you, Salvatore?'

He nodded and tipped his head to one side. 'Of course I do, my darling Liliana. You know how much I love you, and your cooking – no one cooks like you. To have you as my wife, I long for that time.'

I would have liked to think he loved me for more than the food I could prepare for him. Did he look forward to the time we would spend together, to the conversations we would have, to making love to me? But he was clearly exhausted, and I must be grateful that he'd come to Casa Stella to see me. He could have just gone straight to bed and slept. Who knew when he'd last slept for more than a snatched hour here and there? And in an actual bed.

'Well, I shall continue to pray for you every morning and night. And I'll go to Chiesa Santa Maria as often as I can. I can still compile a list of wedding guests, and Mamma can make the cake if we're able to find all the ingredients.'

'There's no harm in doing that, I suppose – if it makes you feel better.'

'I think it will help me to cope with your absence. How long do you think it will take before this war ends?'

'A few months... I'm sure we'll be more or less finished by Christmas. And then I shall come back to you for good.'

How I longed for that day to arrive, but for now I would try my best to be patient.

'So, are you leaving tonight then?'

He nodded, ruefully. 'I am now working with the British army. They will come to pick me up after dark.'

He took another cigarette out of the packet and lit it. I studied him smoking across the table from me and thought if only he loved me as much as his beloved cigarettes. He didn't seem to be able to live without them, and got through as many as he could in a day. But I supposed it was his way of surviving, of suppressing the pain of what he was living through.

I twisted the opal ring once again, a habit I'd developed since he'd given it to me. When I touched it, I felt as though I was with him, wherever he was. If only he had a ring on his finger to remind him of me when he was away. And then it struck me. I knew exactly what I was going to buy him as a Christmas present. I would try to find him a cigarette case. Perhaps they'd have one in a shop in San Gimignano. I could get it engraved with his initials – SR for Salvatore Ricci – because then at least I would always be with him. Not on his finger but in his pocket, at least. And that was better than nothing.

I sighed. 'Your mamma told me about this grand celebration she wanted to have. But alas, we shall have to wait... and I could have prepared your favourite tart with fresh figs from the tree in the garden too.'

'The one with almonds?'

I nodded.

His face dropped. 'You know that tart is one of my favourites of all the desserts you make.'

He pushed his chair back from the table and stood up, fastened his waistcoat, and then raised his chin, as if he were composing himself in an attempt to override the emotions raging through him.

'Let me at least walk back to the oliviera with you,' I said.

He looked at his watch. 'I have time for a walk in the field behind Casa Stella instead, if you do.'

I reached under the table for my shoes and put them on.

'Of course I do. The cannellini beans can wait.'

He smiled faintly, and took my hand in his. We walked along the path that ran along the side of the house, and then he opened the gate that led into the field. There we spent a precious hour together, before he returned me to the doorstep of Casa Stella. We embraced, and he kissed me on the lips, and said, 'Ti voglio bene, Liliana.' I said the same to him, for we did love each other, and we would be together eventually – I had to believe it. Because how else could I get up in the morning?

CHAPTER 9

JEN

Half an hour or so later, Matteo came out of his front door. He'd changed into another pair of shorts and a white polo shirt that enhanced his tan. He pulled up a chair, next to mine, facing the view. Then he picked up the bottle of Chianti and half-filled his glass, before topping up mine.

'So, what do you think of Casa Stella?' he said.

'I like it, very much. How could I not?'

'This is true. How could you not be blown away by this beautiful pink house in the Tuscan hills?'

'I'm grateful to my great-aunt for choosing me to pass it on to. How long did you know Francesca for?' I asked.

He sat back in his chair and crossed one leg over the other. 'My family, the Bianchi family, has known your grandmother's family, the Magginis, for many years.'

Nonna's maiden name had been Maggini, but when she married my grandfather her surname became Farina. My full name was Jen Farina, or Ginevra Farina officially. No one ever called me Ginevra though, apart from Nonna and my parents sometimes. When I'd started school, everyone kept getting

Ginevra wrong, mispronouncing and misspelling it – both teachers and pupils – and so I'd decided that I was going to call myself Jen instead. My parents had reluctantly agreed, even though they would have preferred me to use the Italian name they'd so carefully chosen.

'Your grandparents grew up with my nonna, didn't they? I remember you mentioning this in Cambridge.'

'Yes, your nonna and Francesca used to play here in these gardens as children with my grandfather, Paolo, and my great-aunt, Nicoletta. And our great-grandfathers were friends when they lived in Florence. They bought Corte Paradiso together as a holiday home, and divided the original house into two.'

'When was that?'

'Between the wars, I believe.'

'And now here we are, descended from those families, sharing a bottle of wine – and these houses have seen so much history, no doubt.'

'During the war, both families left Florence once Italy changed sides and came here to live. They shared produce from their gardens, and kept small farm animals between them. Both of our great-grandfathers helped allied prisoners of war after the downfall of Mussolini.'

'Yes, weren't our great-grandfathers killed for helping a British fighter pilot?' Nonna had told me this.

Matteo nodded, wistfully. 'They were very brave – yes, our great-grandmothers were widowed at the same time. It would have been devastating for them both.'

I thought about Nonna, losing her father so suddenly under such horrific circumstances, and well before his time.

'It must have been really hard for both families.'

He went on. 'I have read a great deal about the war. There were eighty thousand POWs released from camps – some of those men were taken on trains to Germany, and they jumped from the trains and hid in the countryside. Others in the north made their way to Switzerland with the help of Italian civilians and partisans. Some made their way to what was called the Gustav Line, which ran south of Rome across Italy. Below that line, Allied soldiers had already taken Italy back from the Germans.'

'What a frightening time to live through.'

'And Italy was bombed from above too by the Allies – many civilians lost their lives this way. But still many of them helped the Allies on the ground to reach places of safety, and to sabotage the Germans as well.'

'I know my nonna went to Cambridge when the war ended. I'm not sure why she stayed, though – perhaps because she met my nonno Giulio.'

'I guess you'll have to ask her.'

'She seems very sad about the falling-out with her sister. I don't know what on earth it was about.'

Matteo shrugged. 'It could be anything.'

'It's related to that ring, I'm sure of it. But I don't know what the story is. I found out when googling...' I told him what I'd discovered about the superstition with opal engagement rings and October.

'Oh, that is interesting. I haven't heard that one before.'

'Neither had I. I think my nonna was given the ring when she got engaged to someone. Then presumably he was killed in the war. Perhaps she left it in Tuscany because she couldn't bear to wear it anymore. But still, this doesn't explain why she fell out with Francesca.'

'It's a mystery,' Matteo said, taking a sip of his wine.

'Oh, I meant to ask if you have the key to a locked cupboard in Casa Stella?'

'I can take a look. Whereabouts is the cupboard?'

'At the top of the stairs.'

'Ah yes, Francesca wanted that cupboard to be locked when

she rented the house out, but I'm not sure what happened to the key. If I can't find it, we can always break into the cupboard together.'

'Thanks, well, if you don't find the key we'll have to do that, I guess!'

'And what about you, Jen?' he said. 'Your family is Italian, but they didn't give you an Italian name?'

'Oh yes, my real name is Ginevra, but I haven't used it since I was small. I got tired of everyone getting it wrong. In the end I told my parents I wanted to be called Jen, short for the English equivalent, Jennifer. They reluctantly agreed.'

'And how long have you been working at the restaurant?'

'Only a few months. I had my own business that failed, sadly, so my family suggested I work at Da Nonna until I got back on my feet.'

'Oh, I'm sorry to hear that. What business did you have?'

'A cupcake business – you know those little cakes with swirled icing on top.' I explained, seeing as they weren't really a thing in Italy. 'There was a real demand for them for a while. Now people seem to want pastries instead – cinnamon swirls and buns.'

'Couldn't you make those too?'

'I considered it, but to be honest the whole stress of running a business by myself' – I didn't add while also planning a wedding that then didn't even happen – 'and trying to find customers became too much, especially after...'

'After what?'

No, I wasn't sure whether I wanted him to know about Harvey. It was embarrassing having your fiancé run off with your best friend. I played with the stem of my wine glass.

'Okay, I think you are not ready to tell me – but whatever it was, it doesn't sound good for you, and I'm sorry if you are sad.'

I smiled, appreciating his concern for my welfare. If we got to know each other better, perhaps I'd tell him.

'No, it wasn't at all a good time for me, but I'm okay. At least, I will be...'

He picked up the bottle of wine and topped up my glass.

'Of course you will be. Because now you are here. Italy will revive you, I guarantee it. Being here at this house will be like recharging yourself to one hundred per cent. Like a phone.'

I chuckled at his analogy. Lately, I felt as though I'd been operating at only half of that, maybe less.

'Do you really think so?'

'I know so. Everyone who stays at Casa Stella tells me what an incredible time they had – guests never wanted to leave. Sometimes they would ask to extend their stay, or they'd rebook as soon as they got home. I have a feeling you might not want to leave either.'

'Hmm, I do have to fly back on Friday for an event at Da Nonna at the weekend, but I can always return.'

'You must – come back and enjoy the rest of August. It costs virtually nothing to live here. Look at the garden – abundant with lettuces and tomatoes and all kinds of vegetables. At the moment, there are figs and plums growing on the trees. Soon we shall have apples. You like to cook?'

'I do, but I haven't done much of that recently.'

'Well, now is the time to begin again then.'

He uncrossed his legs. 'And you can start by going into the garden and finding a beautiful lettuga and a lovely ripe pomodoro so you can make a delicious salad to go with our steaks. I dug up some potatoes yesterday so we can have home-made fries with our bistecca too.'

My mouth watered at the thought of steak and chips and a fresh salad on the side.

'That sounds absolutely delicious.'

'Okay, off you go then, and I'll see you in my kitchen.'

He was being quite bossy, but actually I didn't mind

someone else doing the thinking for a change. Especially if it meant I'd end up with a lovely dinner.

Matteo picked up his glass and made his way towards the door to Casa Luna. I watched him go. I liked that he was so positive and full of energy. His English was certainly good enough for us to communicate properly, but it wouldn't do me any harm to brush up on my Italian. A tap on his kitchen window made me jump – he was waving at me to go into the garden, and then he came to the back door, holding a frying pan.

'Off you go to pick our salad... Ginevra,' he said with a wink.

I laughed and pushed my chair back from the table. I didn't mind someone using my actual name when they pronounced it correctly. The 'r' had rolled off his tongue so beautifully. Rolling Rs was a skill. I thought back to when Nonna had sat with me in the kitchen one day when we'd been making orecchiette, telling me to repeat the letter 'R' over and over again, until I got it right. 'If you're going to speak Italian, you need to do it properly,' she'd said, and then, 'Who ever heard of an Italian who couldn't roll their Rs?' Dear Nonna – she had taught me so much over the years.

I made my way towards Matteo's garden and stepped onto the round paving stones pressed into the grass, passing a lavender bush brimming with bees and butterflies. On my right was the swimming pool, glistening in the evening sun. I couldn't wait to take a dip when I had a spare moment, and to sunbathe on one of the loungers that looked so inviting. Cicadas chirruped all around me. The sun was still warm on my face, even so late in the day, and I studied the rolling hills with roads that twisted and wound in between. There was even a castle in the distance, complete with turrets, surrounded by cypress trees. It was a scene from a fairytale. I headed for the vegetable patch at the end and searched for the lettuces. And then I found a row of the kind with frilly leaves, all so perfectly lined up, and I squatted to pick one that was just large enough for the two of us without any going to waste. Then I found a giant red tomato, lifted it to my nose and breathed in its scent – that smell of a tomato on a vine always so reminiscent of Italy. And I just knew it would be perfectly sweet from the sun. This was going to be the best dinner, and I couldn't wait to get to know Matteo some more.

CHAPTER 10

LILIANA

The weeks passed and autumn came. The leaves on the trees turned a golden yellow and red and brown and fell to the ground. September was usually the time of year when grapes were picked in the vineyards all around us – but the war had brought winegrowers to their knees. Many had halted production. The end-of-summer thunderstorms had brought wind and heavy rain and fork lightning that lit up the sky. And then the temperature dropped. The chill in the air was a relief for us all after months of thick heat that wrapped itself around you like a blanket. Still, we were fortunate that it had been cooler in the Tuscan hills than in Florence.

Before the war, our family and the Bianchis next door had spent the period from Ferragosto – the public holiday on 15 August – to the beginning of September at Casa Stella every summer. Papa would put up a sign saying COMPLETO in the window of our pensione, and then we'd cram our belongings into the car, and make our way along the winding road up into the hills, leaving behind the sticky air. In the countryside, we would savour the cooler temperatures, and la vita lenta, where life moved more slowly. We would spend hours sitting at the table on the terrazza at Casa Stella eating as a famiglia. Extended family would join us for some of that time too, as well as the Bianchis and friends made in the village, such as the Riccis. Everyone was welcome with our Italian culture of convivialità – food was to be shared, and we celebrated the joy of togetherness and good conversation. I missed those days. Mamma, Nonna Paola, Francesca and I still always sat together at mealtimes but hosting large groups at our table had become rare. Our engagement celebration was the only time in recent memory.

Autumn turned into winter and with it came the north wind, the tramontana. And there were long cold dark nights to endure. We had resorted to using olive kernels to light our fire, as well as our small ration of lignite and any fallen branches and twigs that we might find. Every day, I prayed for Salvatore to come back to me. In the morning after waking up and last thing at night – kneeling on the floor with my hands pressed together, elbows resting on the bed. How would he survive out there in sub-zero temperatures? What was he eating, and how was he staying warm? I hoped that some kind Italian civilians had taken it upon themselves to help him and fellow partisans by providing them with shelter and food. Without such help, I couldn't imagine that he would stand any chance of surviving. And that was without the Tedeschi capturing him.

As Christmas approached, there was word, sent via a message from his partisan friends in the area, that Salvatore would return for the special Cena di Vigilia on Christmas Eve when we would eat fish – it was tradition in Italy to celebrate this way – and then everyone would attend midnight Mass together at the Chiesa Santa Maria. I was so pleased to have found a second-hand cigarette case at a bric-a-brac shop in San Gimignano. I had siphoned off a little money each week from my wages in order to pay for it, and I'd had it engraved with Salvatore's initials. I wouldn't be giving Mamma, Nonna or Francesca a gift this year – we'd all agreed that being alive and together was more than enough. But I had really wanted to buy something for the man I loved.

On Christmas Eve, Salvatore's family, the Riccis, invited us to Oliviera Santa Chiara, and Nonna and I spent the day in the kitchen making a panforte – a rich fruit cake from our region, packed with almonds and hazelnuts and candied citrus, all held together with honey and sugar and flavoured with cinnamon – to take with us. We had been conserving orange and lemon peel, almonds and hazelnuts over the past few months. It was a pity that we could not eat baccalà, salt cod, as there were no imports from Norway during the war. Instead, we had to make do with tins of sardines, which we stuffed with breadcrumbs and herbs, and anchovies to make a sauce to go with spaghetti. When we arrived at the oliviera, I offered to help prepare dinner as there was plenty to do.

I was in the kitchen, wearing an apron, the sleeves of my dress rolled up, when Salvatore came through the back door, all bedraggled. At first, I had to do a double-take. Was it really him? His hair was long and straggly, and it looked as though it hadn't been washed in weeks, months even. A thick, dark beard covered his face. His eyes had deep bags underneath, and he had certainly gained a few lines around them during his time away. His shoulders were hunched, and he appeared to be utterly exhausted, both physically and mentally. How I hated to see my fidanzato like this! He could barely get two words out of his mouth. His mamma went up to him, and so did I. We were both competing for his attention – but it was only right that she should get to embrace him first, as he was her son, after all. She ranked more highly than me, at least until we were married. And perhaps after we were married too, from what I'd seen with other sons and their mammas, who refused to let them belong to their wives instead of them. Some mothers-in-law did their best to meddle and get involved with the marriage, almost as if they didn't want it to be a successful union. How I hoped that Salvatore's mamma would not be this kind of mother-in-law to me. Although this was the least of my worries! We needed to actually get married in the first place.

After his mother had embraced him, and he'd shaken hands with his father, he looked at me, and nodded and smiled, and I ran into his arms. He smelt of mud and sweat and tobacco, but I didn't care about any of this. He pulled me to him tightly. Oh how I loved him, my Salvatore. And now he was back home safe and sound, at long last.

'Go and wash and change into clean clothes, Toto, and then come down and we shall drink an aperitivo to celebrate your return,' his mamma said.

He approached the staircase, and rested his hand on the banister. As he trudged up the stairs, it was as if he didn't have the strength to do so without holding on to something for support. My amore seemed to be decades older than he actually was. Watching him, I swallowed. It was so hard to see him like this, but I was sure that in time he would regain his strength.

When Salvatore came back downstairs, he looked like a different man. He'd shaved off his beard, and washed his thick, dark hair, that he kept off his face with a little gel. He wore a white shirt, undone a few buttons at the collar, to show his cross on a gold chain – he never took this off. The white shirt enhanced his olive skin, still bronzed by the summer sun. I was at the stove, stirring a pan of sugo di pomodoro, when he came up behind me, and put his arms around my waist. He pulled me to him, nuzzled my neck, and I could smell the scent of his cologne – oaky, musky – it was familiar to me. It was *his* scent.

'I am so glad to have you back for good, at long last,' I said, turning round to face him.

But his face dropped, telling me that this wasn't the case.

He was going to leave me again, risking his life once more. Would I ever get to marry the man I loved? Would he even survive the remainder of the war?

'You're leaving me again, aren't you?' I said, looking up at him.

He nodded. 'Yes, carina, I'm afraid I am.'

'When?'

'Tomorrow.'

Oh Madonna. I let out a sigh, and tightened the strings on my apron. We would just have to make the most of the time we had. I raised my chin, and pushed my shoulders back.

'So, soon we eat, and after, maybe, we tell everyone we're going to midnight Mass, but instead we go for a walk together in the moonlight?' I said.

'As you wish, carina.'

When dinner was ready, a little while later, we all sat down at the table. Salvatore and I, and both sets of parents and siblings. Although Salvatore and I weren't yet married, our families had already more or less become one. It warmed my heart to be sitting at this table together on Christmas Eve, sharing food that Salvatore's mamma and I had prepared.

The centre was decorated with candles and jars of holly and ivy. Bottles of Chianti had been opened to breathe. We'd put out the plates of stuffed sardines as antipasti.

Salvatore's mamma asked us all to be quiet, and she closed her eyes, and said grace, and then his papa clinked a wine glass with a fork.

'I would like to welcome my son, Salvatore, back to the oliviera. He has informed me that he will go away again tomorrow, but next time he returns it will be for good. Cin cin to that.'

'Cin cin,' we all said in unison, raising our glasses and clinking each other's, locking eyes, and smiling and not missing out one person at the table – for it was seen as bad luck to do so. I couldn't reach Salvatore's youngest brother, Pio, right at the end of the table, and I hoped to get away with leaving it.

But his mamma looked over at me.

'Liliana, don't forget to clink glasses with every person at the table. Otherwise, it is bad luck,' she said. I stood up and followed her instructions, for it was easier than protesting – she was a powerful force, a veritable matriarch.

'What good will that do when she's already wearing that ring,' Nonna Paola said.

Oh no. What was she thinking bringing this up now?

'Nonna,' I said, shaking my head.

'Your grandmother is right,' his mamma said.

'But the decision has been made already,' his papa said.

'Still, it is not the best decision,' Nonna Paola said.

Salvatore and I exchanged a glance across the table. The situation was so awkward. I twisted the ring on my finger.

'Why can't they change the ring?' my mamma said.

Salvatore put his hands together, in a prayer position. 'Signora Maggini, I have already told you that I cannot change it because of the promise I made to my dear Nonna Claudia.'

'It is true,' his mamma said. 'I had no idea about this superstition, otherwise I would have said something before he proposed.'

'If only he'd found a girl whose birthday was in October,' Nonna Paola said, looking across at Francesca.

'Not this again. Nonna,' I said, horrified that she would do this to me, and to Francesca.

'Times are changing,' his papa said. 'And we need to put practicality above superstition. The war has taught me this. Sometimes, we have to use our heads rather than our hearts.'

'Papa is right,' Salvatore said. 'I love Liliana, and we are getting married when I return, and she will continue to wear that engagement ring.'

I was glad that my fiancé was standing up for us. But deep down, I was beginning to feel more and more uncomfortable about wearing the ring. Every time I looked at it, I felt a sense of unease. But I ignored this nagging feeling in my gut. There was nothing I could do – as Salvatore's papa had said – because the decision had now been made. Maybe when we were married, I could surreptitiously remove the ring, and say it kept getting caught in things, or covered in flour when I was baking. I could still wear my wedding ring, which would be a simple gold band. Then I could put the opal ring in a drawer, and in time, hopefully, it would be quietly forgotten about. I could even pretend to lose it or actually drop it in a field somewhere. Perhaps if I continued to feel uncomfortable about wearing it, I would do that. I consoled myself with this thought – it was the only way to make myself feel better about the situation I found myself in. And I wished Nonna Paola would stop suggesting that Salvatore marry Francesca instead – I really didn't like that idea being put into his head. Or hers! She didn't seem to like this suggestion either – for we were close, Francesca and I. We always had been and always would be – as far as I was concerned. She was my sister, after all.

When we'd finished eating Salvatore stood up, and suggested we take a walk before Mass while the mammas cleared up in the kitchen. I was off the hook because I'd been in the kitchen all afternoon preparing our meal. We explained to everyone that we'd see them there.

We went outside, and the air was crisp. We wore our coats and boots, and hats and gloves. The sky was filled with stars, and the moon was full, shining down on us like a giant lamp, lighting our way. We followed the path behind the farmhouse that led to the frantoio – the building where the olives were pressed with a large stone. Salvatore unlocked the door with a key from his pocket, and then we went inside, falling against that door as he kissed me with so much passion. I had never known him to be like this with me before.

'I want you so much, Liliana.'

I felt the same, but we weren't married. We would be committing a sin.

'I want you too, Salvatore, but we can't.'

He pulled away, and said, 'You are right, of course.' And then I remembered, I still had to give him the cigarette case.

'Salvatore.'

'Sì?'

'I forgot to give you your Christmas gift – something special.'

'Oh?'

I took the cigarette case out of my pocket. It wasn't wrapped up or anything, and I gave it to him as it was.

'It's a cigarette case with your initials, SR, on it, look.' I showed them to him.

He nodded and smiled. 'Thank you, Liliana. That's thoughtful of you. I shall treasure it.'

'I know how much you love your cigarettes. Now you'll always have me with you, like I have you with me when I wear your engagement ring.'

He slid the cigarette case into his pocket.

'That is true.'

Salvatore seemed to be pleased with my present, but I felt a little dismissed. Did he know how much trouble I'd gone to finding it, and then getting it engraved? But then I realised his thoughts were elsewhere – he just wanted to hold me in his arms and that was understandable, of course. He would be going away again tomorrow and he wanted to make the most of every second with me.

He took my hand once again, and my head was all over the place. Had I made a mistake? What if he left in the morning and didn't come back this time? What if I'd missed my chance to have him make love to me? Would I regret it? Of course I would. Salvatore led me through into the room where the olives were pressed, and explained the whole process to me, and I nodded and said the right things as I pretended to listen, but all the time wondered if I should ask him to take me – here in this room, right now, before I changed my mind. It wouldn't be long before he came back – the war would surely end in the spring, for the Tedeschi had almost been driven out of Italy altogether. And we would get married as soon as he returned. So, if we made love now, it would be all right. The Lord would understand, wouldn't he?

'Salvatore,' I said.

He turned to look at me. 'What is it, carina?'

'I think we should make the most of this time we have together.'

His eyebrows shot up. 'Really, are you sure?'

'I love you, Salvatore, and we shall be married very soon. Besides, if it wasn't for this war, we would be husband and wife already. We aren't doing anything wrong, are we?'

'No, carina. Well, if you're sure...'

I nodded, moving towards him.

'You will certainly be sending me on my way with a spring in my step,' he said, with a laugh. And then he leant down and put his arms around my waist and kissed me.

CHAPTER 11

JEN

I took the lettuce and tomato, with vine still attached, into Matteo's house and set them down on the kitchen worktop. He looked up and smiled.

'Ah, there you are, Jen. Oh aspetta, look! You have a ladybird on you...'

He leant forward and gently touched my shoulder. I did my best not to be distracted by the scent of his now-familiar citrus cologne as he leant in close to me. He showed me a tiny ladybird resting on the tip of his finger. I noted that he had very nice hands, bronzed by the sun. When I looked up at him, our eyes met – but I thought nothing of it. We were only just becoming friends and it wasn't that long since Harvey had run off with Amanda. I had no interest in pursuing any kind of relationship for the foreseeable future. But a new friendship suited me just fine. Besides, I didn't know what his actual situation was anyway. Google had told me about his ex, Natalia Valentini, the presenter on the TV show he produced, so clearly he was capable of attracting exceptionally high-calibre women. He didn't seem like the kind of man who'd be single for long, but I doubted he'd be interested in me, even if I was into him.

'How about that?' he said, lifting his thick eyebrows and bringing me out of my thoughts. 'You need to make a wish now.'

'Is that what you're supposed to do when a ladybird lands on you?'

He nodded. Thinking about it, I'd heard this somewhere before, but a long time ago – in the playground during my primary school days.

'My mamma says ladybirds bring good fortune and prosperity. You should always make a wish if one lands on you, before setting it free to grant someone else one.'

This was a lovely idea, but I wasn't sure I believed it.

'Oh, well I wouldn't know what to wish for,' I said.

'There is nothing you want, nothing that could make your life better?'

I considered his questions. Lately, I'd been so busy working at Da Nonna that I hadn't had a chance to step back and re-evaluate what I wanted from my life. Getting married certainly wasn't on my agenda anymore, even though I would turn thirty in a few months. If I ever accepted a proposal of marriage again, it would be with the right man. But I was in no rush.

'Hmm,' I said, unsure of what to say.

'Okay, how about this... try to clear your mind for a moment...' Matteo said, the ladybird still sitting on his finger.

'All right.'

'Now close your eyes and take a deep breath. What did you want when you were a young girl?'

I felt a little silly, standing in front of him with my eyes shut, inhaling as if I were in a yoga class – vulnerable, almost. What had I always wanted? I thought back to our house near Jesus Green – our happy family home, always filled with the aroma of cooking, laughter, and so much love and warmth. I counted myself lucky to have been born into such a wonderful family. Nonna had spent a lot of time in the kitchen with me, passing on her recipes. She had brought her own recipe book from Italy.

Her nonna Paola also had her own book – the one I needed to try and find. And so, together we'd started my recipe book. I still had it, languishing somewhere in the flat because I hadn't used it in so long, not since using it to write my blog posts for *Jen's Italian Bites*. More recently I had been thinking about my dream again: to have a cookbook with my name on the front.

I opened my eyes to see that Matteo was studying me intently. When I met his gaze, he swallowed and looked away.

'Ginevra, just think of *something*,' he said, rolling his eyes, the corners of his lips upturned. 'We have dinner to make, and I am hungry...'

'When I was a little girl, I used to cook with my nonna – she taught me so many recipes – and I always wanted to have my own cookery book published, taking inspiration from my Italian heritage.'

'Va bene, that's your wish – I have decided for you.'

He moved towards the back door, and gently shook his finger. The ladybird fluttered away, off into the Tuscan hills, perhaps to grant someone else a wish... Oh come on, I didn't believe it, did I? Weren't wishes supposed to be a secret, like when you blow out candles on a birthday cake? If Matteo knew my wish, how could it come true?

Talking of superstitions reminded me of the opal ring.

'Superstitions are often important to Italians, aren't they?' I said.

'They are, especially for the older generations. I can be superstitious every now and again, usually when it's something that can bring buona fortuna, like with the ladybird,' he said, with a laugh. 'I like to ignore anything that might supposedly bring me bad luck. But my nonna...' He shook his head. 'She allowed superstitions to run her entire life.'

'I couldn't imagine living like that.'

'Me neither. Anyway...' He patted his stomach. 'Let's make dinner. I need to eat something, Ginevra.'

I went to the sink and rinsed the mud off the lettuce and shook it dry in a colander. In the cupboard, I found a salad bowl with a pattern of lemons and blue swirls on it. I ripped the lettuce leaves into the bowl. I sliced the tomato and laid it out on a plate in a circular pattern. Outside the back door, I crouched down and picked a handful of basil leaves from the terracotta pot. Raising them to my nose, I closed my eyes, and inhaled their sweet and slightly spicy aroma. I removed the leaves from their stalks, and arranged them over the sliced tomato. Then I dressed the salad with olive oil, vinegar, salt and black pepper. So simple, but I knew it would taste wonderful with ingredients grown under the Tuscan sun.

Standing back, I admired the side dishes I'd created. Even though it hadn't taken me long, this small exercise had been fulfilling.

Matteo lit the hob and within seconds the oil in the deep-fat fryer started to hiss and spit. He carefully dropped in handfuls of chips and then pressed the steaks onto a griddle.

'How do you like your bistecca to be cooked?' he said.

I told him medium.

'Okay, Jen. You go outside and enjoy your wine, and take in the view. I'll bring out our dinner soon – it's almost ready.'

When I stepped outside, I was struck by how peaceful the garden was, the only sounds coming from cicadas, bees buzzing on a pot of hydrangeas nearby and a car engine in the distance. Aside from those sounds, I could hear the hissing of chips frying and the steaks sizzling on the griddle through the open kitchen window. It all smelt so inviting and I couldn't wait to eat. The bougainvillea flowers on the veranda looked so vibrant, and I let out a happy sigh. I placed the salad bowl and plate on the table and covered them with a tea towel to protect them from flies. Then I set our places so we were facing the view, using napkins and cutlery found in the drawer of an old dresser. My life had certainly changed since

Matteo turned up at Da Nonna the previous Saturday. How had I got through the summer with no outside space and all that racket coming from the flat downstairs? As Matteo had pointed out, it would cost me so little to be here. I'd got into the habit of being super frugal lately because, after losing the business, I'd been so cautious about buying anything unless I absolutely needed it. Although wages at Da Nonna were just above the minimum, I hadn't spent any money while working there, apart from on bills and loan repayments, and I made decent tips. It was only my first evening here, though, and I would see how the next few days went before making any decisions.

Matteo brought out two plates, piled high with steak and chips, and I couldn't wait to tuck in. He topped up our wine, and said, 'Buon appetito.'

I cut into the steak – he'd cooked it perfectly. There were lines from the griddle, and it was tender on the inside with just a touch of redness. I couldn't bear to eat meat when it was bleeding onto the plate. The chips were perfectly thin and crispy, and absolutely delicious, too. I used the wooden servers to put salad and tomatoes onto my plate. The lettuce was refreshingly crunchy and the tomatoes so delightfully sweet from the sun – how different everything tasted when plucked straight from the garden. We didn't speak as we ate, although Matteo paused to compliment me on my outstanding salad.

'The dressing is perfetto, not too much oil, not too much vinegar, just enough seasoning. You have got the balance just right,' he said.

I thanked him and smiled to myself. In the distance the sun was sinking in the sky, and the clouds were tinged with pink. Being there in that moment gave me the sudden urge to go shopping and buy ingredients to combine with those in the garden – and make more delicious meals. Would Matteo want to eat them with me? I was sure he wouldn't object to being cooked for, and I felt some need to impress him. I would so love to prepare a whole meal and have him compliment my cooking.

'So tomorrow I'll drive you to Florence to see my cousin, Fabrizio, the solicitor.'

'Oh yes, I'd forgotten about that,' I said. 'Don't you need to work?'

'There is no filming tomorrow, it is the day before Ferragosto, after all.'

I knew how important Ferragosto, 15 August, was to Italians. It was a national holiday dating back to Roman times when Emperor Augustus gave workers a day of rest. There were always celebratory fireworks once it got dark. The whole of Italy would stop to celebrate this special day in their calendar. And then they'd often take the rest of August off work too.

'And then I shall take some time off for the rest of the summer,' he said. It appeared Matteo was following this tradition too. I liked the idea of him being around for longer.

'You're here at Casa Luna for all that time then?'

'Well, filming doesn't start again until the beginning of September. I shall go and see my parents sometimes – they live on the other side of San Gimignano.'

'What is San Gimignano like?'

'Oh, it's a beautiful medieval town with incredible panoramic views of the Tuscan hills. We can go one evening before you return to Cambridge, to drink wine with the view. I know an enoteca that you would love.'

I liked the idea of this.

'Sounds great. So, where do you live when you're not here?'

'I have an apartment in Florence, but I often come here at weekends. And in the summer when I have time off work, I stay here.'

'I don't blame you – it's so quiet and relaxing.'

'Corte Paradiso is rather an apt name for where we are, isn't it?'

'Yes,' I said, looking at the sun setting before me, feeling as though I was sitting in a painting. 'It's truly how I'd imagine paradise to be. So, I saw from your business card that you are a TV producer, for what kind of programmes?' I asked, already knowing the answer from Google.

'I work on home improvements mostly. My biggest show is *Rifare la casa*, meaning to do up your house.'

'And you enjoy it?'

'Yes, but I have ideas for my own shows that I'm working on. My dream is to come up with an idea that I can sell to TV companies all over the world. I have been trying for a while now, but perhaps I just need some kind of inspiration,' he said, taking a sip of his wine, and looking over at me. 'Hopefully soon it will come to me...'

'I'm sure it will,' I said.

As we ate, the light faded, and Matteo went inside, and came back out with a candle and mosquito burners – coils in small terracotta pots that he placed at the edge of the terrace. I'd seen my grandparents use these in Riccione. You lit the coil and it would burn for ages, ideally keeping the mosquitoes away, although sometimes they didn't seem to do much.

'So you want to have your own cookery book?' he asked, passing me a can of insect repellent.

I nodded my thanks, and sprayed the parts of my body that were exposed – my neck, arms and ankles mostly. All those places mosquitoes loved to gorge on.

'Yes, I sent some ideas to literary agents, and I didn't have any luck.'

'Perhaps you could try another way, like doing something on social media?' he said.

'I used to have a recipe blog, back when they were popular, but that kind of fizzled out. And I've had a go at posting photos with recipes on Instagram, but that never really got much attention.'

'Have you thought about making cooking videos?'

I burst out laughing. 'Are you serious?'

'Certo. You know like Jamie Oliver and that woman, Nigella, on television, preparing recipes and talking about them as you cook – and then you post them on Instagram and TikTok and YouTube and so on...'

Nonna and I used to pretend we were making our own cookery show called *Jen and Her Nonna* when I was a child, but the reality of actually talking on camera – the horror! I shook my head.

'I don't think so, but thanks for the idea, Matteo.'

'But why not?'

'I wouldn't know where to start.'

'Ma Ginevra, you are sitting next to someone who knows all there is to know about filming. I'm a producer now, but I started as a director. You just need a ring light and a tripod when doing it yourself. And a phone, obviously.'

'But I don't have a ring light or a tripod.'

'You can buy them online very cheaply. In the meantime, you can borrow my equipment.'

'But me talking on camera, I don't know... I'm not sure I am brave enough.'

'Of course you are, and you would look so good on camera. You have the face...' He looked away, perhaps feeling he'd overstepped. I could feel myself blushing. I swatted away a mosquito that was buzzing round my ear, despite our efforts to keep them away. Was he saying he found me attractive? If he did, that would be all right with me... Even if we were just friends, I could still relish his mild attempt at flirtation. Who didn't love a bit of attention from someone they found attractive? I paused while considering my response. Our eyes met – oh the pressure for me to say *something* to break the awkward silence that had fallen between us.

'Thank you... that's nice of you to say,' I finally said, quietly, running a hand through my hair. I needed to wash it but had forgotten to bring my straighteners with me. Was I ready for Matteo to see my natural curls? I usually only showed that look to the people I was close to – those I trusted. It was my way of taking off my mask.

'I will help you.'

Goodness, he was being persistent. Why did he care so much?

'Really, you'd do that?'

'Yes, perché no? I am on holiday now until September. Why don't I help you make a few videos, to get you started? We can post them and see how you do.'

'Are you sure you don't have better ways to spend your time?'

He shook his head. 'My plans for this summer fell through, so I am a free man, here to relax. Actually you'd be doing me a favour as I will get bored if I don't have anything creative to do.'

I wondered if these plans had been with Natalia Valentini, before their relationship had ended.

'Don't you need to work on your show ideas?'

'I can do that too. Perhaps filming you might wake me up and give me the inspiration I need.'

'Okay, but only if it does help you in some way too.'

'We start the day after tomorrow.'

'Really? That seems so soon.'

'Yes, you need to think of a few of your best recipes. You will need to get the food for them – from the garden, and from the shops in the village. Choose a good recipe to start with.'

'Well, all right then.'

'And domani, Firenze,' he said.

We raised our glasses and clinked them together, saying, 'Cin cin.'

'I can't wait.'

To have Matteo, a local, take me to Florence, was a rare

opportunity, and I knew that. I wasn't sure about making the cooking videos, but it was kind of him to be so encouraging. The thought of seeing myself talk on camera was terrifying, but I was prepared to give it a go. He was certainly bringing out my sense of adventure. What was it Nonna had said? Failing is part of life, and I'd certainly done my fair share of failing lately. But perhaps if I picked myself up and kept on trying, I might eventually succeed at something – who knew? All I could do was try. I couldn't wait to tell Nonna how it was all going – she'd be so interested to know. I would send her a postcard before returning to Cambridge, as promised, with an update on my adventure in the Tuscan hills.

CHAPTER 12

LILIANA

That night, on Christmas Eve, after Salvatore leant forward and pressed his lips to mine, we became lost in the heat of the moment. We were fuelled by Chianti and the adrenaline rush of it being his last night at the oliviera for some time – who knew how long it would be before we saw each other again? What if we *never* saw each other again? After that thought overcame me, I realised that I must make the most of that night with him. We had to make love, and we'd already waited for so very long – if it wasn't for the war, we would be already married. So really, we weren't doing anything wrong. It was the war that had put us in this situation where our patience was being tested over and over again.

We took off our coats and made a bed with them on the stone floor. The only light came from the moon through the window. And then we lay down, and Salvatore, my amore, made love to me, so tenderly, yet with so much passion. I had no doubt in my mind that we were absolutely made for each other. Afterwards, he held me in his strong and capable arms – so very tightly – and in them I felt so safe. In that moment, nothing else in the world mattered. It was just us. And then the next thing I knew he was tapping me on the shoulder, waking me up from the deepest, most satisfied sleep I'd ever had.

'Carina, svegliati,' he said, softly.

I sat up with a start. Where was I? Oh yes, I was in the frantoio. With Salvatore.

'What time is it?' I said, rubbing my eyes.

'It is four o'clock in the morning. We need to go back to our beds. You wouldn't want your mamma and nonna to know you were here with me, would you?'

I shook my head, vehemently. 'No, certainly not. They would be livid, and so ashamed of me.' Was I ashamed of myself? I should be, I knew that. But in my heart, I felt as though I had done the right thing – for Salvatore and me. I pulled on my dress over my head, and fastened the buttons. Then I rolled my stockings up my legs, and, standing up, put on my boots and did up the laces.

Salvatore got dressed. He picked my coat off the floor, and gave it a shake to remove the dust, then he held it so I could slip my arms through the sleeves. He took my hand.

'Andiamo. I'll walk you back through the village.'

We went outside, and he locked the door to the frantoio. The stars still twinkled in the night sky and the full moon lit our way as we progressed along the path, and down the side of his family's farmhouse to Via del Bacio. It was oh so quiet – the only sound was the occasional rustle in a bush of some animal or other, probably a fox or a deer.

We walked along the road – no lights were on in the houses. There were no streetlamps, and we had no torch. We were lucky that the moon was full that night, otherwise we would have struggled to find our way – although Salvatore had told me that his night vision had improved since he'd been living in the woods and caves while working with the partisans.

When we reached Casa Stella, Salvatore let go of my hand, and pulled me into an embrace. He squeezed me to him tightly. And I savoured that moment.

'Thank you for tonight, Liliana. I shall go on my way a happy and satisfied man.'

He kissed me on the lips, and then he left, and I watched him walk back along Via del Bacio towards the oliviera, his boots making a soft tapping sound.

I didn't know what to think or feel. Joy and sadness battled against each other inside of me. I had been so happy to have experienced him making love to me. But now he was leaving and there was no guarantee he'd come back next time. And if he did, he might be seriously injured. He might lose a limb or even be blinded. I shuddered at these thoughts and pushed them out of my mind. So far, he had been lucky to survive. He just needed to come back one last time. And then he would be here in Cintaldo with me for the rest of his life, our lives. All I could do was continue to pray – and, seeing as we had committed a sin, I would go to the Chiesa Santa Maria and confess everything to Padre Luca. He would no doubt say something to alleviate my guilt – which had already begun to set in. It was a pity that I'd missed midnight Mass – a service I attended with my family every year.

I opened the gate, as carefully and quietly as I could, and, as it creaked, I hoped that the sound wasn't waking anyone up at Casa Stella. Inside, I lit a candle, tiptoed through the kitchen and the hall, then upstairs to my bedroom, where I removed my clothes. I then pulled my white cotton nightdress over my head, and climbed into bed. I was so very tired. When I closed my eyes, I thought back to my time with Salvatore in the frantoio, playing it in my head like a film. I just knew that I would replay this moment every night before drifting off to sleep. That was until he came back and we created brand-new memories in its place. I would remember every single second of our first time vividly for the rest of my life. That was why I'd committed a sin, for that memory with my amore, the man I loved more than anything else in the world.

CHAPTER 13

JEN

The next morning, Matteo and I left for Florence after breakfast. I couldn't wait to see the Renaissance city for the first time. It was another balmy day, and I wore a floaty floral dress. I'd bought it in Italy the previous summer when visiting my grandparents, in a little boutique near the seafront at Riccione – and whenever I wore it, I always felt as though I was on holiday. Matteo drove with the windows down, which created a lovely breeze. We made our way along the country road with the most beautiful scenery before us, cicadas chirruping in the undergrowth on the grass verges scattered with pretty wild flowers. The radio played some old Italian song that I recognised in the background, 'Quando, Quando, Quando'.

On the faster road, Matteo closed the windows and switched on the air conditioning – refreshingly cool on my face. We didn't speak much, but it wasn't awkward or anything – there wasn't some desperate need to fill the air with small talk. Besides we'd spent hours chatting the night before. As I was wearing sunglasses, I had the advantage of being able to sneak sideways glances at him whenever I liked without him noticing.

When we reached the city, Matteo drove us down a narrow

street, the car rumbling on the cobblestones. I looked up in wonder at the tall, crumbling buildings painted in lemon yellow and terracotta with green and brown shutters – in places the paint was peeling off, but this all added to their charm. Most of the properties appeared to be residential but there was the odd bar and café or other small business tucked in between. Matteo reversed into a parking space on the street and switched off the engine.

'Ecco, we have arrived.'

We got out of the car, back into the sweltering heat, and he gestured for me to follow him along the pavement until we reached a building with a sign saying AVVOCATO BIANCHI. He pushed open the door, and I was glad to be blessed with air conditioning again.

Matteo approached the reception desk, and spoke to a woman who seemed to recognise him. She did a lot of smiling and spoke to him warmly, and then she picked up the phone and gestured for us to take a seat. Before long, a man dressed in a navy-blue suit came down the corridor towards us, and raised his arms in the air.

'Matteo, ciao, come va?'

We stood up, and they shook hands, and chatted for a moment.

Then he said, 'Scusami, Fabrizio – allow me to introduce Jen Farina, Francesca's great-niece. Jen, this is the cousin I mentioned.'

Fabrizio stepped forward and proffered a hand.

'Piacere, Jen.'

I smiled and said the same in return.

Fabrizio ushered us into a room, where we sat down at a big table. He then presented me with some papers and a pen.

'I have provided you with both the Italian and English versions – as we do this kind of thing for British expats all of the time. Basically, the contract says that the opal ring and the house now officially belong to you.'

For a moment, I considered whether I should be getting this paperwork checked by a solicitor in Cambridge before signing, but how much would that cost me? And I'd have to find a solicitor in the first place. I decided to trust Fabrizio – his family had known mine for many years. They'd helped each other through the war, and our great-grandfathers had even died together. Nonna had confirmed all of this, so I couldn't foresee any problems.

I signed the parts marked by sticky arrows. Fabrizio then checked my signature, and handed me my copy.

'And there you are. Now you are the owner of Casa Stella at Corte Paradiso. How lucky you are!' Fabrizio said.

'I really am.' I thanked him effusively, seeing as he'd done all this work without asking for a penny. I would have to leave a present for him with Matteo.

'And I know Casa Stella myself, of course,' Fabrizio went on. 'Our family has been spending summers at Casa Luna, next door, since I was a young boy. And now of course, Matteo keeps the place going.'

We all stood up and did a lot of hand-shaking.

'Grazie, cugino,' Matteo said to Fabrizio.

Fabrizio shrugged. 'It is totally my pleasure. Now, what are you doing domani sera for Ferragosto?'

Matteo stroked his chin. 'I hadn't thought about it.'

'Come over to my place? Rosa is throwing a party.'

'Can Jen come, too?'

Fabrizio looked at me. 'Certo. Perché no?'

'Sorry, Jen. I was assuming you'd like to go. Will you come?' Matteo asked.

Wow, I'd only been in Florence for five minutes and was already being invited to a thing as Matteo's kind-of-date. I hoped Rosa – Fabrizio's wife or girlfriend, I presumed – didn't mind me tagging along, and that she'd be friendly towards me, though.

I nodded and smiled. 'Yes, that would be lovely. Grazie, Fabrizio.'

'Okay, come over tomorrow at around seven,' Fabrizio said to us both.

After saying our goodbyes, Matteo and I found ourselves back in the heat. He led me across the road so we were walking on the shady side – an advantage of the tall buildings was that they created shade.

'Right, shall we go and get a panino? I'm hungry,' he said.

I nodded. 'Same.'

'I know just the place – there is a bakery called Pasticceria Mancini where they make the most incredible panini. And after, I'll show you the Ponte Vecchio.'

As we made our way along the pavement, I was careful not to trip up as there were cracks in the paving stones – many of them were crumbling away and in desperate need of repair. Mopeds buzzed along beside us, and by now more people had appeared, many walking down the street purposefully, some pulling along suitcases, the wheels rumbling. Florence was thriving, and slightly hectic, but I liked it, and I was excited to see more.

We sat outside the Uffizi art gallery, on a stone bench – we'd managed to find some shade. Our view was of the area where artists sat at their easels and sold paintings of Tuscany – many were of fields of sunflowers, and Florence landmarks such as the Duomo and the Ponte Vecchio.

Matteo passed me a paper bag, and I reached inside to find a hot panino with cheese and ham wrapped in foil. We both bit into our panini – mine was absolutely delicious, and I could taste mustard mayo, a condiment often used in Italian sandwiches, which I loved.

'We'll have to come back another day if you want to see the Uffizi. Otherwise we'd need to queue for ages to get in,' he said. 'It's best to book in advance.'

I didn't really feel like queuing in the heat. 'Ah, okay.'

'But after this, let's get an ice cream and I'll show you the Ponte Vecchio, which is just over there,' he said, pointing to the right.

When we'd finished our panini, Matteo took me to a gelateria, where we selected cones – I asked for a scoop of chocolate ice cream, and Matteo chose pistachio. I paid seeing as he'd bought the panini. We then ambled along, beside the River Arno, with all the bridges crossing from one side to the other. Then there it was – the Ponte Vecchio, the yellow bridge with arches and adorable little buildings going across it. It was even more impressive than I'd seen in photographs and there was quite a crowd of people who apparently thought the same – posing for photos and trying to get the best angles with their phones. I couldn't wait to take a few of my own.

On the bridge, we stood under the arches, tourists bustling around us, and I studied the river. Matteo was looking down at the ground, and he seemed sad. I wanted to ask what was wrong but wasn't sure he'd want me to.

'There are some jewellery shops to look at, if you like,' he said.

I didn't have money in my budget to splash on jewellery.

'Yes, we could window-shop as I'm quite broke at the moment,' I said.

We walked along and looked through the windows – I caught my reflection, and ran a hand through my hair as it had been blown about by the breeze. And then *our* reflection as we stood next to each other, side by side. He let out a long sigh. What was wrong all of a sudden?

He pushed up his sunglasses, so they were resting in his hair. 'I bought a pair of earrings in there for my ex-girlfriend for her birthday.'

Was he referring to Natalia Valentini?

'Oh?'

His eyes glazed over, and I considered what the story was there. It didn't feel appropriate to press him any further. Had his plans for the next two weeks actually been with her, and when they split up, in June, according to Google, they'd been cancelled? He would tell me what he wanted me to know, I guessed, when he was ready. I took out my phone, and snapped a few photos of the arches, and the view from the bridge, down the river. I also took a few selfies to choose from, to put on Instagram. Just to show Harvey I was living my best life.

But then Matteo went on...

'Yes, she took the earrings back and got a refund.'

'She didn't like them?'

He shook his head.

'Esatto. She said they weren't her style, and that I didn't know her at all. Not long after, our relationship sadly ended.' And then he exhaled. 'I could never do anything right, however hard I tried. Besides, there was always the problem of geography with her wanting to buy a place together in Milan and me preferring to live in Florence, and spending weekends and time off at Corte Paradiso,' he added with a shrug.

Why was he telling me all this? I guessed seeing the jewellery shop had reminded him. He needed to vent, and I happened to be there. Or was he trying in a roundabout way to let me know that he was single?

He looked down at me.

'Sorry if that was too much information for you, Ginevra.'

At least now I would feel able to tell him about Harvey, if and when the opportunity arose.

I shrugged. 'It's okay, really. Sometimes talking can make you feel better – a problem shared and all that.'

He threw me a smile, and slipped his sunglasses back onto his nose.

'Shall we drive back to Corte Paradiso and open some wine? I have a bottle of Brunello di Montalcino. We can celebrate you being the new owner of Casa Stella. How about it?'

I knew that Brunello di Montalcino wasn't cheap, and it just so happened to be one of my favourite Italian red wines – so warm and sumptuous.

'Ooh that sounds perfetto to me.'

CHAPTER 14

LILIANA

After Salvatore had left once again, the months passed, so very slowly. I often thought back to our time together in the frantoio and relived it all in my head, usually before drifting off to sleep every night. I could only hope for more nights like that one – and tried to suppress the thought that they might never happen. For he might be shot when hiding in the woods, or blown up by a grenade, or caught in crossfire. He might lose a limb like Tomasso Levi who lived down the road, who had lost both of his legs. His life as he'd known it was over – and now he was an invalid, confined to a wheelchair, and the woman he'd hastily married before leaving was now destined to be his nurse forever. Her life as she'd known it was over, too. He was unable to have children, now he was paralysed below the waist, and so she would never get to be a mother. All of her dreams and expectations were shattered. What if I became like her? What if my life was hugely impacted by him being maimed in a similar way? It was selfish of me to even entertain this thought, for he would be the one who suffered most of all. We weren't married, so I hadn't committed to anything, and perhaps his mamma would look after him. But who would care for him after she died? If he lost his legs like Tomasso, I would take it upon myself to be his nurse, for it would be my duty, my destiny. I would have to swallow the bitter pill that children could never be an option for me, and that my husband would never make love to me like he had in the frantoio on Christmas Eve.

We endured a bleak winter. And life seemed harder than it had ever been. Getting out of bed on those days when the temperature was below zero was more of a struggle than ever. All I wanted to do was roll over and go back to sleep, to stay under the warmth of my blankets. I couldn't remember ever feeling so tired, and put this down to living through a war taking its toll, to saying goodbye to Salvatore again and again, and the constant worry that he might not return. But still I had to get up and go to work every day at the castello in order to earn my keep, and provide my family with everything that they needed to get by.

Snow covered the Tuscan hills. Frost created pretty patterns on the outside of the windowpanes and ice formed on the inside. One morning when I was looking out of the kitchen window, I saw a wolf in our back garden, standing there boldly, and looking me straight in the eye. I couldn't believe it as there were so few wolves in Italy at that time, and they were often to be found in the Apennines. What was he or she doing here in the garden at Casa Stella? And then it struck me: the wolf was a sign from the Lord himself. We would often say, 'In Bocca al Lupo' – it meant literally into the mouth of the wolf – but we used this term to wish someone good luck. Rather than see this beautiful creature with its grey and white fur as a sign of impending danger, I chose to see it as a symbol of protection against adversity – Salvatore was alive and well, I was sure of it. The wolf returned every day, standing there in the snow, leaving paw prints in its wake, those amber eyes looking directly into mine so intently, it would leave me feeling a little shaken. Even though I knew that it could kill me, I wasn't afraid – well, I didn't venture into the garden when it was out there though, of course... but when I saw that wolf, I would feel reassured. 'Salvatore is all right,' I would mutter to myself, closing my eyes and making the sign of the cross. He would come back to me, I was sure of it.

Throughout that long, hard winter we continued to keep our fires going with olive kernels, and branches and twigs collected off the ground, when we could find them, along with our small ration of lignite. There was no electricity at Casa Stella and we used candles for light. Those long, cold days when the sun sank below the horizon early dragged on and on, until at last spring came. How relieved we all were when the snow finally melted. Daffodils, snowdrops and crocuses popped up in the garden. After returning from the castello each day, I began to spend my time nurturing the vegetable patch again. We needed to produce as much food as possible from our modest piece of land. We often exchanged vegetables with the Bianchi family next door, and sometimes we'd sit together – *a tavola* on one of our terrazzas and share our harvest.

Winter was over at last, but there was still no word from Salvatore. I didn't know if he was dead or alive. Every now and again, I would go to the oliviera to ask his mamma if she'd heard from him. Usually he would pass messages to other partisans and eventually word would get back to his family to reassure them he was still alive. But the last time they'd heard news was in February, and we were approaching May. Who knew what could have happened since that last message was sent? I tried to keep myself busy, in the garden, and in the kitchen. I even knitted and sewed – I made a jumper for Salvatore as a present for when he returned, as well as a scarf and a hat. I went foraging in the fields and woods for mushrooms, asparagus, garlic, dandelions, and sorrel. I'd find snails under the rocks in our garden, and we'd fry them with a little butter and a sprinkle of salt. I milked our goat and collected eggs from our chickens. Salvatore's family supplied us with olive oil, and it was the beautiful golden colour that meant it was of the highest quality. The men in the village who were past fighting age would sometimes go into the woods and hunt wild boar, and bring the beast back to us. We'd roast it on a fire together in one of our gardens – and prepare dishes to go with it. The next day we'd make wild boar ravioli and another day a hearty stew. Signor Conti at the fattoria would often give me unpasteurised milk, still warm, from his sheep, and I would make ricotta at home. Every now and again, he would give me mozzarella made from the milk of the buffalo he kept on his land. It was melt-in-the-mouth delicious, and we'd slice it up and serve with tomatoes and basil leaves, drizzled with olive oil and vinegar, and sprinkled with seasoning. If we had enough salami, we added a couple of slices of that too – cut extra thin to make it go further.

One morning, on my way back from the fattoria, I went to drop off a bottle of unpasteurised milk at the oliviera. The door to the farmhouse was open, and I followed the voices to the kitchen, where everyone would congregate round the table during breaks throughout the day while Salvatore's mamma stood at the stove.

'Buongiorno,' I said, cheerily, placing the milk on the side.

But his mamma was not standing at the stove that day. She was sitting at the table along with his papa and three brothers, and they were all wearing glum looks on their faces.

His papa, Giorgio, gestured for me to join them.

'Vieni, Liliana. Help yourself to coffee,' he said.

The silver moka pot was on the side, and I filled an espresso cup before pulling up a chair. My heart was thumping. I sensed there was news from my amore, and that it wasn't good news. Was my Salvatore dead?

'Tell me, what is it?' I said.

There was a pause while they all looked at each other, tension hanging in the air. Then his papa spoke.

'We have news about our Salvatore. He is alive, but...' He cleared his throat before picking up his espresso cup and taking a sip.

I placed my hand on my chest. But what, had he lost a limb? Had he lost his sight? My breath shortened, and my eyes began to well with tears.

'But what?' I wrung my hands together under the table. 'Please tell me he's all right.'

Giorgio sighed. 'He is at the hospital in Florence.'

I nodded. So he was in good hands, hopefully.

'We don't have all the details yet. He has been hurt. I shall take his mamma and brothers to visit him later today.'

I gulped. 'When can I see him?'

'We shall go first, and then, dopo, you can go. Maybe tomorrow?'

If we were married already, I would be going first. Composing myself, I sniffed.

'I can take the bus in my lunch break.'

The next day, with Lady Enid's permission, I left the castello while she and the professor ate the lunch I'd prepared, to take the bus to Florence. I would return later that afternoon. The thought of visiting Salvatore in hospital was so nerve-racking, but also I couldn't help feeling excited about seeing his face, about him taking my hand in his. My stomach ached with so much longing. I'd been suffering from nausea lately, and had put it down to nerves. I had been living through a war, after all, and the constant fear of losing the man I loved. My body was probably struggling to cope with it all. But now he was back, and everything was going to work out. It had to.

At the hospital, Salvatore was in a ward with other

wounded men, and I located his bed. He was sitting up, staring into space, when I approached. His hair had grown even longer since Christmas, and once again a thick, dark beard covered his face. There were nurses and doctors in white coats busying themselves all around me with clipboards and pens, going from bed to bed, their voices a murmur. I pulled up a chair and sat down beside Salvatore's bed. The crown of his head was wrapped with bandages, and his left leg was covered in a plaster cast and raised into the air with a piece of rope. Seeing him like this, oh so vulnerable, tugged at my heart. But at the same time, I was grateful to see him alive. He had survived until the very end of the war, and now all he had to do was recover. Then we could get married at long last. Surely he would recover from these injuries? It had to be a good sign that he was conscious.

'Amore mio, I am so glad to see you,' I said, reaching for his hand and giving it a kiss.

He pulled his hand away, and scrunched up his eyes.

'Who are you?' he said.

I sat up straight in my chair.

'What do you mean?' I said. Was he teasing? He did like to do this sometimes. I smiled and rolled my eyes, playing along. 'It's me, Liliana, your fidanzata, you silly fool.'

He wrinkled his forehead. I couldn't help noticing how the war had aged him – he had lines on his face that a man of his age should not have.

'I have no idea who you are,' he replied, dismissing me with the wave of a hand.

All right, this wasn't funny anymore.

'Come on, Salvatore. Stop messing around. It's me, the woman you love.'

He said nothing. Those dark-brown eyes that had once been filled with love for me were now so cold and hard. But how could this be?

I twisted the opal ring on my finger, willing it to remind him of who I was. Then I swallowed, and leant forward in my chair, touching his hand with mine. He pulled his hand away once again, as if he were repulsed by me, as if I were a mere stranger.

'Salvatore, don't you remember giving me this ring when you proposed? We're supposed to be getting married now that you have returned – now the war is over after all these years of waiting.'

I stood up, and leant over the bed, and showed him the ring.

'This ring belonged to your Nonna Claudia, don't you remember? And all the fuss Nonna Paola made about it being unlucky?' Then I added quietly, 'Supposedly,' shaking my head. Had Nonna Paola been right after all? Should I have listened to her warnings?

He lay there, so very still. Frustrated by his lack of response, I tapped him on the arm.

'You have to answer me. Tell me this isn't true, that you're playing a joke on me? This just isn't funny anymore, Salvatore. Come on, dai...' I was almost shouting now, and other patients were looking over, watching the whole spectacle. They had nothing better to do and I was no doubt providing them with their entertainment for the day. 'You can tell me the truth now – that you remember me, that you are my fidanzato...' Then I lowered my voice. 'Surely you recall our night together in the frantoio. How can you forget what happened between us?' I leant over and whispered into his ear. 'Don't you remember the night you made love to me, when you said we'd be married within weeks?'

He clenched his jaw.

'You are mistaken.'

'But Salvatore, I gave myself to you. What will I do now?'

He inhaled as if gathering his thoughts.

'You must have confused me with another man. Please leave.'

So that was it then. I stood up and took my handkerchief

out of my pocket. Tears streamed down my face. I wiped them away with my handkerchief, but they kept on coming. Pushing my shoulders back, I tried to compose myself. I approached a nurse, hoping she could shine a light on my situation.

'Excuse me,' I said.

She smiled. 'How can I help you?'

I pointed in Salvatore's direction.

'That man doesn't remember who I am. But we're engaged,' I said, showing her the opal ring on my finger.

She looked over at him, and tipped her head to one side.

'I am sorry, signorina. He does have a head injury. Sometimes in that situation a person will lose their memory – it's called amnesia.'

I clutched my forehead.

'What am I supposed to do now?'

She shook her head.

'I don't know. It happens, I'm afraid,' she said, her tone of voice sympathetic. 'His memory might come back, but then again it might not.'

She gave my shoulder a squeeze and walked off, leaving me with those words hanging in the air. Words that devastated me to my core. I wanted to ask her more questions. Was there anything I could do to make him remember me? Watching her approach a patient's bed, I considered going over and pressing her further. But clearly she was run off her feet, and it wouldn't be fair on the patient she was attending to.

Should I go and talk to Salvatore again? When I looked over at him, his eyes were firmly shut and he appeared to have fallen asleep. There was no point in staying in this miserable hospital ward any longer. I could come back another day. Perhaps after I left, he might remember me. I glanced at him one more time, and passed through the door, down the stairs and through the exit into the street. Even though there were people walking by, I couldn't help leaning against the wall and weeping as if the world were about to end. By now, my handkerchief was soaked through with my tears. An elderly woman in a headscarf passed by and threw me a look of pity. I shouldn't be acting like this in public. Mamma and Nonna Paola would be horrified. But these horrendous circumstances were dictating my emotions. How could my fidanzato – the man I'd given myself to – not know of my existence? What was I supposed to do now?

I tried to breathe deeply. He had to remember me. He *had* to... I couldn't go on without him. Especially with the knowledge that my courses hadn't been since before Christmas Eve, just over four months ago. My diet hadn't been as nutritious as it should be – we were living on the bare minimum with food supplies at their lowest. And I prayed this was the explanation. Because the other one was too dreadful to bear should Salvatore never remember me: I could be carrying a baby inside of me. And that baby would be his.

CHAPTER 15

JEN

By the time we'd pulled into the drive at Corte Paradiso I was tired, and ready for a shower. It was quite overwhelming to think that I now owned Casa Stella – how totally bonkers was that? I'd gone from being a jilted bride, the owner of a failed business and the tenant of a flat with no outside space, and above a noisy band, to being the owner of a rather charming house in the Tuscan hills with a handsome Italian neighbour to boot. It was quite mind-boggling really. Would I want to spend more time here, or rent the place out, as Matteo had originally suggested? I wasn't sure yet, although I'd already become fond of the house since arriving only the day before. I was still thinking about whether to come back before the end of August, especially as Matteo would be next door for company. If he was working, I might feel differently. On the drive back from Florence, I'd thought about what he'd said about his ex, Natalia, when we were standing on the Ponte Vecchio. It still wasn't clear why he'd confided in me about his previous failed relationship. Maybe, in the heat of the moment, when he spotted the jewellery shop, he'd needed to get off his chest how he was feeling, and I just happened to be there.

Matteo parked the car, and we agreed to meet again after we'd had a chance to wash and get changed. I went inside and up the stairs, where I put the paperwork from Fabrizio in a drawer in my bedroom. I then had a lovely long, cool shower and put on a pair of shorts and a T-shirt. It was still warm outside, and the temperature wouldn't drop for another hour or so. I went downstairs and checked my phone at the kitchen table. I'd posted a photo of the Ponte Vecchio on my Instagram story, and Harvey had liked it. Why had he done this? Even though he was now with Amanda, it made me smile that she'd have no idea about it. But then the smile dropped from my face when it struck me that he would almost definitely have been doing the same thing with her when we were engaged. The thing about liking Instagram stories rather than posts was that no one else knew about the liking – the action of pressing the love heart – apart from the two of you. Well, I enjoyed the satisfaction of seeing him like my stories far too much to block him – that would stop him from seeing my posts and stories altogether. No, this way I was getting one up on Amanda, the 'best friend' who had betrayed me. And it felt kind of good – even if I would never want Harvey back.

I heard the scraping of a chair on the terrace, and looked up to see Matteo through the window. 'Ginevra, vieni,' he said. 'I have the Brunello.'

Ah, the Brunello di Montalcino. We stocked it at Da Nonna, and it was very pricey. It wouldn't be so expensive here, but still it was at the higher end of Tuscan red wines.

I went outside, and the bottle of wine was there, open, to breathe, I presumed, and there were two beautifully large bulbous wine glasses. But there was no sign of Matteo. I sat down and admired the incredible view – it was just so mind-blowingly stunning. How I wished I could paint, but in the meantime I would take a lot of photos – and even set my phone to panoramic view for some of them. The photos wouldn't do the view justice, but I just wanted them to look back on as a memory of my time in Tuscany. I posted the best one on my Instagram story – with the castle in the distance, surrounded by cypress trees.

Then I heard the sound of running water, and spotted a hose running from a tap under the kitchen window, along the terrace and into the garden. Matteo was standing on the lawn, watering the plants bare-chested. Oh my. I drew in my breath.

'There you are!' he called over. 'Due minuti.'

'Okay,' I called back. Looking at the bottle of wine, I decided it would be rude to start drinking without him.

Instead, I watched him through my sunglasses. He had really muscular arms – those biceps... Did he work out? Or was he one of those men who was so physically active that his body just stayed toned like that? When he'd finished he went inside, then reappeared, pulling a white T-shirt over his head.

'So, are you ready to try this Brunello?' he said.

I removed my sunglasses and put them on the table.

'Definitely.'

He poured some into each of our glasses and we clinked and said, 'Cin cin'.

And then I took a sip. Wow, it was just the right temperature, so warm and sumptuous.

'And congratulations on the house,' he said. 'Are you excited?'

'I am,' I said. 'It feels like a new beginning – and it all came out of nowhere.'

I thought back to the previous Saturday night when he'd come into the restaurant. And now here we were, sharing a lovely bottle of wine, and celebrating together. We'd spent the day in Florence. And tomorrow we were going to his cousin's Ferragosto party. My life had suddenly taken an about-turn – and I was savouring every moment.

'So, did you come up with any ideas for tomorrow's cooking video?' he said.

'I haven't had a chance to, really,' I said. In fact, I had decided I wasn't brave enough. Talking to camera and posting a video of me online – how on earth could I do something like that? All I wanted to do was back out.

'Okay, well there's still time.'

'You don't have to do this, really Matteo.'

'Ginevra, have you changed your mind?'

I looked away, fidgeting with the gold stud in my ear. Now I felt bad. We had agreed to do it, after all, and I was not keeping my word. It wasn't like me to be flaky.

'Maybe...' I eventually said.

He laughed. 'Oh, come on... Ginevra, I have won several awards for my work. Let me help you make just one video, and then you decide.'

When I looked back at him, he met my gaze. How could I say no to those chocolate-brown eyes as they pleaded with me? And he was being kind, offering his time and expertise gratis. I needed to seize the day, as Nonna would say, however daunting it was.

I blinked.

'Well, if you really don't mind...'

'I really don't mind. In fact, I want to help you, after everything you say you've been through recently. Making cooking videos could actually change your life.'

I burst out laughing. Yeah right. I doubted that very much, but his optimism was kind of infectious. I didn't have anything to lose.

I pressed my palms together. 'Okay, let's do it.'

'Brava! What's the first recipe that comes into your head?'

I thought for a moment.

'My nonna's meatballs.'

'Perfetto. Who doesn't love polpette?'

'Well true, apart from vegetarians, obviously.'

He chuckled. 'Obviously. But I'm sure there are vegetarian and indeed vegan versions you can make too.'

'I could suggest alternatives for anyone who doesn't eat meat or dairy.'

He sipped his wine and topped up our glasses.

'Allora... in the morning, when the butcher opens, you can cycle into the village and buy the meat. We have tomatoes, basil and oregano in the garden for sugo di pomodoro. In the meantime, I'll set up my kitchen for filming. We'll use my ring light.'

'That sounds like a plan. Thank you.'

'I can film on your phone and, after, I will show you how to edit the video.'

What ingredients did I need, apart from the meat? Parmesan, breadcrumbs, mustard. I would buy those items too.

'So, we are all set?' he said.

I nodded, smiling. 'But can I just ask...' The wine was making me bolder. 'What's in it for you?'

'I get to eat the polpette, yes?'

I burst out laughing.

'Fair enough. We can have them for lunch, or dinner, whatever you prefer.'

'Lucky me,' he said with a wink.

CHAPTER 16

LILIANA

On the bus back from Florence, I sat by the window, looking out at the Tuscan hills. Hot, thick tears ran down my face, and I couldn't stop them however hard I tried. The last thing I felt like doing was going back to the castello, but Lady Enid was expecting me. I'd promised to make gnocchi for dinner and the professor would be disappointed if I didn't keep my word. When I reached the castello, I went into the kitchen, put on my apron and tied the strings. I mashed a couple of boiled potatoes, made a dough with water and a little flour. Then I divided up the dough, rolled it into sausage shapes and cut off small pillow-shaped pieces, pressing them with the back of a fork, to make my gnocchi. There was an art to making pasta and this activity never failed to soothe my soul. I allowed myself to just focus on breathing while creating little potato dumplings to be proud of. Cooking was an escape on a difficult day such as this one. The challenge of making meals taste mouthwatering with minimal ingredients during the wartime years had kept me going at times. And today I needed to get lost in this activity more than ever.

I chopped up two large tomatoes and boiled them with

water, basil, oregano, seasoning and the stock that I kept on standby, in a pan on the side. The garden at the castello was impressive, and the professor and Lady Enid paid a contadino to tend to it. He was allowed to take some of the produce to share with his family. Castello dell'Uva had once belonged to an Italian count, who had died penniless, and then had been promptly purchased by a Florentine landlord, who rented it out to wealthy expats from England. There was a little land for cows, sheep, goats and chickens. The landlord leased the land to a farmer who provided the professor and Lady Enid with meat on occasion – and often she was generous enough to give me some of these provisions to take home. I had benefitted greatly from working for this kind English couple.

I went into the drawing room, where Lady Enid was sitting in an armchair, reading the *Corriere della Sera* newspaper, a glass of brandy in one hand, and a cigarette in the other. The professor would no doubt be in his study, working on the Etruscan book. He spent hours in there, writing, and seemed to enjoy spending a great deal of time alone. Lady Enid was the same – they spent most of the day on their own projects, coming together at mealtimes and in the evenings, after supper, where they would have what appeared to be intense conversations about important matters of the day by the fire. She often wore trousers, which was highly unusual for a woman, but she considered herself to be an intellectual who didn't need to conform. They had no children, and I'd wondered what the reason was for this. Did they not want them, or had they tried and failed to conceive?

'Buonasera, Lady Enid,' I said.

She looked up from the newspaper.

'Buonasera, dear Liliana. How was your visit to the hospital?'

I drew in my breath, still not having recovered from the shock of Salvatore not recognising me. Now the task of putting this information into words, and then saying them out loud, was immensely daunting, as well as rather embarrassing. Who would want to admit that their fiancé had forgotten about their entire existence?

'Is everything quite all right?' she said.

I adjusted one of the pins holding up my bun.

'He has lost his memory, signora.'

She took a sip of her brandy and frowned. 'What... are you telling me that he doesn't know who you are?'

Tears once again pricked my eyes, and I took a handkerchief out of the pocket of my dress – it was a clean one that I'd found in my bag. I nodded, and dabbed my eyes, trying my best to be stoic.

'Oh dear, how terribly sad. Perhaps his memory will return,' Lady Enid said. She drew on her cigarette. 'It happens, you know. Next time you visit, he might remember you.'

'That's what the nurse said. But it could take some time, or it might not happen at all.'

And there was the strong possibility that I was carrying his child. I didn't have the luxury of time on my side. And I couldn't ask the village doctor to confirm, because I feared he would tell Mamma her daughter had conceived out of wedlock. I couldn't ignore that Salvatore's baby was probably growing bigger inside my womb with every minute that passed.

She tapped her cigarette over the ashtray. 'I am truly sorry. How utterly devastating for you, Liliana.'

Lady Enid had no idea that my actual situation was even worse.

'Yes, it is very upsetting.'

'I can't even imagine... who would want to be in your shoes?'

Her glass was almost empty, and I refilled it from the bottle of brandy.

'Thank you, my dear. Well, as I said before, if anything

changes we'd be delighted if you came back to England with us. Cambridge is a beautiful city.'

I'd forgotten about her proposition. When she'd first mentioned this, it was the day after Salvatore had proposed. But now the engagement was bound to be off, unless his memory suddenly returned. Somehow I couldn't imagine it would though. I twisted the opal ring on my finger. No, I wasn't someone who gave up so easily. I would try again. I'd go back tomorrow and talk to him, bring up memories that we'd shared together. Perhaps that would make a difference.

'Thank you, signora. I shall consider your kind offer carefully.'

'Well, you don't have very long. We're booked on a ship that leaves Livorno next week. The professor's friend, Hugo Edwards, who I mentioned before and works at the Foreign Office, has arranged our passage. We are most fortunate as it's almost impossible to travel back to England currently – there is such a long list of British soldiers who need to return.'

'Would I be able to go on that ship too?'

'I'm sure we could ask him to add you, pretend you're a relative or something – I doubt it will be a problem. Hugo is rather influential, after all.'

I thought for a moment. This did appear to be my only option currently... unless I went to live in a convent until the baby was born. But I couldn't bear the thought of that – I might as well be incarcerated, and the nuns were bound to judge me for what I'd done to end up in my situation.

I would try talking to Salvatore one more time, and then I would inform Lady Enid of my decision.

'Would it be all right if I went to the hospital again tomorrow?'

'Absolutely, go and see him again first thing in the morning, before coming here.'

'All right, thank you. I'll do that.'

'I'm sure, after you left the hospital today, his memory will have come flooding back – how on earth could he forget you? And then everything will be all right.'

'I do hope so.'

The telephone rang, and she picked up the receiver. This was my cue to leave.

'Pronto,' she said.

I gave her a nod, and left the room, and went back into the kitchen. I took a red onion and started to chop it up to add to a side salad. So, tomorrow, I would go back to the hospital and try again. I shouldn't give up hope just yet. Once again, I found myself crying, and it wasn't helped by the onion. I went to stand over the sink, looking out at the garden, tears now streaming down my face. There was a strong chance that Salvatore was no longer my amore. Who would he belong to instead? I doubted it would be long before he found another woman to take my place – another woman to wear the opal ring that was on my finger. And it would be *she* who got to live with him on the oliviera as his wife, preparing all of his meals. Well, he wouldn't ever find a woman who could cook as well as me – that was for sure. For being a skilled cook was my gift – and he couldn't take that away from me. Perhaps this gift was what would save me – by taking me to England, where I could find a way to have the baby without anyone in my family finding out. Then, I could find my way back to Tuscany as if it had never happened. If I went to Cambridge, I'd wait until I'd had a chance to settle in, and then I would bring up the subject with Lady Enid. She didn't seem like the kind of person who would judge me, and I just hoped she would help me come up with a plan should I need one.

When I got back to Casa Stella, Mamma, Nonna Paola and Francesca were sitting at the table on the terrazza, making cappelletti, pasta shapes that looked like little hats. While telling them what had happened at the hospital, I burst into tears. I had to stop every now and again to catch my breath, and blow my nose with my handkerchief.

'Don't worry, Liliana. I'm sure his memory will return,' Mamma said, as pragmatic as ever.

'It's that ring – it has brought you bad luck already,' Nonna Paola said, making the sign of the cross. 'Oh Madonna.'

Mamma threw her a stern look, and she shrugged.

'Mah, what do want me to say – I told you so,' Nonna Paola said, waving her arms in the air.

'You don't have to be so smug about it,' Mamma said. 'Liliana loves that boy with all her heart. What will she do if he has forgotten her? Her future will be in tatters. There are barely any men left her age who are alive, never mind who are unmarried.'

'All you can do is go and see him again, and hope he will remember you – jog his memory by being there next to his bedside,' Nonna Paola said. 'Talk to him, see if he remembers your voice.'

'Yes, I have agreed with Lady Enid that I'll go back to the hospital tomorrow, before going to the castello.'

'Va bene, that's all you can do,' Mamma said. 'We shall all pray for you.'

If it took days or a week for his memory to return, that would be all right as then we could get married. But it could take months, or even years. Or he might never regain his memory at all. I wasn't in a position to wait. If there was a baby growing inside of me, my best option would be to go to England with the professor and Lady Enid. Then I could have the baby there, and return to Tuscany afterwards without anyone finding out.

. . .

The next morning, I couldn't eat breakfast as my stomach ached. I felt as though I was going to be sick. I selected my favourite navy-blue dress. I hadn't worn it for a while, and it was uncomfortably tight at the waist. I sighed as I studied myself in the mirror. There was no longer any doubt in my mind that I was carrying Salvatore's child inside of me. I applied a little make-up, not too much, just enough to make me look more fetching – with red lipstick as it was in fashion. And then I walked into the village, and waited for the bus at the stop on Via del Bacio, outside the pasticceria. Perhaps my visit the day before had somehow jogged Salvatore's memory and kicked his subconscious into action – I could only hope this had happened.

On the bus, I rehearsed what I was going to say to him in my head, picturing him lying there while I spoke, softly but firmly. This time I would be prepared. The shock of him not remembering me had left me so dumbfounded, I'd probably said all of the wrong things all at once. I needed to be calmer and more measured.

At the hospital, I went up the stairs to his ward once again. He was in the same bed with his leg still elevated and bandages wrapped round the crown of his head. How I hated to see my amore like this.

I pulled up a chair and sat down, and he glared at me.

'Salvatore, it's me. I've come back to see you.' I put my hand on his and gave it a squeeze. But he pulled his hand away. A wave of nausea swept over me.

He knotted his eyebrows together. 'What do you think you're doing?' he said, his tone of voice so brusque, I couldn't bear it.

How was this actually happening? For some reason I'd convinced myself that perhaps he had just needed another day to remember me. I'd been so optimistic on the bus journey here. But now it was as if I were a balloon and he'd popped me with a pin. I hadn't seen his family since visiting him the day before.

Presumably he couldn't remember any of them either. His mamma, who doted on him, would be inconsolable. Selfishly, I only cared about how his amnesia affected me. Seeing his mamma in an emotional state would make the situation even harder to endure.

Then he opened his mouth to speak. What was it – had I become familiar to him again? I smiled. 'Yes, go on...'

'Will you pass me a cigarette, and light it for me?'

'Oh, yes, of course.'

'They're on the bedside table.'

But then I caught sight of something familiar – it was the cigarette case that I'd given to him at Christmas, in the frantoio, with the light from the moon shining through the window. I reached forward and picked up the case, and ran my fingers over the initials, SR for Salvatore Ricci. I opened the case and took out a cigarette and placed it carefully between those perfect lips that had touched mine on Christmas Eve. I picked up the box of matches, struck a match, and lit the cigarette for him.

He gave me a nod.

'Grazie, signorina.'

And now he was calling me signorina as if I were a mere stranger. I had just passed him a cigarette from the case that I had given to him as a special present. Did he not realise this?

'Do you know who gave you that cigarette case?'

He shook his head. 'I don't remember.'

I swallowed, my heart breaking into pieces. 'It was me, the night you made love to me.'

He looked at me, and for a split second I thought I could see a flicker of recognition in his dark-brown eyes. But then, he sighed.

'I am sorry, signorina. You are wasting your time here. I don't know who you are, I'm afraid. Now, go on your way...'

He pointed a finger in the direction of the door.

'But no, I want to help jog your memory. I need you to remember me. You don't understand, I can't—'

'I'm sure you will manage just fine,' he said. 'You seem like a strong and capable woman to me.'

'Don't you want me anymore, Salvatore?'

'It's not that I don't want you, I don't know who you are. I can't marry a woman who I don't know, even if the doctor is telling me that I have amnesia, and she is telling me that we are engaged. I can't do that. It wouldn't be fair to you.'

'Maybe, in time, your memory might come back?'

He shrugged. 'Maybe, maybe not. Dopo la pioggia, il bel tempo.'

'After the rain comes better weather. How does that help me?'

'You must have hope. We've lived through a long war and now good times will come for you, I am sure.'

When I stood up my legs were like jelly, and I put a hand on the chair to steady myself. I leant down to kiss him gently on the cheek, a lump in my throat.

'I will always love you, Salvatore,' I whispered.

He looked up at me, his eyes surprisingly earnest for a split second. They appeared to be watery. Why did he suddenly seem sad? Perhaps he felt bad because he couldn't remember this strange woman who was saying they were engaged.

I left the hospital, and as it was a sunny day I walked to the Ponte Vecchio and stood there on the bridge that had been spared when the Tedeschi retreated. Florence was in a state of devastation after all the recent fighting – so many bridges had been blown up and there was rubble everywhere. But I looked up along the River Arno, and decided yes, dopo la pioggia, il bel tempo. I had to have hope, because what else did I have? If Salvatore didn't want to be with me, I had to find a way forward. I would go to England with the professor and Lady Enid, and I would find a way to have the baby and give it away.

And then I would come back and pretend nothing had happened. I could possibly write to Salvatore from England and give him one last chance to remember me. For now I needed to get away from everyone who knew me before my stomach grew any bigger. I stood there, on the Ponte Vecchio, ignoring the sight of bridges that had been destroyed – and focused on the beauty of what I could see. I told myself that everything would be all right because it had to be – and there was no point in being glum as that wasn't good for the baby. I needed to find a way to be optimistic for the future. Perhaps in the next few weeks, Salvatore's memory would return and, somehow, I could salvage the situation. In the meantime, I would be going to England.

When I got back to Casa Stella, after working at the castello, and agreeing everything with Lady Enid, I sat down with Mamma, Nonna Paola and Francesca at the kitchen table.

'I have something to tell you all,' I said. 'I'm going to England next week with the professor and Lady Enid.'

Mamma gasped. 'What? But... but why would you abandon us like that?'

'Because Salvatore doesn't remember me, and they offered me this chance to go somewhere new, and it will only be for a few months... and then I'll come back, in the autumn.'

'Why in the autumn?'

I couldn't say that this would be after I'd had the child.

'They'd like me to be their cook until the end of the summer, so they have a chance to find my replacement. I'll need to teach that person how to cook like me.'

'Oh well, I suppose we can manage without you for a few months,' Mamma said.

'I will be sorry to see you go,' Francesca said.

'Can I ask one of you to return this ring to Salvatore?' I said, removing it from my finger and placing it on the table. The milky-white stone caught the light from the candle, almost taunting me. As if to say, you lost this battle.

Nonna Paola shook her head. 'It's all because of that ring that this has happened. What did I tell you?'

'You are not helping poor Liliana. It is hard enough – she has lost her future,' Mamma said to Nonna Paola. 'Yes, don't worry about the ring. We'll make sure he gets it back.'

'Grazie, Mamma,' I said.

When I arrived in England, I would tell Lady Enid about my situation. I trusted that she'd help me find a home for unmarried mothers where I could give birth and arrange to have the baby adopted. Of course, I didn't want to give my baby away, but what choice did I have? There was no way that I could keep a baby without being married. And there was certainly no sign of that happening in the near future.

CHAPTER 17

JEN

The next morning when I woke up, I couldn't help feeling excited about my plans for the day. Matteo and I were going to make my first cooking video. It all seemed totally ridiculous, but somehow he kept bringing out my adventurous side – and I needed to embrace it while I could. I had been stuck in a rut lately. I was usually a glass-half-full person, but recent events had set me back – as they would anyone. It was time to leave Harvey and Amanda in the past and move on with my life. I got out of bed and went to open the windows. And then I pushed open the shutters and leant out and took in the glorious view – green luscious hills for as far as the eye could see with thick forests, rows of vines and grand-looking houses.

My life here in Tuscany could not be more different from the one I'd been living back in Cambridge. I was used to traffic passing at all times of day and night. But here, it was so quiet and there was a certain stillness that was almost soporific – the only sounds a tractor chugging in the distance and a moped buzzing past on the road that led through the village, set against the backing track of cicadas. Taking a minute to listen to them was always so soothing.

Still wearing my white cotton pyjamas, I went down to the kitchen to make an espresso with the silver moka pot. I opened the French doors and took the pot and my tiny cup and saucer onto the terrace. The sun was already shining brightly, but the heat hadn't built up yet – so I could sit there without getting too hot and just enjoy being. I looked at the pool, crystal blue, and sparkling in the early-morning sun. I couldn't wait to get out there and work on my tan. There was no sign of Matteo, and I expected he was having a lie-in. I didn't really want him to see me in my pyjamas anyway.

After knocking back two espressos, I went upstairs to shower and change into shorts and a T-shirt. Now it was time to go and get the meat for my polpette, and I found Francesca's old bicycle behind the shed. As I wheeled the bike down the garden, I could see Matteo pottering around in his kitchen. He spotted me and came to open the door.

'Buongiorno, Ginevra,' he said, brightly.

'Buongiorno,' I said, throwing him a smile.

'Do you feel ready to make an incredible video together today?'

I laughed. 'I'm not sure it will be incredible, but we can certainly try.'

'Brava,' he said, and then he threw me a wave. 'A dopo.'

'Ciao,' I said, climbing onto the bike as he went back into his kitchen.

Goodness, seeing him first thing in the morning wasn't a bad start to the day. I cycled along the gravel drive. Although it was a bumpy ride, this failed to dampen my good mood. I negotiated the potholes as if I was doing some kind of puzzle. On either side of me were cypress trees and it was all rather idyllic. The sky was a deep-blue colour with wisps of cloud. The cicadas were so loud here in the nearby undergrowth, and birds darted between the trees. A stag beetle buzzed past my ear, making me start, and then it landed on the edge of the road, flapping its wings. I couldn't have felt more immersed in nature.

And then a negative thought crept into my mind – the whole idea of making this video seemed totally ridiculous. Who on earth did I think I was, Nigella Lawson? But Matteo had been very encouraging, and a part of me was intrigued to see how it might all turn out. Besides, I did really like spending time with him, and if all else failed I would at least get to do that. And he seemed like a solid and trustworthy type – I kind of knew that he wouldn't let me down.

When I reached the end of the drive, I joined the main road that passed through the village. It wasn't busy, with just the occasional car or bus going past on its way to San Gimignano. I took a right and cycled past a church, Chiesa Santa Maria, and Bar Tosca with a few tables and chairs scattered on the pavement. After that, I passed a row of local shops until I reached the macelleria, the butcher, at the other end of the street – Via del Bacio, literally meaning street of the kiss – how very charming. The butcher was next to the sign for an olive farm – Oliviera Santa Chiara, run by a Signor Pio Ricci. The sign said you could do a tour and a tasting – that was something to think about. I leant my bike against a wall and went in to buy pork and beef mince for my meatballs. Next, I bought a hunk of Parmesan from the deli next door. In the pasticceria, I breathed in the aroma of bread and cakes, which was just heavenly. I selected a loaf of bread and brioches with pistachio cream.

I returned to Casa Stella, and put the bike back behind the shed. Matteo was sitting at the table on the terrace, sipping from a cup while scrolling his phone, his face deep in concentration.

'Ah, there you are,' I said.

He looked up and smiled at me, before putting his phone down on the table.

'I have something for you,' I said.

'Per me? Davvero?'

I reached into my tote bag and took out the paper bag of pastries.

'Actually, I have something for each of us. These brioches have pistachio cream inside.'

'Ah, Ginevra.' He rubbed his hands together. 'My favourite. Grazie. Pull up a chair. I'll get some plates and another coffee cup.'

He leapt up and went inside, and came back with everything. I placed the pastries on our plates.

'Well, this is a real treat. I was just thinking about what to eat for breakfast,' he said.

'I went to the butcher and got the meat for the polpette.'

'So, after this, we begin?'

'Really, so soon?'

'Why not? It will take time to set up.'

'Okay.'

'Have you thought about what you might wear?'

I shook my head.

'I haven't, no. Can't I wear this?'

He shrugged.

'You can, certo.' He stroked his chin. 'Or you could wear colours that look good on camera – perhaps... that dress you wore yesterday?'

So, he'd noticed the floral dress I'd worn on our trip to Florence.

'I'll go and change into that after breakfast.'

I picked up my brioche, and bit into it with a crunch. It was so crispy that flakes fell onto my plate. The pistachio cream in the centre was delicious and I savoured every mouthful. I should suggest to Dad that he sell these pastries in the coffee shop at Da Nonna. How I wished every day could start like this.

. . .

When we'd finished our breakfast I went to change into my dress, and then I met Matteo in his kitchen. He'd already set up the ring light and got out all the equipment that I might need – a frying pan, a saucepan, a big mixing bowl, a grater, et cetera. He was really trying to help me, and I was grateful. I had brought over my bag of ingredients, and I laid them out on the worktop.

'So, let's begin,' Matteo said.

'Okay… what shall I do?'

'I'll film everything, and we can cut the parts we don't need later. Every time you take a new step in the recipe, explain what you are doing.'

I stood at the kitchen island with him opposite me, holding the phone. Number eleven lines formed between his eyes as he focused on his task. I could sense that he really wanted this to go well for me. His support gave me a warm feeling, and it was motivating to have someone so in my corner.

'Just pretend you're talking to a friend,' he said. 'If you like, I can ask questions to direct you. We can take out my voice later.'

'That sounds like a good idea,' I said.

'Allora, Ginevra, what do you need to do first?'

I opened the bag from the butcher and glanced at the phone.

'I'm just going to put the meat into the bowl.'

'Tell me, what meat is it?'

I explained that it was half beef and half pork.

'Okay, let's start with a short introduction. Something like… I'm Jen Farina, and this is my new account. Follow me for recipes from my Italian heritage, passed down from my grandmother, and her grandmother before her.'

I repeated his words.

'Excellent. You come across well,' he said. He pointed to the lens on his phone. 'Don't forget to smile and look directly at the camera when you're speaking. Let's just record that bit again.'

Fixing a grin on my face, I followed his advice.

'Bellissima. Now describe what you're doing. Take the meat out of the bag and show it to me, explain why you are using half pork and half beef. Tell us you cycled into a charming village in the Tuscan hills this morning to buy it at the macelleria. Filming this video here in Tuscany will probably get you more attention than at home. It adds to the authenticity as well as your credibility.'

I followed his direction, appreciating that he wasn't speaking to me in a bossy way – his tone of voice was both respectful and helpful.

'This is looking really good already, Ginevra.'

We did seem to make a great team.

I put all of the ingredients into a bowl – breadcrumbs made from the loaf, the Parmesan, mustard, garlic, oregano, basil, an egg, seasoning – and got stuck in with my hands to make the meatball mixture. Then I shaped the mixture into ball shapes and put them on a plate.

'Now I need to put these in the fridge for a bit while I prepare the sugo di pomodoro, the tomato sauce,' I said.

'Okay, explain that you are using tomatoes picked from a garden in Tuscany. Your viewers will love that. Another time, we can film you out there, too.'

I did this, and chopped up the tomatoes on the wooden board while Matteo zoomed in with the phone. I added freshly crushed garlic, basil and oregano and put everything in a saucepan with a little water. As we went on I began to relax, and found it easier to talk, and just pretended I was explaining everything to Matteo and he wasn't filming me.

'Now we take a break while the sugo simmers.'

Matteo made a pot of coffee, and we went to sit outside while he showed me what he'd filmed already. I was surprised to find that I didn't come across too badly, at all. And I seemed to actually know what I was talking about.

'So, we cut this down, and add subtitles so viewers can watch on silent. And obviously we need to film the rest of the recipe, and you eating the finished product – that is crucial in cooking videos, I find. But what do you think, so far?'

'I think it's... actually not too bad at all!' I said.

'You seem surprised, but you are a natural, Ginevra – I knew you would be, that's why I kept on encouraging you. Now we finish filming and then we edit. You need to write the recipe in your phone notes and later, if you are happy, we can post the video on Instagram, TikTok, Facebook, YouTube – evenings are best when more people are likely to be viewing. So, we post tonight before leaving for the Ferragosto party?'

'Okay, but I need to set up accounts that I don't have.'

'You have Instagram already, yes?'

I nodded. Had he been looking? The thought of him looking me up online, as I had with him, was interesting.

'I'll show you how to do the rest. It won't take long.'

'Do you think this will actually lead to me publishing a cookbook?'

'If we are successful, yes, why not? But you need to post a lot of videos, and build up your brand and fanbase. Then who knows what might happen?'

Whether the videos were a hit or not, I was enjoying cooking again. But also Matteo was helping me to feel part of something. I'd felt so alone lately, and the way he referred to us as 'we' was heartwarming. He genuinely seemed to be rooting for me. I was excited to see what might happen when we posted this video. I doubted I'd ever be the kind of person who went viral, and I didn't see myself as an 'influencer' (it wasn't really me), but I so enjoyed the act of being creative. It made me feel truly fulfilled. If I didn't put myself out there, how would I ever know?

CHAPTER 18

LILIANA

A week later, early one morning, I hugged Mamma, Nonna Paola and Francesca goodbye in the kitchen. We were all sobbing, but I had to go. I picked up Papa's suitcase, for he didn't need it anymore, and I was depending on it to bring me some luck. Perhaps he would watch over me in some way on my journey to a foreign country. A jeep waited outside Casa Stella in the dark, the engine running, and I stepped up inside. The professor sat in the front, and I joined Lady Enid on the back seat. A British officer was at the wheel, and he got out to put my suitcase in the back for me.

'Right, chaps, let's get you to Livorno so you can sail on back to Blighty,' he said, cheerfully, and then we set off up the drive, and through the village, along Via del Bacio, until we reached the main road.

And then it struck me – I was going to have to speak English all of the time. There would be no Italians for me to communicate with in Cambridge. How would I manage? I could get by when communicating with the professor and Lady Enid, but my vocabulary was limited. I rested my hand on my stomach, a habit I'd adopted when no one could see. Closing my eyes, I prayed that everything would be all right for me and the baby. I just needed to give birth, and then I could return home and be with my family again. Giving my child up would be heartbreaking, but what choice did I have? In the meantime, I needed to be brave.

We travelled to England by ship – from Livorno to Portsmouth. I hadn't been on a ship before, and I was seasick the whole time. Conditions were cramped, and I shared a cabin with Lady Enid, who pretended I was her younger sister. At Portsmouth, we took a train to London, and then another train to Cambridge. When we arrived, it was late at night. It had been an exhausting journey, and particularly so as an expectant mother.

A taxi took us from the station to a rather lovely street lined with tall, grand houses, a few storeys high. The driver pulled up outside one of the houses, and we got out and walked up the steps to the front door. There was a sign that said BENTLEY HOUSE. The maid, who was a woman around my age, greeted us at the door.

'Welcome to Bentley House, Miss Maggini. I'm Nancy, the housekeeper.'

Apparently, she'd been taking care of the house in the professor and Lady Enid's absence. Inside, the hall floor was black-and-white tiles, and the walls were covered with paintings and photographs. Nancy led me up a servants' staircase at the back of the house, to the top floor, where she opened the door to a small room. I followed her inside and put down my suitcase.

'This is your bedroom, Liliana,' she said.

From what I could see from the streetlamps, the window overlooked a large patch of grass, edged with trees.

'I imagine that's a pretty view, in the daylight,' I said.

'Oh yes, that's Parker's Piece. If you cross it, you'll be in the centre of Cambridge. But don't worry, I'll tell you where everything is in the morning.'

'Thank you, Nancy,'

'I understand you're going to be the cook. Do come downstairs when you're ready – there is vegetable soup for your supper. You can take over the reins from tomorrow,' Nancy said.

She left, and I heard her go down the stairs. I noticed a small fireplace with a few lumps of coal beside it. A blanket and sheets were folded neatly on the bed. I made the bed and went downstairs to the kitchen. The baby had become heavier over the past week, and each stair was an endurance. I was oh so tired and my legs felt as though they were made of lead. How would I live and work in this house while pregnant? I would just have to do my best. With any luck, I would manage to sleep well in that room.

When I'd eaten soup and bread and cheese at the table in the kitchen with Nancy, I went upstairs and climbed into bed and lay there thinking. Would I be all right here in this strange city in another country? Would Lady Enid understand when I told her about the baby and help me? When should I tell her? Should I wait until it was really so obvious that I was pregnant, I couldn't keep it a secret any longer? I had left my new address with Mamma, Nonna Paola and Francesca, and I hoped they'd write to me. I would write them a letter in the morning. Apparently, once I'd served breakfast, I could have a couple of hours off to go and get food. Nancy would hopefully tell me where to go, and then perhaps I'd explore this new city before returning and preparing a light lunch for the professor and Lady Enid. They weren't particularly demanding, and I was sure that I could cope with this job. I had to, as there was nowhere else to go.

The next morning, I found Lady Enid in the drawing room. It had vast windows and looked out onto the large green called Parker's Piece – it was quite a view. I hadn't slept very well.

Even though it was spring, my bedroom had been chilly. Perhaps Nancy could find me an extra blanket and a few more lumps of coal so I could keep the fire going for longer. My bed was next to the window, and it was rather draughty. When I'd woken up, I'd felt all disorientated. I'd had a dream about running through that field of sunflowers with Salvatore. But this time he'd proposed with a sapphire ring instead. If only... And then unwelcome thoughts came. What was I doing in this strange country where everyone spoke a different language? How would I manage? I had survived a war, I supposed, the horrific death of my dear papa and being occupied by the Tedeschi. This new world I found myself in, with a baby inside of me, wasn't going to be easy to navigate, but surely it would be easier than what I had already endured? I was having to mourn the loss of Salvatore as well, even though he was very much alive... but I was dead to him, as in I didn't exist in his eyes.

I found myself picturing the kitchen at Casa Stella, with Mamma and Nonna Paola and Francesca sitting at the table, drinking their morning espressos, poured from the moka pot. They would be talking about what food they were going to prepare and eat that day, for their whole lives revolved around what the next meal would be. Food was everything for us Italians. Closing my eyes, I pictured myself sitting there with them, and a tear ran down my cheek. No, I had to be strong – for myself, and for the baby. I had to trust that everything would work out, that everything would be all right. Because how else could I move forward, and get through every day?

I put on the black dress and white apron brought from Italy, and went downstairs to the kitchen in the basement. Nancy hadn't arrived yet. She lived out, with her family, at the other end of Cambridge, apparently, and cycled in every day. I found a knife and cut myself a slice of bread, and sat down at the table. There was no moka pot, and I wondered where I might find one. I poured myself a glass of water from a jug on the table.

There was a little light through the window at the top – above ground, but there was no view, just the concrete wall at the front of the house. When I had eaten, I went into the drawing room to see if the professor and Lady Enid had made an appearance. He had taken up residence in an armchair with winged back, smoking a pipe, and she was sitting opposite. They were conversing about poetry, from what I could make out.

'Good morning,' I said.

'Good morning, Liliana,' Lady Enid said. The professor gave me a nod.

'What can I get you for breakfast?' I asked.

'Do you know, I think I'll have a boiled egg,' Lady Enid said.

'Same for me, please,' the professor said.

'Bring it to the table by the window when it's ready, and a pot of tea for two,' Lady Enid said.

'Right away. Can you suggest where I buy provisions this morning?' I asked.

'Oh yes, of course,' Lady Enid said. 'There is a charming Italian delicatessen on King's Parade called Da Nonna. That's if it's still there. Many of these businesses were impacted during the war when Italians were interned. That was until the armistice, when they became our allies. It might have been destroyed by a bomb, for all we know.'

From everything she was saying, it seemed most unlikely this place was actually going to be there. But the opportunity to have some time to myself while exploring Cambridge was too good to miss.

'Where will I find King's Parade?' I said.

'Nancy will give you directions. And she can provide you with English money.'

'What shall I buy?'

'That's up to you. I trust you entirely, Liliana.'

'Very well. I'll set off after making those eggs.'

I returned to the basement, with no idea how to serve a

boiled egg. I hoped Nancy would arrive soon so she could enlighten me. Otherwise, perhaps there was a recipe book somewhere. I had brought my own from Tuscany, but it only included Italian dishes. After serving breakfast, I would walk into Cambridge and try to find this Italian delicatessen Lady Enid had mentioned. Was it really a shop run by actual Italians? I relished the thought of seeing people from my own country. It would certainly make me feel more at home.

CHAPTER 19

JEN

That evening, Matteo drove us to Florence for Fabrizio and his girlfriend Rosa's Ferragosto party. I had bought a bottle of Vin Santo in the village to thank Fabrizio for sorting out the contract for Casa Stella. Matteo drove with the windows down and the radio on, playing Italian pop music. Earlier, after we'd finished making the cooking video, he had helped me to edit it, and then I'd posted it just before we left the house. I hadn't dared check to see how it was doing, and maybe would need a drink before I could do so. When we reached the centre of Florence, Matteo parked in the street and then led me to an old yellow crumbling building with tall windows and green shutters. Many of the windowsills had boxes bursting with brightly coloured flowers. He rang the intercom, and then came Fabrizio's voice and we were buzzed inside, through the big old heavy door, to a musty-smelling foyer with pigeonholes. We climbed flight after flight of stairs, our footsteps echoing up to the ceiling high above us, until, at long last, we approached the top floor. By then my legs ached and I was gasping for a drink.

'There are a lot of stairs, but it will be worth it,' Matteo said.

The main reason I needed a drink though was to help

calm my nerves – I had no idea who any of these people at the party were. Would they be friendly towards me? My conversational Italian was okay, but sometimes I'd get stuck due to my limited vocabulary. Would I end up looking like an idiot?

When we reached the top floor, the door was wide open.

Matteo called out, 'Ciao, ragazzi,' as we entered.

Inside, the apartment was filled with antique furniture and paintings and old photographs on the walls. The sound of voices was coming from the kitchen. As we got closer, I saw Fabrizio, perched on a stool at the island, and a woman, presumably Rosa, arranging a selection of cheeses on a wooden board. A door opened onto a terrace with the most impressive view over the terracotta rooftops of Florence – the Duomo cathedral with its big dome and stripey tower in the distance, and the rolling Tuscan hills beyond. Church bells rang nearby, setting the scene perfectly.

'Come on in, welcome!' Fabrizio said, getting down from the stool to shake hands with Matteo. He came over and double-kissed me. I handed him the bottle of Vin Santo.

'This is to say thank you for sorting out the contract,' I said.

'Ah grazie, Jen. I love Vin Santo.'

'This is such a lovely flat,' I said, scanning the room.

He smiled at me, warmly.

'I'm glad you like it. This is my girlfriend, Rosa,' he said. She was now slicing a loaf of bread and placing it into a basket.

'Piacere,' she said, smiling and throwing us a wave. She then came over to double-kiss Matteo and then me. 'Welcome... andiamo fuori.'

Rosa stepped outside and we all followed. Fabrizio gestured for us to sit down. There was a round marble-topped table, and comfortable-looking chairs with squishy cushions.

Fabrizio poured glasses of red wine for everyone, and they both sat opposite us.

'So, did you know that Natalia got that job presenting the *Grande Casa* show?' Rosa said to Matteo.

So, Rosa knew Natalia then. Were they friends? It then occurred to me that Natalia might turn up. Oh no, I couldn't handle that if she did – it would be really awkward. Even though nothing was going on with Matteo, it still felt as though we had some kind of bond and were there together, as a pair.

He shook his head. 'I had no idea.'

'Well, she only found out yesterday. I'm surprised she didn't message you, though.'

'It doesn't matter,' he replied, dismissing her with the wave of a hand. His tone of voice implied that he really wanted her to change the subject.

'I do think she misses you...' Rosa said, persevering.

He threw her a look as if to say, *do you really have to do this in front of Jen*, and she sighed and rolled her eyes.

'Rosa is my ex-girlfriend's make-up artist,' Matteo said. 'And so that is the reason we are talking about her.'

Ah, now it all made sense. She worked for Natalia and was naturally protective.

'Oh, I'm sorry, Jen, is it? You don't mind me keeping Matteo updated, do you?' Rosa said to me.

'Not at all.' What else could I say? I hoped they'd change the subject soon, though.

Rosa was making me feel uncomfortable, and I almost wanted to leave, but I couldn't because Matteo had driven me there. If I got up and left, where would I go? I couldn't ask him to leave his cousin's place. I would have to grin and bear it. But then, thankfully, a group of people came through the door and joined us on the terrace. Ah what a relief. Perhaps Rosa would now forget about Natalia and be distracted by these other guests. Then hopefully the rest of the evening might be easier.

Fabrizio came round with a bottle of wine, and Matteo put his hand over the glass, and said, 'No, grazie, cugino.'

'Aren't you staying at your flat?' Fabrizio said.

Matteo shook his head. 'I have to drive Jen back to Casa Stella.'

'Can't she stay at your place too?'

Matteo looked at me. 'You don't have anything with you, do you? And that's assuming you'd want to stay here in Florence *stasera*.'

He was asking me to stay at his flat? How could I say no? It would mean he could have a drink or two, and properly let his hair down.

I shrugged. 'That's okay, I can stay if it means you can have wine. You might have to lend me a few things, though.'

'Okay, done – don't worry, I have everything you need. You can take my bed, and I'll sleep on the sofa,' he said, gesturing to Fabrizio to fill up his glass.

Another hour or so passed and I drank a couple more glasses of wine. Fabrizio brought out bowls of crisps and olives with cocktail sticks. And then there were fireworks, lighting up the Florence sky in an array of pretty colours. We all watched in wonder.

When the firework display had finished, Matteo stood up and said to me, 'Shall we go?'

I nodded. 'Sure, yes of course.'

We thanked Fabrizio, and Rosa. I did worry she might have made the assumption that Matteo and I were seeing each other, which couldn't have been further from the truth – although I was now going to stay at his flat. I doubted anything would happen though, and it shouldn't. Even if I wanted it to, I wasn't ready to move on yet, and it didn't sound like he was either.

We went back down all of the stairs, and then outside onto the street – which was alive with groups of young people talking loudly and laughing and generally having a good time. The temperature had dropped a little and we walked along the street, which was dimly lit. There was noise all around coming from open windows and roof terraces and balconies. And surrounding streets. A few fireworks were still going off and the atmosphere was buzzing – Florence felt alive. I felt alive. I was in Florence on Ferragosto – a day I'd always experienced in Italy with my family in Riccione. I loved the way Italians tended to embrace la vita lenta, a slower pace of life during those last two weeks of August – rejecting the world that had become too hectic in recent times.

Would Matteo offer me a drink back at his place? Or would we just go to bed? It was getting late, after all. As I walked, I was thinking all this over when I tripped over an uneven paving stone. Matteo grabbed my arm just in time, stopping me from falling flat on my face.

'Thank you,' I said, grateful that he'd come to my rescue.

'Prego. Are you drunk, Ginevra?' he said, his lips upturned at the corners.

'Oh no. I didn't even drink that much. It's just that the pavement is so uneven and it's quite dark with barely any street lighting.'

'Take my hand.'

I slid my hand into his and, somehow, I was suddenly walking along the street in Florence holding the hand of a handsome Italian man. I couldn't help feeling proud to be associated with him like this. As we passed other people, they threw us glances, and I smiled to myself rather smugly that they were assuming we were a couple when we weren't at all. Would I want to be part of a couple with Matteo? I wasn't sure, but it was fun pretending for the night.

'I have an idea,' Matteo said.

'What's that?'

'There's a really beautiful garden in a small boutique hotel in the next street. I'd love to show it to you, and we could get a drink?'

'Sounds good.'

In the next street, Matteo took me through the reception of a hotel called Pensione Firenze and we said 'Buonasera' to the man behind the desk. He led me down the hall and through a door into a pretty garden with trees in giant terracotta pots and a crumbling wall, lit with fairy lights. A bell tower rose up from behind the wall, glowing from floodlights placed beneath. Around the garden were tables and chairs, most of them occupied with people eating and drinking. What a charming little garden he'd brought me to! And who would have known it was there.

Matteo suggested we sit down and a waiter came over.

'Have you ever had a limoncello spritz?' he said to me.

I shook my head.

'You have to try. Shall I order one for each of us?'

I nodded. 'Okay.'

He spoke to the waiter, who said, 'Certo, signore,' before scurrying off into the bar with his tray and white tea towel.

He returned with two tall wine glasses containing a yellow drink and straw, and placed them on the table. He then put down bowls of crisps, olives and nuts. We thanked him and said, 'Cin cin.'

The lighting was dim, with only a candle on the table between us, and we locked eyes as we clinked our glasses, and then I took a sip. It was perfect – chilled, lemony, sweet but not too much, and so refreshing.

'Be careful, it's strong,' Matteo said. 'Did you check your video to see how it's doing?'

'Oh, no... I'm not sure if I'm brave enough.'

'Shall I check from my phone?'

'Okay.'

He got out his phone and ran his fingers over the screen. It buzzed, and his face dropped.

'What's the matter?' I said.

'Oh, it's nothing,' he said, tapping the screen. 'Just a message from someone that I don't want to hear from.'

Was it Natalia? I didn't dare ask, and it would spoil the good time we were having if we started talking about his ex.

'Oh,' was all I could manage.

'Anyway, let's look at your video,' he said, his face in deep concentration.

I watched his face, waiting for the reaction... and then it completely lit up.

'Ginevra, brava!'

'What, how is it doing?'

'It has over a thousand likes and... aspetta... thirty thousand views.'

'What? Are you joking? Surely not. How is that possible?'

'I think TikTok likes you. Let me look at Instagram... yes, it's not quite as many views and likes, but not a bad start at all.'

'Wow, this is amazing.'

'You know what this means?'

'What does it mean?'

'We have to make more videos, and soon. You need to make the most of this opportunity. Tomorrow, you make your next recipe.'

It was exciting to think that my video had done well, and I couldn't wait to make the next one. The bell rang in the church tower next to us as if to congratulate me, and really that moment couldn't have been any more perfect.

'Shall we go?' he said.

We left the hotel and he took my hand in his again, and we made our way around all the people on the pavement. And then I spotted a photo booth.

'Why is there a photo booth in the middle of the street?' I asked.

'Ah yes, the tourists often like to use it. Would you like to try?'

It would be nice to have a photo of us as a souvenir.

'Yeah, why not.'

He pulled back the curtains, and we went inside and squeezed together onto the stool. I couldn't help breathing in that citrus cologne – his signature scent. Matteo pressed all the relevant buttons and paid. Then there were a few flashes, and we went back outside and waited.

After a few minutes, the photos came out of the machine and I picked them up. Wow, we looked really good together... For a moment, I almost wished we were an actual couple.

'Ah, they are really lovely,' I said.

He leant on my shoulder and studied them. 'Yes, they have come out well.'

We walked past the Duomo, all lit up and looking pretty, and, a few streets later, Matteo stopped outside a big old door and took a key out of his pocket.

'This is my place,' he said.

In the lobby, he pressed the button to call the lift – very luxurious – and I was grateful as I couldn't face any more stairs. It pinged its arrival, and we stepped inside. There was a mirror, and we stood there in silence, unable to avoid our reflections as we stood side by side. The tension was palpable but we'd both had too much to drink and we were getting over exes. Now wasn't the time. We reached Matteo's floor with a bump, then we got out and he unlocked the front door to his flat.

Inside it was all very modern and plush, with tall windows overlooking the rooftops, a big open-plan kitchen-diner-lounge with balcony, and then a hall leading to presumably a bedroom and bathroom. I liked it.

'So, I am sleeping on the sofa. Let me show you the

bedroom. I can give you pyjamas, a spare toothbrush, and there are women's toiletries if you need.'

This was awkward. I scratched my head. Although I needed to remove my make-up, I didn't feel inclined to use what was presumably Natalia's stuff. But I would have to, maybe in the morning, as I could barely keep my eyes open. He handed me a pair of men's pyjamas.

'This flat is air-conditioned, so you will need them,' he said, with a laugh. 'Buonanotte, Ginevra, sleep well.'

'Goodnight, Matteo.'

He leant forward and kissed me gently on the cheek, and then pulled away, and walked down the hall. He stopped and turned around.

'By the way, well done with the video.'

I went inside the bedroom and closed the door behind me. What a night. I reached into my bag for the photos from the booth and studied them with a happy sigh. Both of us looked as though we were enjoying ourselves. I would treasure these photos, for sure. It had been a long day, and I'd drunk far too much booze. But as I drifted off to sleep, I realised that I did quite like Matteo. I thought back to that moment in the lift when we'd been looking at each other in the mirror. There was definitely chemistry there, but would anything actually happen between us?

CHAPTER 20

LILIANA

When I got back to the kitchen, I was grateful to see that Nancy had arrived. She was wearing her maid's uniform of a black dress, and she put on her white apron and tied the strings at her waist.

'Good morning, Liliana,' she said.

I nodded and smiled. 'Good morning, Nancy. I am glad you are here, because I need your help.'

She frowned. 'Why, what's wrong?'

'They want boiled eggs, and I have no idea how to serve them.'

'Ah, you need *Mrs Beeton's Household Management*,' she said, going over to a shelf in the corner and picking up a heavy-looking book. She brushed the dust off the cover with her hand and passed it to me.

'How will this help?'

'It's a book with every British recipe you will ever need,' she said.

I thanked her. Although I'd attended school until the age of ten, and could read enough to get by in Italian, I wouldn't be able to understand this book written in English. But I was too embarrassed to say anything.

'Would you mind showing me, just this once?' I asked. 'Seeing as I have to make them now.'

Nancy nodded, and picked up a small saucepan and filled it with water from the tap. Then she placed it on the stove and struck a match to light the hob.

'When the water boils, you place two eggs in the pan, and time them for around six minutes – that is the professor and Lady Enid's preferred time. There's a clock up there on the wall.'

She opened a cupboard and took out two tiny cups without handles.

'These are egg cups. You need to put the eggs in these when they're ready, and smack the top with a spoon so they crack. Use the grill to toast some bread and spread it with butter, then you cut it into long thin strips. We call them soldiers.'

'Oh, all right, thank you,' I said, hoping I'd remember everything.

She studied me with kind eyes.

'Liliana, it's your first day in a strange country, and you must be tired. Why don't I go and check on the fire in the drawing room, and then I'll stand over you while you prepare them. Just take them out of the water after six minutes, and I'll be back.'

'I am most grateful, thank you, Nancy.'

She scurried off up the stairs, and I placed two eggs very carefully in the pan of water that was now boiling.

When she came back, just as I was placing the eggs in the cups, she guided me through everything else, and we put it all on a tray together with a pot of tea, jug of milk, bowl of sugar, and cups and saucers. I carried it upstairs, set it out on the table, and returned to the kitchen.

Nancy gave me some English notes and coins, and drew out a little map of how to get to King's Parade on a scrap of paper. I was excited to see Cambridge, and I removed my apron, went outside, and walked down the steps. Parker's Piece was before me with a grand building at one side, and it was lined around the edges with trees, blooming with spring blossom. I crossed the road to the other side, and took the diagonal path to the other end.

When I'd crossed Parker's Piece, I found myself on a busy street with lots of cars passing and people filling the pavements – and the grand building that I'd seen from a distance was a plush-looking hotel, called the University Arms. As I walked past, the doorman gave me a smile, and I smiled back. Clearly, he could see I was wearing a maid's uniform – and we were two servants acknowledging each other, united in some small way. This feeling gave me a lift as I made my way along the wide pavement, past a cinema opposite, and an old university building on my right. Looking at the piece of paper Nancy had given me, I crossed the road and made my way along Downing Street, with grand old sand-coloured buildings on either side. 'Go to the end and turn right,' she'd told me, 'and then you'll be on King's Parade – the most beautiful street in Cambridge. There's King's College with a grand chapel that looks like a cathedral. You'll be blown away, I know it.'

I reached the end of Downing Street, and took a right, and there before me was King's College – it was indeed a beautiful building, with a chapel attached to it, all built in sand-coloured bricks. It looked very grand. I continued along King's Parade until I reached Da Nonna, opposite the chapel itself. For some reason, I felt a little nervous because I would have to interact with other people in this foreign country. But weren't they Italian? Presumably then they would speak my language? Unless they were second generation, but even then, I'd heard, Italian immigrants would teach their children the language as they grew up, so they would usually be bilingual.

Gathering myself together, I took a breath, and pushed the door open. A bell jangled to announce my presence as I entered. Instantly, I was transported back to my country. The aroma of freshly ground coffee was the first thing to hit me. There was a counter and a few tables in the corner, occupied by people who looked Italian – going by their dark-brown hair, and the way they spoke to each other, using their hands to gesticulate, I had no doubt they were from my home country. For a moment, I found myself thinking once again of the kitchen at Casa Stella – of Mamma, Nonna Paola and Francesca, all sitting around the table, talking and sharing small details about our day.

'Buongiorno, how can I help?' A voice coming from behind the counter brought me back to the present, and there was a man standing there. He looked Italian, and was around my age, maybe older. He wore an apron over a white shirt, with a few buttons undone at the collar. Nestling within his chest hair was the familiar gold chain with a cross pendant, just like Salvatore's. Seeing this, I found myself unable to put two words together. The baby was making me feel more tired than usual. My head ached and I really needed to sit down for a minute.

'You look very pale. Are you all right?' the man asked.

Nodding, my mouth dry, I swallowed. 'I'm sorry. Buongiorno, I...'

'Aspetta, you are Italian?' he said, his manner friendly.

'Yes,' I said.

'Why didn't you say so? Come in, sit down. Let me get you an espresso. You look tired.'

He came out from behind the counter, and gestured for me to follow him to a table by the window, with a view of the chapel. It was an impressive building to look at.

'Are you sure?' I said, adjusting the collar on my dress. 'I don't know if I have enough money for an—'

'Look, it's your first time here at Da Nonna, and we like to make our customers welcome. Come, sit down, I shall give you an espresso on the house.'

'Are you sure?'

'Sì, certo. Sit down, relax. Enjoy the view,' he said, sweeping his arms in the direction of King's Parade.

He was being kind, and I was so grateful.

Behind the counter, he switched on a machine, and it made a fizzing and spitting noise. A minute or two later, he brought over an espresso in a tiny cup with a saucer, a glass of water, a bowl of sugar and, on a plate, a small cantuccini biscuit.

'Grazie mille,' I said. 'You are molto gentile.'

'My mamma baked this biscuit this morning, and I can guarantee it will pick you up.'

I smiled. 'It looks delicious.'

'What is your name?' he said.

'Liliana.'

'I am Giulio. Welcome to Da Nonna. When you have finished, I'll come back, and you can tell me what you need and how I can help. Okay?'

I nodded. Giulio went back behind the counter, and I watched him go. He moved around the room in a very masculine way. He had dark curly hair which fell over his face, and a Roman nose, and he had the warmest dark-brown eyes with long eyelashes. I liked him instantly, and hoped we would become friends. The thought of knowing someone here in this strange city, in this strange country, would make such a difference to my everyday life.

I downed my espresso and ate the biscuit – it was warm and crunchy and delicious and just what I needed. Then sure enough, Giulio came back over and pulled out the chair opposite.

'I have a secret to tell you,' he whispered.

'What's that?'

'This is the best table in the room – we only give it to special people.'

I smiled. 'How do you know I am special?'

'As soon as you walked in, I just knew, I am going to know that girl for a very long time.'

I could feel my cheeks flush, and once again I was lost for words. Why was he being so nice to me? After all I'd been through lately, his friendly demeanour was so comforting. And then I was suddenly aware of my expanding stomach, and my swollen ankles – of Salvatore's baby growing inside of me. What would he think if he knew I was carrying an illegitimate child? That I had lain with a man without being married. He would not be so friendly, I was sure of it. He couldn't find out. I could not let this man know of my situation. He would be horrified.

Suddenly conscious of the sin I'd committed, I found myself asking, 'Can you tell me where to find the Catholic church?'

'Certo, there are a few here in Cambridge, but we do have the most beautiful Catholic church you'll have ever seen – in this country, anyway. It is called Our Lady of the Assumption and the English Martyrs, and it is on Hills Road. Let me take you there – what are you doing on Sunday?'

I hadn't expected him to offer to show me where it was, and to attend with me. It would be helpful to have someone to sit with. And then I'd have to return another time on my own to go to confession, and to light a candle for Papa.

'I was actually hoping to attend Mass.'

'Perfetto. Come with me, and my famiglia. They will be happy for you to join us.'

Would his family mind? I might feel as though I were imposing, depending how friendly they were.

'Really, are you sure?'

'Veramente. My mamma is heavily involved with the

church, and she's always delighted to welcome new congregants, so do not worry. Now, tell me, what is it you wanted to buy?'

He held out a hand, and helped me up from the table, and led me over to the counter. There before me was a selection of Italian food. I felt so fortunate to have walked into Da Nonna that morning. Already, I felt less alone.

CHAPTER 21

JEN

The next morning, I woke up in Florence, in Matteo's bed – but he wasn't in it. He'd kept his word and slept on the sofa in the living room cum kitchen-diner. How lucky he was to live in such a plush flat in the centre of Florence. The room was pitch black because the shutters were closed, and I clicked on the lamp on the bedside table. I lay there, looking around, curious to find out more about this man who'd entered my life only ten days previously, out of the blue. There was no clutter to be seen – just the usual bedroom furniture such as a fitted wardrobe and chest of drawers, and, on the wall, blown-up photographs of Tuscan scenes in black and white. How often did someone enter your life and become immediately significant in some way? At a time when you really needed someone in your corner. Someone to shine a light on you and point you in the right direction. As Matteo was doing. Would he stay in my life or was all this just temporary? If he owned the house next door to Casa Stella, I guessed we'd stay in touch. And it was the opal engagement ring that had brought him to me, as well as Casa Stella. But really it had started with the ring, because Francesca wanted it to be passed down the female line – and I was next in this line in our family. She hadn't had children and Nonna had only given birth to sons – four of them, including my dad, Giulio junior.

I didn't know much about Matteo, apart from what he did for a living, and that he'd been kind to my great-aunt during her final years – this particular fact told me an awful lot about him. How many men his age in his position would have done the same? It was impressive how he'd done all of that for her with no expectation of anything in return. And he'd even come to find me and Nonna in Cambridge. Yes, he'd been in London on a business trip, but still, it wasn't a bad effort at all. On top of all that, he'd arranged for Fabrizio to do the paperwork, and he'd driven me to his office in Florence. He'd left food and wine for me at Casa Stella for when I arrived, and it had been his idea to make cooking videos. I'd had the privilege of a TV producer film my first video for me. And already the video was doing well. This had given me a confidence boost, and I was feeling inspired to make more of them – ideas were popping into my head all the time of recipes to make. I was actually excited. Matteo had been good to me, and I was grateful.

I unplugged my phone from the socket above the bedside table where it had been charging overnight. I unlocked the screen and started scrolling. This wasn't the best habit, and I needed to break it. But there were so many things to check. Harvey had liked my photo of the firework display from the night before on my Instagram story. And most importantly, he'd liked the cooking video. There were so many likes and comments from people I didn't even know! Harvey couldn't be happy with Amanda – why else would he be doing this? I still couldn't bring myself to block him though, as it did kind of mean I had one up on Amanda. Yes, he was doing that thing that men liked to do – just to let you know they weren't quite ready to let go of you yet, and 'I'll keep love-hearting your Instagram stories to remind you of my existence for a little while longer.' But my heart had definitely moved away from him since coming to Tuscany. Even if Harvey asked for my forgiveness and apologised for what he'd done – as I'd fantasised about over and over again – there would be no way back now. I couldn't imagine he would though, even if he wanted to. He would be too proud to admit he'd made such a big mistake.

Yes, my heart had moved away from Harvey now. But was it ready to be with someone else – the man whose bed I'd slept in last night? I remembered Rosa going on and on about his ex, Natalia. I had seen photos of her before, but I checked Google again to remind myself. She was absolutely *stunning*! She had dark-brown hair in a bob and an hourglass figure with a narrow waist and breasts like peaches, and gorgeously bronzed skin. Long legs that went on forever. And a face that was on a par with Monica Bellucci's, round and angelic. She was your typical Italian beauty, that was for sure. It just wasn't fair. There was no way I could compete with that. I zoomed in on a few of the photos just to verify all of this. Yes, there was absolutely no doubt that she was beautiful. And this confirmed that Matteo would have zero interest in me. He obviously not only went out with women who looked like film stars, but they had to be high profile, too. I was neither of these things. Not with my untamed curls that Matteo hadn't even seen yet. No wonder he hadn't even tried to kiss me. He'd probably caught me checking him out in the mirror in the lift, and thought, 'Oh no, she fancies me. I'd better back off a little.' Not that he had even been that forward in the first place. He was just being a good host – helping me because I was Francesca's great-niece, doing that Italian thing of welcoming strangers, and making sure they had enough to eat, and that they knew where everything was. That was all he'd been doing.

When I looked down at myself, I realised that I was wearing a pair of pyjamas – his pyjamas – they were white with navy-blue stripes, and huge on me. I'd rolled the top down as they were so long and too wide for my waist. But they were comfortable and I'd slept very well in them.

A knock came at the door, and I clicked my phone off to hide that I'd been looking into Matteo's love life, and then he pushed open the door a little, and peeked his head round.

'Are you awake?' he said, softly.

'Yes?' I said, brushing a few tendrils of hair off my face, and sitting up straight, suddenly feeling rather self-conscious and aware of my appearance. I must look dreadful, with mascara probably running down my face from the night before.

He pushed the door fully open, and stood there, studying me as if he found me charming in some way, a grin from ear to ear. He wore a fluffy navy-blue dressing gown, and his hair was all ruffled – and he looked damn sexy.

'Buongiorno, Ginevra!' he said. 'How cute do you look in my pyjamas?'

I smiled. Did I really? He was one of those chirpy first-thing-in-the-morning people. Normally, I found this kind of person irritating, especially when groggy from the night before. But for some reason I didn't mind him being like this.

'Buongiorno, Matteo,' I said, my voice croaky. I desperately needed a coffee.

He perched on the end of the bed, and there it was, his citrus cologne – I could smell it from there.

'Did you sleep well?'

I had indeed slept like a log in his comfortable double bed, wearing his pyjamas.

'Yes, I did.'

'I'm going to that bakery, Mancini's – it is the best – to get pastries. Va bene?'

'That sounds amazing.'

'Help yourself to a towel in the bathroom if you want a shower. And when I get back, we sit on the balcony and drink coffee and eat pastries, okay?'

I smiled, and thanked him, and he gave me a little wave, and said, 'A dopo,' as he left the room, closing the door carefully behind him. I got up and went to pull open the windows, and then I pushed open the shutters – and wow, it was my *A Room with a View* moment, for, as we were on the top floor, I could see the city of Florence and the Tuscan hills in the background. All the pretty rooftops with their terracotta tiles, and the Duomo, and beyond to the River Arno, and all the bridges that crossed it to the other side – with of course, the Ponte Vecchio, painted in yellow with its arches standing proudly.

I inhaled. I was actually living the dream. I looked down to see Matteo come out of the front door and walk down the street. I watched him until he was out of sight and then went into the very nice en suite, all white marble with swirls of grey. I made the decision to use Natalia's cleanser, and stepped into the shower, and allowed the water to wash over me. I couldn't help feeling optimistic about the future. I was inspired to be creative, to produce delicious things to eat, and to make my cooking videos – until I got the cookbook deal I so craved. Suddenly I was determined to get what I wanted from my life. I'd got my mojo back and it was in the house where Nonna had once lived. The house that had been a refuge for her family during the war. It had saved them and now it was saving me.

When Matteo came back with brioches filled with coffee cream, we had breakfast on the balcony. He made us espressos using his coffee machine and brought out a bowl of cantaloupe melon, the orange flesh cut into cubes. This breakfast was just what I needed with my sore head from the night before. I wanted to ask him more about Natalia. Did he still like her? I didn't feel bold enough to be asking him this though.

'So, when we've finished eating, we drive back to Cintaldo. We can sit by the pool if you like.'

Lying in the sun sounded like just what I needed.

'I'd love that,' I said.

Half an hour or so later, we got in the car, and he put the roof down. I found myself glancing at him through my sunglasses. And he threw me sideways glances when stopping at traffic lights. The tension from the lift was still there. I wondered if anything might happen before I went back to Cambridge. Maybe a day by the pool would bring us closer together. I would wear my red bikini as it made my boobs look bigger than they actually were. He took the turning to Corte Paradiso, and pulled up in front of Casa Luna. But there was another car parked there – a red convertible Mercedes with the top down.

'Oh mio Dio,' he said.

'What is it?'

'It's Natalia – she is here... she's been trying to call me, both last night, and this morning. She left a voicemail, but I haven't listened to it.'

Oh great. We got out of the car.

'Hey Matteo,' a voice came from by the pool – and then, there she was, walking towards us. And what a vision, in a white bikini that left little to the imagination, her hair pulled up into a high ponytail.

'Ciao, Natalia. What are you doing here?' he said. He seemed exasperated, and I didn't blame him. Who needed an ex turning up out of the blue?

'I have a problem...' She set her eyes on me. 'Who is this woman?'

'This is Ginevra, from England, she is Francesca's great-niece.'

She stretched out her hand and smiled, warmly, which surprised me.

'Of course, I remember now. Ciao, piacere.'

I said the same.

'Allora, Matteo...' she continued. 'I need your help. Because I am shortlisted for Best Presenter at the upcoming A Casa Mia Awards in Milan on Thursday night. I want you to come with me, and stand on the red carpet. Pretend we are still together.'

'What, are you serious?' he said.

'Please, I really need you to do this for me.'

He raised his arms in the air. 'I thought we were done with this kind of thing?'

Fluttering her eyelashes, she spoke in a baby voice. 'Please, Matteo. I am begging you to be there for me this one last time.'

He let out a long sigh. 'Okay. Va bene.'

'Good. And a photographer will be arriving shortly from *Ciao Now* magazine. He will take photos of us in the pool with our arms around each other, looking as though we are in love. My agent says we need to create a buzz for the launch of the new series.'

He rolled his eyes, stroking his chin. 'Do I have a choice?'

'Not really,' she said, playfully. She turned to look at me. 'I am sorry about this, Ginevra. I hate to interrupt your plans.'

She didn't seem like someone you could say no to.

'It's fine, really,' I said, brightly. 'You go ahead.'

'Grazie, Ginevra,' he said, throwing me a grateful look. Then he turned to Natalia. 'We'd better tidy up the pool area and prepare, I guess.'

I threw them both a cheerful wave as I unlocked the door to Casa Stella. I couldn't help being frustrated that I wouldn't get to lie by the pool with Matteo after all. What was this pretending to be with Natalia actually about? Some kind of PR exercise, it appeared. But I wasn't going to let any of this dent my inspired mood. I made a cafetière of coffee and sat in the living room, compiling a list of cooking videos to film.

I would cycle into the village and buy the ingredients before the shops closed for lunch. I'd ask to borrow Matteo's ring light and tripod and have a go at filming content myself. How hard could it be? I would need to rise to the challenge if I wanted to stand on my own two feet. Matteo wouldn't always be next door to help me. Although my head ached a little from the night before, I couldn't help feeling motivated to create something to be proud of. I would get lost in my very own project for the remainder of the day. I could sit by the pool with Matteo tomorrow instead. Or even later this afternoon. Surely Natalia wasn't going to hang around for the whole day?

CHAPTER 22

LILIANA

I returned to Bentley House with sugo di pomodoro and orecchiette like those we made by hand at Casa Stella, outside at the table on warmer days, talking and laughing together. When I left Da Nonna and stepped back onto King's Parade, it struck me that meeting Giulio and being in a place that felt familiar to me had brightened my day a little. The baby didn't feel quite as cumbersome as I walked, and I almost had a spring in my step. I looked forward to going to church with Giulio and his family on Sunday. He'd offered to come to the house and pick me up beforehand so we could walk there together. I was impressed by what a gentleman he was. I looked forward to meeting his mamma and brothers there. His papa had sadly been killed during the war, just like mine.

When I got back to the house I put everything in the kitchen, and then set to work preparing lunch. Giulio had told me about Market Square around the corner. There I'd bought a chicken, potatoes and carrots. On the way back across Parker's Piece, I'd found myself thinking about Salvatore. How I missed him. Would I ever get past the sadness that hung over me constantly and followed me around like a black cloud? Not only was I devastated to lose my amore, but also it didn't help to be separated from my family when I needed it most. Perhaps Salvatore's memory might have returned since I left Italy? Would Mamma write to me if it did? I had thought about writing to him since arriving in Cambridge. I could send him a letter, giving myself one last chance to tell him about the baby, and see if it changed anything. I allowed myself to daydream about him getting his memory back... I would return to Italy and we'd get married straight away. I would actually get the wedding I'd dreamt of all these years. But more importantly, I would then get to keep our baby after all. My decision was made: I would write a letter to him that very day and post it at the earliest opportunity.

After lunch, the professor and Lady Enid went upstairs for their siesta – they were continuing to follow this Italian tradition even though we were now in England. I wasn't complaining, because it meant some time off for me. Carrying the baby meant I was always tired by lunchtime, and I went upstairs for a welcome nap. Lady Enid was a good employer, and she only cared about me buying the food, preparing it, serving it and keeping on top of the kitchen. The rest of my time was my own. Nancy was the housekeeper here and so I would not need to do any of the cleaning.

When I woke up, I checked my watch and saw I had half an hour before I'd be back on duty. Now was my chance to write my letter to Salvatore. I took out my pad of writing paper and envelopes and fountain pen, and sat down at the desk in the corner of the bedroom.

Dearest Salvatore,

I am writing to you from Cambridge in England. The English couple who I worked for have brought me back with them –

because they enjoy my cooking so much. I am thankful because they have saved me. You see, Salvatore, amore mio, I am carrying your child – our child. I am hoping that since I last saw you at the hospital your memory will have returned. If it has, you will recall the very special night we spent together on Christmas Eve in the frantoio. You made love to me with so much passion – we agreed that it wouldn't be long before you were due to return and that it was a risk we were prepared to take. You seemed so down when you came back to the oliviera that day that I wanted to give you something to help you get through the rest of the war. I wanted to give myself to you completely.

If you do remember, please write back and tell me to come home to you. Tell me that we will be married at the Chiesa Santa Maria as we always planned, and that I shall be your wife. Tell me that I will get to live on the oliviera with you, and that our child will grow up with you and me as their mamma and papa. Tell me that I won't have to give our baby away to strangers.

If I don't hear back from you, I shall have to ask my employer, Lady Enid, to send me to a home for unmarried mothers or such like. And then our baby will be adopted, and he or she will never know you or me. Imagine how heart-wrenching that would be? I pray that you will remember me... remember us.

I love you with all my heart, amore mio.

Yours always,

Liliana

I read back the words I'd written. Yes, I'd said everything I needed to say. But I would read the letter again the following day before posting it. I could always change it if need be. It was so important that I got this letter right. What if his memory hadn't come back – how would it feel for him to receive such news about an unborn child, fathered by him? Surely, it would be utterly devastating? Would he tell his family and then mine? Should I take that risk? I would mull it all over before making my decision. I shouldn't be hasty and there was still a little time to play with. Perhaps going to Mass would bring some clarity – how I hoped it would. Whatever happened, I wouldn't want to look back and wish I'd done things differently. I wouldn't want to have any regrets. One usually regretted what one didn't do rather than what one did do – Nonna Paola would sometimes say this. But I needed to be careful not to make the situation worse than it already was.

The next morning, Giulio came to collect me to go to church. When he knocked on the front door, I was waiting in the hall, wearing my finest for Mass – a maroon dress, which once again was rather snug, but it just about fitted – and stockings and shoes with a low heel. I would need to think about adding panels to my dresses, or perhaps buying larger ones – if I could find the money. I picked up my handbag from the console table and opened the front door to see him standing there, wearing a suit and tie. He looked very dapper, and he had a great big grin on his face.

'Buongiorno, signorina,' he said.

I smiled and said, 'Buongiorno, signore,' in return, and walked down the steps towards the gate. He stood aside, and opened it for me, and I passed through to the other side, onto the pavement.

'This way,' he said, making for Parker's Piece. 'It's only a five-minute walk or so.'

As we walked, he asked me about where I was from in Italy, and I told him my story, omitting anything to do with Salvatore, of course. He told me how his parents had come to England from Calabria in the early 1900s.

After we'd crossed Parker's Piece, we turned a corner, and I was struck by a magnificent church a few hundred yards away. It stood tall and proud, tucked into the nook of a crossroads. I couldn't help looking up at it in wonder.

'What a majestic building,' I said.

'Isn't it.'

We crossed the busy road at the traffic lights, and approached the main door, where the priest welcomed us with a warm smile and a handshake. Being in a church again was a comfort. We went inside, and Giulio led me to a row where I presumed his family were sitting, all together – his brothers, like him wore suits and ties, and his mamma wore a brown dress. He introduced me, and they all nodded and smiled. His brothers were called Marco, Paolo and Luigi, and they were all younger than him. We sat down in the pew, and I was on the aisle. Organ music played, and the priest appeared in the pulpit and spoke to us. Being in church made me feel at home again – although the priest spoke mostly in English, with a little Latin, at least the experience of going to Mass was familiar to me. Being there lifted my spirits.

Afterwards, Giulio introduced me to his family.

'Piacere, Liliana,' his mamma said, proffering a hand. I shook it, and she smiled at me warmly, and truly it made me happy to be in the presence of an Italian matriarch again. 'You must come for lunch one day,' she said, as if reading my thoughts.

'Thank you, I'd like that very much, Signora Farina,' I said.

'We live in a house near Jesus Green, at the other side of Cambridge. Giulio can make the arrangements with you.'

The Italian way of welcoming strangers in need *a tavola*, was familiar to me too. My family had done this at Casa Stella during the war with so many people – partisans and Allied prisoners of war – and in the end it had been Papa's downfall. But we thrived on la convivialità, on sharing food with others when welcoming them into our homes.

'I would appreciate that very much – thank you for your kind invitation.'

She threw me a wave, and walked off with Giulio's brothers in the direction of Parker's Piece.

Giulio stood there, and looked down at me, scratched his nose.

'Do you mean that, would you like to come and eat with my family at our home?'

I nodded. 'Yes, of course. Your mother is very kind.'

'She likes to have people round, and I said you were here in Cambridge, all alone, just arrived from Italy. My family understands how it feels to come to England as a stranger – to know no one.'

'Well, I shall have to see when I can get some time off, on a day that suits your mamma.'

'Certo. We have all the time in the world.'

I wasn't sure we did. If I sent the letter to Salvatore, and he replied to say he remembered everything and to go home and get married – I would be gone. And Giulio would then wonder where on earth I'd disappeared to. If I got to know him and his family, they would be confused by my sudden departure. And if Salvatore didn't ask me to go back to him, I would be returning to Tuscany after I'd had the baby, for certain. Was it a good idea to get to know Giulio more than as someone who went into his family's delicatessen, or who attended Mass at the same time?

'Thank you for inviting me to Mass with your family, Giulio.'

'It is nothing. Will I see you at Da Nonna tomorrow?'

I nodded.

'Si, senza dubbio.'

'Shall I walk you back to your house?'

I shook my head. 'Oh no, I shall be fine, thank you.'

'Va bene. Arrivederci, Liliana.'

He turned and ran to catch up with his family, and I watched him go. And then I made my way back to Bentley House, back to my life as a cook so I could prepare lunch for the professor and Lady Enid. And then I would reread the letter I'd written to Salvatore, and decide whether to rewrite it, or even to send it. Was it the right thing to do? Surely, if his memory returned, he would be in touch straight away? Mamma would tell him where I was – she had my address. I would think on it some more, and make my decision the next day.

CHAPTER 23

JEN

An hour or so later, I cycled into the village to get pancetta for my next cooking video before the shops closed for siesta. In Italy there was always that rush to get anything you needed before lunchtime. Often, shops wouldn't open again until around four o'clock. I was going to make spaghetti carbonara, a simple recipe using few ingredients, and delicious too. The story went that this recipe originated in Rome when it was liberated in 1944. American soldiers had asked Italians what to do with their bacon and powdered eggs rations, wanting something to remind them of the bacon and egg breakfast they'd have at home. And so spaghetti carbonara was born. If the butcher had any guanciale, pork cheek – the traditional choice for an authentic Roman carbonara – I'd buy that instead of pancetta. If I could get my hands on a piece of pecorino, I would buy that, too. Otherwise, pancetta and Parmesan would do just fine.

I'd come up with several recipe ideas for my cooking videos that morning, sitting on the sofa, looking out at the Tuscan scenery. Spaghetti carbonara could be part of a pasta series. I would go on to make ragù, pesto with all that basil from the terracotta pot, and the dish that Matteo and I both loved – cacio e pepe. For viewers who were looking for more of a challenge, I could make handmade pasta shapes such as orecchiette like Nonna had taught me. Then there was gnocchi, made using potatoes, and ravioli, filled with wild boar or beef. I could make lasagne the proper Italian way with hard-boiled eggs, but also a simpler version. I liked the idea of making further series of risotto, salads, desserts, cakes and biscuits, soups, stews. The list was endless! In my head, I could visualise a whole cookbook, laid out with beautiful photographs of all these wonderful Italian dishes. I would just keep on manifesting my dream until hopefully one day it would become true. I couldn't wait to tell Matteo about all my ideas when we next got to spend time together. Hopefully Natalia wouldn't stick around for too long. Surely she'd need to get back to Milan? And then Matteo and I could sit together on the terrace with a bottle of Chianti, and I'd impress him with my spaghetti carbonara.

I went to get Francesca's bike from behind the shed and climbed on, putting my feet on the pedals. There was now a van parked next to Natalia's Mercedes. Over by the pool, I could see a couple of men in T-shirts and shorts setting up screens and big lights. Wow, it was a professional photo shoot. How could I expect a man who lived this kind of life to be interested in me? It was a big shame that Natalia had sabotaged my day. All I could do was shut this thought out of my mind, and try to enjoy the scenery as I cycled along the gravel road. But this time, I wasn't blown away by the beauty of my surroundings, or by the sound of the cicadas. This time, the beauty almost seemed to taunt me, as if reminding me that my day had gone downhill. But no, I must go and get my food. Then I would attempt to make a cooking video all by myself. Remembering that I needed to borrow Matteo's equipment, I stopped cycling for a moment to WhatsApp him.

Hi, I'm just cycling into the village to get supplies. Would you mind leaving your ring light and tripod in my kitchen? Grazie.

I waited. The grey ticks went blue. And then 'typing'...

Si, certo

He still had a copy of my key, and I had one of his, just in case he or I locked ourselves out. I managed to buy both pecorino and guanciale, and when I got back from the village I wheeled the bike behind the shed and the photo shoot seemed to be in full swing. Envy tugged at my gut as I looked over to see Matteo and Natalia in the pool with their arms around each other. How I wished I was in her place. Seeing the pair of them like this, I was truly jealous, even though they were supposedly just pretending to still be an item. I did like Matteo as more than a friend. But with Natalia in the picture, there didn't seem to be much chance of anything happening between us. I reassured myself that, later, she'd go back to Milan. This thought spurred me on to get in the kitchen and start on a meal to really impress Matteo with that evening.

In the kitchen, I saw that he'd left the ring light and tripod on the table. I went to change into the floral dress, seeing as it had worked so well last time. I touched up my make-up and brushed my hair. It really did need a wash, and I'd been getting by with dry shampoo for the past few days. I'd have to wash it after swimming, and reveal my natural curls to Matteo. I switched on the ring light and adjusted the tripod to the right height. And then I began filming, stopping and starting as I went. I followed the format that Matteo had suggested before. First, I introduced the recipe. Then I chopped up the guanciale from the deli into cubes, saying that you could also use pancetta or any bacon really. I separated the egg yolk from the white and then whisked the yolk and mixed it with grated pecorino. I dropped the spaghetti into boiling water, giving tips on how to cook it – not for too long, so it was al dente, literally meaning to the tooth. So the pasta was slightly hard when you bit into it. This was how Italians considered that pasta should always be cooked.

While the spaghetti was boiling, I fried the guanciale until it was golden and crispy, then I added the cooked spaghetti to the pan followed by the egg and cheese mixture and a little water from the pan. This was not done over the heat as it was important that the eggs didn't become scrambled – the heat from the pasta would cook them just enough so you should end up with a creamy sauce. Cream was often used when making carbonara in England, but it wasn't needed. Of course, you could add it if you wanted, but you shouldn't include it if you were making carbonara the authentic Italian way.

By the time I'd finished cooking and filming, stopping and starting the camera as I went, I was exhausted. And my mouth was dry from all the talking. I poured myself a large glass of water, and then I sat at the table for my final take – me tasting what I'd made, and saying, 'Mmm, that's delicious, so authentically Italian.' Perhaps this would be my catchphrase? I'd say it at the end of all my videos and see how it went. While eating the pasta, I watched the video back. I hadn't done a bad job, all on my own. I would have a go at editing it with a coffee on the sofa. And then I'd add subtitles and the recipe details from my phone notes, as well as some text on the video itself at the beginning – my hook. Matteo had told me that I needed a good hook, because that was what kept viewers watching, meaning the video would get shown to more people. Something like 'Did you know this is *actually* how you make carbonara?' And then towards the end, 'You don't need cream at all.'

I made a pot of coffee and went into the living room. There on the sofa, I set about editing my video. I knew it would take some time, but I needed to be patient and get it as good as it could be. When I'd finished, half an hour later, I couldn't wait to show it to Matteo. He was bound to be so proud of me doing it all by myself without his help. But then a message popped up from him in WhatsApp.

We've just finished the shoot and Natalia is taking me for dinner in San Gimignano to say thank you. It's too late to drive back to Milan tonight so she's going to stay over. See you tomorrow?

She was staying over. Envy tugged at my stomach. Did that mean they'd sleep together? I hoped that I wouldn't hear anything through the walls...

Sure, of course.

What else was there to say? I couldn't help including a full stop rather than a friendly emoji to reflect my disappointment. Should I post the video tonight without him checking it first? I wasn't sure. I'd have a shower and change into something more comfortable and clear up the kitchen. Then I'd look at it again and make my decision. It had been so thrilling seeing all the likes and views come in last time and I wasn't sure if I could wait another day to see it all happen again. How I wished that I would get to have wine with Matteo on the terrace tonight – we'd spent the past three evenings together and now I would be alone. But still, after they'd gone out, I would have a glass of wine and look at the view and decide whether to post my video or not. I should make the most of being in Tuscany as before long I'd be back in Cambridge – working at Da Nonna all day and night and going home to a flat I didn't like living in. Unless I decided to come back to Casa Stella again before the summer was over. Should I? I wasn't sure... it would depend on whether Matteo was actually seeing Natalia or just pretending for PR purposes. Perhaps they'd fall into bed together after tonight's romantic dinner out? Being at Casa Stella wouldn't be quite the same if Natalia was visiting all the time – I'd just end up feeling like a third wheel.

That evening, I waited for the sound of the car engine to start and then, through the kitchen window, I watched them go. Now I could sit on the terrace with a glass of Chianti. Once again, it seemed as though the idyllic setting was taunting me. The temperature was cooler than on previous nights and a light breeze brushed my face. It would hopefully keep the mosquitoes away. Admittedly, I was relieved to have some respite from the heat, even though when I'd arrived on that wonderful balmy night everything had been so perfect. I found myself picturing that evening again, smiling to myself as I sipped my wine. Perhaps tomorrow we could have another evening like that. But what if Natalia decided to stay tomorrow too? And then he went to the awards in Milan on Thursday? Why hadn't I savoured every single minute of his company more? I had wondered if he might kiss me before I returned to Cambridge – but no, I pushed that thought out of my mind. Right now, he was probably kissing Natalia in San Gimignano with a phenomenal view of the Tuscan hills as their backdrop. They were probably dining in a fancy restaurant with white tablecloths and someone going between the tables playing a violin while they gazed into each other's eyes.

I watched my video again – it wasn't bad at all. Matteo had told me that early evenings were often a good time to post, when people were enjoying some downtime on their phones after work or on the train home. I took a deep breath. Should I be brave? What if Matteo was with Natalia all day tomorrow and he couldn't check it anyway? I wasn't feeling patient enough to wait for another day or two. I pressed the button to post my video on TikTok, and then went through all the other apps and did the same. After that, I put my phone on the table. I'd have another glass of wine – pluck up some Dutch courage – before checking to see how it was doing.

The sky flashed. What was that, lightning? And then a rumble. Oh, it was a thunderstorm. There were often dramatic thunderstorms in Italy towards the end of August. I'd watched one approach across the sea from my grandparents' summer house in Riccione the previous year. I felt droplets of rain on my shoulder. Time to go inside. Fork lightning lit up the whole sky and then a crack and bang. I picked up my glass of wine and phone and went back into Casa Stella, closing the French doors firmly behind me. There I sat on the sofa, watching the thunderstorm play out in the night sky, and then heavy rain came, bringing more flashes and rumbles. I thought of Matteo and Natalia out in San Gimignano. They'd be stuck there until the storm moved on. Oh dear.

I refilled my wine glass and took a big sip. Right, I couldn't wait any longer to check how my video was doing. My heart racing, I clicked into the apps and... wow, the views and likes numbers were huge! My gut fizzed with excitement. This was hugely motivating. It made me want to record more videos and get more attention. Would this new direction lead to my cookbook deal? All I could do was keep working through my list of recipes. As Matteo had said, filming the videos in Tuscany was probably adding an authentic Italian touch, pleasing the algorithms and gaining me views.

A message flashed up from Mum, interrupting my thoughts.

Ciao, cara... we're back home. How is the house in Tuscany? I can't wait to hear all about it. We're looking forward to seeing you at the 80th anniversary lunch on Sunday for Da Nonna. Can I ask you a favour?

Oh yes, the lunch on Sunday. The reason I'd booked my return flight for Friday in the first place.

Hi Mum. Tuscany is amazing. What's the favour?

Can you make 80 of your tiramisù cupcakes for guests to take home? Thought it would be a nice touch

I thought my cupcake-making days were over, but I knew it would mean a lot to my family if I made them. I'd have to do it on Friday night when I got back to the flat.

Okay can you drop the ingredients round my flat and I'll make them when I get back on Friday night? Can you order cake toppers with number 80 in gold?

Sure I'll get those ordered. Send me a list and Giuseppe will drop everything round

Grazie, Mamma. A dopo

Ciao. See you on Sunday. Don't be late!

I went to get a glass of water from a bottle in the fridge, and made my way upstairs. I would have an early night. I only had two days left at Casa Stella and hoped I'd get to see Matteo tomorrow. If not, I was more than capable of entertaining myself. I could get the bus into San Gimignano and amble around. This was something I'd planned to do anyway. And then I could make more cooking videos. If Natalia left, I would lie by the pool. It would be nice to leave Italy with a bit of a suntan, at least.

CHAPTER 24

LILIANA

That evening, after making supper for the professor and Lady Enid, I sat on my bed and unfolded the letter I'd written to Salvatore. As I read my words, imagining what it would be like for him to read them, tears ran down my face. How could I have been so foolish, giving myself to him on Christmas Eve? It had only been one time, but it had been enough to get me in trouble and now here I was, living in a foreign country, feeling quite alone. Although I'd met Giulio, and already considered him to be a friend, I wished I could confide in him. He seemed like a wise person, and I would relish the opportunity to ask for his advice. But I had no one to talk to. There was Nancy, I supposed, but I wasn't sure if she'd be interested in my woes. She seemed nice enough, and not a judgemental type, but we hadn't had a chance to get to know each other on a personal level. Our conversations always seemed to be related to matters concerning the professor and Lady Enid.

The following morning, I walked to King's Parade, to Da Nonna, and Giulio came to open the door, gesturing for me to sit down at the same table by the window. I couldn't help noticing that there was a small jar, containing a red rose with velvety petals, and a sign saying RESERVED. I was touched by the trouble he'd gone to for me.

'I have exciting news,' Giulio said.

'What is it?'

'We have Parma ham, olives, and pecorino – all from Italy. Would you like to try with some bread my mamma baked this morning?'

I would love this reminder of home more than anything.

Nodding, and smiling, I said, 'Yes, that would be really lovely.'

'And an espresso for the signorina?'

'Yes, please.'

'Subito...'

He got up and went to the counter, and played around with the coffee machine for a few minutes, before bringing over an espresso. He then disappeared into the kitchen, and I spooned in sugar from the bowl already on the table.

A few minutes later, he reappeared with a plate containing thin slices of Parma ham, triangles of pecorino and green olives.

'Be careful – the olives have stones in, of course.'

'This looks wonderful.'

'Ah wait un attimo...' He leapt up and went into the kitchen, before coming back with a basket of sliced bread.

He sat down opposite me.

'Well, tuck in.'

'Are you going to help me?'

'If you insist.'

I picked up a slice of ham and rolled it up and ate it. It was so delicious. We sat there together in silence until we'd worked our way through everything.

I picked up the napkin and wiped my mouth, fully satisfied.

'I can't wait to eat that kind of food again when I return to Tuscany.'

'What, you are going back? When?'

'Oh, in the autumn. I'm only here for a few months.'

'Ah, I see. For some reason, I'd understood that you would be here for much longer.'

I shook my head. 'My stay was only ever meant to be temporary.'

He met my gaze, and then unfolded a napkin on the table and refolded it, very carefully.

'So would you like to take some of these things back to the house?' he finally said.

'Yes, please.' I took some coins out of my purse and handed them to him.

'I shall go and prepare everything. Aspetta.'

He went off and organised everything into a bag, and called me over.

'I have added in a couple of those cantuccini biscuits that you like.'

'Grazie, Giulio. You are too kind.'

He looked across the counter at me.

'It is my pleasure. Do you have any suggestions for other biscuits we could make, apart from cantuccini?'

I thought for a moment. 'My nonna Paola makes the most delicious large amaretti biscuits with an almond in the centre. They are soft rather than crunchy, and melt-in-the-mouth delicious.'

'That is a good idea. And if we make them bigger, we can charge more money. Grazie, Liliana. I shall have to ask you for more recipe ideas.'

He went over to the door and opened it.

'Will you come back tomorrow?'

'Yes, every day, apart from Sunday, obviously.'

'And I shall still see you then because we'll go to church together.'

'Oh, we're going together again?'

'Of course we are. I shall escort you like before. And we'll have to work out a date for you to come over to the house for lunch, that's if you would still like to do that. My mamma keeps asking after you.'

I nodded and smiled, and he closed the door behind me. He waved at me through the window as I walked away. Everything had seemed so challenging for such a long time, and Giulio had brought a little light into my life. And I was so grateful. I thanked the Lord under my breath, for taking care of me. I'd expected to be so lonely and sad in Cambridge, but it was as if Giulio had been sent to keep an eye on me – to make sure I was all right. But then it occurred to me – was spending more time with him such a good idea? I was getting bigger each day, and soon it would be impossible to hide that I was with child. Already, it must look as though I was putting on a great deal of weight. If we started spending more time together, he would surely notice if I didn't go to the deli every day anymore? This thought worried me. I would just have to speak to Nancy. I needed her as my ally. At some stage, I would ask if she minded going to the deli on my behalf, giving him a reason why I'd stopped going there. Perhaps I could have influenza that dragged on for a few months – that was realistic enough, wasn't it?

On the way back to Bentley House, I thought again about the letter I'd written to Salvatore. I didn't think I could go ahead with sending it to him, after all. I would keep it in case I changed my mind. But having mulled it all over I had decided that, if his memory came back, he would get in touch with me anyway, and then I could tell him everything. If I sent that letter and it fell into the wrong hands, or if he told his family and word got back to mine, I would be so ashamed. No, I would not send it. Instead, I would hope and pray that his memory returned before the baby came. In the meantime, I would have to speak to Lady Enid. Soon it would be impossible to hide that I was with child, and I was becoming more tired with each day that passed. I needed to ask for her advice. Afterwards, I would ask Nancy to help me hide my pregnancy from Giulio – how I hoped she'd agree to cover for me so he didn't find out. I would be devastated if he did.

After I'd made lunch, I went to the drawing room to speak to Lady Enid about the baby. The professor was lecturing – he tended to spend quite a lot of time at St Catherine's College, meaning that Lady Enid was often in the house on her own during the day. She seemed sad now that we were back in England, and I wondered if she was missing Italy. She was sitting at the desk by the window overlooking the garden, writing letters. As usual, there was a glass of brandy by her side.

'Lady Enid, I have something to tell you,' I said.

She turned round in her chair to look at me.

'Oh yes, what is it, Liliana. Have you been settling in here in Cambridge?'

'I have a problem, and I'm hoping you can help me find a solution.'

She frowned. 'Pray, do tell.'

'I'm... I'm with child.'

'I beg your pardon?'

I repeated myself.

She put a hand over her mouth. 'But Liliana, what happened? Who may I ask is the father?'

I told her about Christmas Eve, how I'd foolishly assumed Salvatore would come back and marry me, and how I hadn't expected to conceive that night.

'And then he came back, but he had no idea who you were?'

I nodded, tears stinging my eyes, as the reality that I'd been shutting out of my mind came back into it.

'I'm not one to judge, as you know – I understand how one

can get caught up in the throes of passion. But now, we need to decide how you are going to deal with this.'

'Yes, exactly,' I said. 'Do you have any ideas? I was thinking that there are probably those places for unmarried mothers, here in England?'

'Well, yes there are, indeed. Ghastly places...' She thought for a moment. 'And how long have you known? Did you know before...?'

'Yes, and when Salvatore couldn't remember me, coming here was my only way out of the mess I found myself in. I am truly sorry, Lady Enid. If my mother or grandmother had found out the truth, they would be horrified.'

'Of course, I understand your position entirely.'

Lady Enid placed a cigarette between her lips, lit it and took a drag. She exhaled. 'Well, you have two options, as far as I can see. The first is to go into one of those ghastly homes for unmarried mothers. There you will have the baby and give it away to complete strangers and you will never see it again.'

The thought of doing this was unsettling, but I couldn't see an alternative. What was the second option?

'And what else might you suggest I do?'

'Well, as you know, the professor and I haven't had any children – and that is because we haven't been able to. I always wanted to be a mother, and we did talk about adopting but, with the war, the opportunity never came. I had thought it was too late for us...' Her voice trailed off.

I blinked and my heart lifted with hope. Surely, she wasn't suggesting...? This would be ideal for me, to know that my child would go to a good home – that Lady Enid and the professor would be their parents. Did she really mean this?

'What are you saying? That you would take the baby?'

'I would have to speak to the professor, but yes, it's a possibility. If he agrees, of course – and he will, I'm sure of it. Now we're back here in Cambridge, he'll be at the college all the time, lecturing and writing books, and having drinks with his colleagues – he likes to socialise more than me. And I was already beginning to feel that my life here could be a little empty. This would be our last chance to have a child of our own. We did talk about trying to adopt when returning to England, so this would be ideal for us – and so much easier than going through the official channels.'

I wanted to wrap my arms around her and hug her, but that wouldn't have been appropriate. She was saving me. That was if the professor agreed.

'That would be wonderful, if you were able to do that, Lady Enid. Do you think the professor will agree to it?'

'Of course he will! He always lets me do what I want. And he'll be pleased that I have a distraction while he's so busy at the university.'

'Thank you, Lady Enid. You have no idea what this means to me.'

'So, you carry on working for as long as you can – I shall confirm everything as soon as I am able. In the meantime, if you start to find your tasks too difficult, do come and tell me.'

'I appreciate that very much.'

'And we'd have to talk about what happens after the baby. Would you want to continue working here?'

'I will go back to Tuscany, signora.'

'Oh, well, that would work rather well – it saves matters becoming complicated.'

I guessed she meant it would save me having to find another job – as there was no way I could continue to work at Bentley House. I would have to leave my baby behind, but at least they would be in good hands.

'Well, I had better get back to work.'

'Very good. We shall talk about this again,' Lady Enid said.

I left the drawing room and made my way back below stairs. The next thing on my list was to speak to Nancy. Already, I felt as though a weight had lifted from my shoulders, despite the weight I was still carrying inside of me. Lady Enid and the professor adopting my child would be the best possible outcome for me, considering the circumstances. As I made my way down the stairs to the kitchen, I couldn't help smiling to myself as I adjusted the strings on my apron. Everything was going to be all right, after all. I just knew it would be.

CHAPTER 25

JEN

The next morning, when I pushed open the bedroom shutters, I was glad to see the sky was back to being a deep-blue colour. The only signs of last night's storm were a few puddles where rainwater had collected in dips on the terrace. I made a cup of tea and sat in bed, checking my latest cooking video. My notifications showed that Matteo had 'liked' it – so he had actually watched it then. This gave me a warm feeling. The second video had done quite well, but not as well as the first one. Perhaps I should have waited for him to check it before posting. Too late now. Oh well, now he was otherwise occupied, I would just have to keep making the videos on my own. Something was driving me to do all this – since arriving in Tuscany, I suddenly felt hugely motivated to make something of my life. Being at Casa Stella was certainly good for me. I jumped into the shower, then dressed, hoping Natalia would leave soon so I could sit by the pool. And then I made my way downstairs. When I switched on the light on the landing, I spotted the cupboard at the top of the stairs. I needed to ask Matteo about the key again.

In the living room, I saw out of the window that Natalia's

red Mercedes was still there. By the time I'd had breakfast and made my next video, she would hopefully have departed for Milan. Not wanting to bump into Matteo and Natalia, I chose to eat breakfast inside that morning. Besides, the table and chairs on the terrace would be wet from the night before. I made a pot of coffee, and generously spread Nutella onto a slice of bread. As I sat at the kitchen table, with a view of the gardens, I found myself daydreaming. Being here in this house had calmed me. Usually, I would scroll through my phone when eating – an awful habit I'd got into. But I didn't seem to need my phone as company here – I was more than content with my own thoughts. My mind wandered to the moment when I'd first seen Matteo standing by the front desk at Da Nonna. Deep down, I'd sensed that he would impact my life in some way as soon as I saw him. And he certainly had – but it was the ring as well as Casa Stella that had brought him to me. I still couldn't work out exactly why Nonna had gone to England at the end of the war. And what on earth could had happened to estrange her from Francesca? Perhaps the answers might be inside that cupboard. Why was it locked? And what could be in there that was so top secret?

I got up and rinsed my plate in the sink, and slotted it into a space in the drying rack. Time to set everything up for my next cooking video: a simple pesto recipe with suggestions on what you could do with it. I opened the back door to crouch down and collect basil leaves from the terracotta pot, noticing a slight chill in the air after the storm. It would be baking hot again by noon, no doubt. As I picked a basil leaf and held it to my nose, breathing in its scent, there they both were, approaching the table on Matteo's terrace. A pastel-pink silk negligee hung off her perfect frame, and he wore shorts with no top. My gut lurched. Had they slept together? I couldn't be sure. They weren't being all touchy-feely or anything. He used a towel to dry the chairs and gestured for Natalia to sit down. She was holding a moka pot and espresso cups and saucers. I was about to sneak back inside and quietly shut the door, but Matteo spotted me – *oh damn*. Natalia pulled up a chair at the table, lit a cigarette and studied her phone. But Matteo came over and squatted down so he was at the same level as me. I did all I could to not look at his bare chest.

'Ciao, Ginevra. Tutto bene?'

I stood up and he did the same.

'Yes, well...' I scratched my nose. 'I was just picking some basil for my next video.'

He grinned, revealing his perfect white teeth, and our eyes met.

'I saw the one you posted last night. Brava. And now you make another?'

I nodded. 'Yes, thought I might as well carry on.'

'Very good. Will you be joining us by the pool when you have finished?'

That would be so awkward. I shrugged while thinking about what to say.

'Maybe,' was all I could manage.

He wasn't telling me when Natalia was leaving, if she was leaving today even. For all I knew, she might be sticking around for another whole day and night.

He slid his hands into the pockets of his shorts, and we stood there looking at each other. It was a shame Natalia had been at Casa Stella when we got back from Florence. On the car journey back, I'd been so hopeful that Matteo and I might grow closer.

'Okay, a dopo, Ginevra,' he finally said, before walking back to the table and sitting down. Natalia glanced up at him, tapped her cigarette over the ashtray, and then returned her attention to her phone. I couldn't help feeling a little sad – that should be me sitting there with him.

I went back inside and put the basil leaves on the kitchen

worktop – so pungent, they filled the whole room with their glorious sweet and peppery scent. But then I found myself drawn to the window. I couldn't help hiding behind the curtain, and watching surreptitiously as Matteo poured out espressos for them both. Now she was talking and waving her hands around, the cigarette resting between her fingers, and he was nodding along.

I sighed. All I could do was record my video, and then later I might get to lie by the pool. If she left this morning, Matteo and I could have spaghetti pesto for lunch. I smiled to myself at this thought. I felt some ridiculous need to impress him with my cooking. Maybe he was my muse. I chuckled to myself at this thought.

I went upstairs to check my appearance, but when I looked in the mirror I realised that I really needed to wash my hair – it was looking so greasy. All right, I would just have to sport my natural curls for the remainder of my time in Tuscany. I jumped in the shower and washed it, and then decided to allow it to dry naturally while I set up the video.

Back in the kitchen, I found a large pestle and mortar made from white marble in one of the cupboards. Wow, what a find – it was covered in scratches and had clearly had plenty of use over the years. Had Nonna used this when she was staying at Casa Stella? Had her mamma used it, and Nonna Paola, who she often mentioned? I adjusted the tripod to the right height and put my phone in it. Then I raised the level of the ring light and switched it on. Time to begin. I pressed record. Into the pestle and mortar, I added garlic cloves, basil, olive oil, grated Parmesan and toasted pine nuts. Making pesto this way was far more satisfying than using a blender. I stopped and started filming when needed with the little Bluetooth gadget that Matteo had given to me – it looked like a mini remote control. I talked through examples of what the pesto could be used for. Then I spread it on toasted bread and covered it with grated

Parmesan before heating it under the grill. I also boiled a pan of spaghetti to show this option. I tasted both dishes, saying, 'Yum… so authentically Italian,' and then the video was done – all ready to be edited.

I went into the living room to take a sofa break. Through the window, I could see that Matteo and Natalia had moved to the sunloungers by the pool. She wore that same white bikini, and he was sporting navy-blue swimming shorts with a pattern on them. She was still smoking and talking in an animated way, and he was still nodding along. She didn't seem to be going anywhere in a hurry. I would use this opportunity to go into San Gimignano, as a visit was on my lists of things to do. It was only ten minutes away by bus. I checked the timetable online, bought a ticket, and made my way along the gravel drive to the bus stop outside the pasticceria on Via del Bacio. Matteo and Natalia were too engrossed in conversation to notice me pass by, much to my relief.

I'd read online that San Gimignano's tall towers had been built as displays of wealth and they'd represented the power of the families they belonged to during the medieval era. I remembered seeing them on the horizon when we returned from Florence. I wanted to amble around the town with no fixed plan – my favourite way to explore. I saw myself soaking up the atmosphere, grabbing an ice cream, and then buying a postcard for Nonna, and finding a nice little café to write it in.

I waited at the bus stop, taking in the charming village and the surrounding hills. Was this really my life? I inhaled, thinking how much I'd love to come back after the anniversary lunch. But I wouldn't want to if Matteo and Natalia were back together and she was there. The bus came and I got on it and sat down. Before long, the towers came into view – so imposing, a medieval Manhattan almost. The road twisted and wound and went uphill, then, before long, the bus was pulling up in the town centre. I stepped down onto the pavement, and before me was a striking archway, the Porta San Giovanni, which I knew to be the entrance to the main part of town. Next to the archway, I was struck by the most incredible view, signposted as a *punto panoramico*. I could see for miles and miles. It was so impressive and inspiring. I took some photos for Instagram, including a selfie with the view as my backdrop. And then I just stood there for a few minutes taking it all in.

As I passed through the archway, I found myself on Via San Giovanni, bustling with cafes and shops and people walking by, their voices echoing up around the tall medieval buildings. Spotting a tabacchi, I went over, and selected a postcard of the towers. Inside, I paid for it along with a postcard stamp for the UK. Then I walked up the hill to Piazza della Cisterna, a square bustling with people. Before me was an ice cream parlour that I'd seen online called Gelateria Dondali. I went inside and asked for a cone with a scoop of pistachio. I sat on a step nearby, in the shade, and savoured every mouthful of that ice cream. Groups of tourists went by – British and American mostly. I got up and continued to walk up the hill, browsing shop windows, until I came across an adorable-looking pasticceria with a handful of tables outside in the shade. I ordered a coffee and an almond biscuit dusted with icing sugar and found a table outside. Right, time to write Nonna's postcard. What should I say? I couldn't remember the last time I'd written one. I was totally ignoring the fact that she'd probably see me before it arrived at home – but that was beside the point. She'd asked me to send her a postcard from a place that held special memories for her, and so I was keeping my word.

To Nonna,

I've been having the best time at Casa Stella. What a house and the views of the Tuscan hills are absolutely breathtaking! You'll be pleased to hear that I'm cooking again using ingredi-

ents from the garden and the village shops. I do love it here. Still haven't found Nonna Paola's recipe book but I'm hoping it's in a cupboard Matteo needs to find the key for... watch this space.

Love, Jen x

While I was sticking on the stamp, my phone buzzed. A message from Matteo. I closed my eyes, hoping they were words I wanted to see.

Ciao, where are you?

Oh, had Natalia left then?

I'm in a café in San Gimignano

Natalia has gone back to Milan

Okay, and...? Did that mean we were spending the evening together then? While I was working out how to reply, another message flashed up.

Shall I come and meet you? We can go to that lovely enoteca I mentioned for a glass of wine

That would be really nice to have a drink with him.

Sure, why not?

Va bene. I'll meet you in half an hour at Enoteca Pietro next to the punto panoramico

There seemed to be several panoramic points in San

Gimignano, according to all the signs I'd seen when walking around. I would find the enoteca on Google maps.

Perfetto

When I searched for Enoteca Pietro, it was a ten-minute walk away. I was glad Matteo was coming to meet me, although still confused about what was going on between him and Natalia. Should I ask him? I didn't really feel confident enough to do this, and it was rather presumptuous too. I wasn't sure if he saw me as any more than a friend. I ordered another coffee – there was no rush. I was in Italy living la vita lenta, the slow life, and I could get quite used to it. I'd find a postbox for Nonna's postcard en route. It wouldn't matter if I was fashionably late, just by five minutes or so... in fact, I'd rather he arrived first.

When I arrived at Enoteca Pietro, Matteo was established on a stool at a high table with a glass of red wine, facing the view – it was truly stunning as we were on a big hill, completely surrounded by countryside. I couldn't think of a better place to have a drink with him.

'Ciao, Ginevra,' he said, waving me over.

He climbed down off the stool, and came to double-kiss me – still smelling of that divine citrus scent.

We sat down. The waiter came over, and Matteo ordered a glass of Chianti for me.

'So, Natalia has gone back to Milan then?' I asked.

'Yes, because she has to go and get ready for the awards ceremony tomorrow night.'

Was he going too? And would she be returning to Corte Paradiso? Although I was desperate for answers to these questions, I didn't feel brave enough to ask. Perhaps a few sips of wine would embolden me.

The waiter brought my wine along with a complimentary bowl of olives.

We clinked glasses and said, 'Cin cin'.

I took a sip and the wine was exactly the right temperature, and full-bodied and earthy. It was one of my favourite Italian reds – and always seemed to slide down very easily.

He studied me, and his eyes narrowed.

'Your hair looks different,' he said.

He'd noticed then.

'Oh yes, I washed it and don't have my straighteners with me.'

'What, you spend time making it straight when it looks like that naturally?'

I nodded.

'But your curls are so pretty – bellissima.'

I could feel my face reddening. What a compliment. I didn't know what to say.

'I keep meaning to ask...' he said.

'Yes?'

'We did talk a little in Florence, when I told you about Natalia and those disastrous earrings from the Ponte Vecchio.'

I raised my eyebrows. 'That was kind of mean of her.'

'I was upset, yes, but I am getting over it. That afternoon, you said you had been with someone until recently. What happened?'

I guessed now was the time to reveal all about Harvey. What would Matteo think of me? A woman who'd been more or less jilted at the altar because of my best friend? For some reason I felt embarrassed, as if I'd done something wrong when it was the two of them. But somehow I found myself wanting to tell him.

'Well... I was engaged.'

'You were?'

'Yes, and it didn't work out.'

'Tell me, what happened, did you change your mind?'

'No, I didn't change my mind.'

'He did?'

I found myself playing with a strand of my hair, twisting it around my finger.

'He ran off with my best friend, Matteo.'

His eyes widened.

'No? Mio Dio. I don't believe it. How could he do that?'

'I know.'

'And what a terrible friend to do that to you. I'm so sorry you had to deal with that. Are you all right?'

His reaction was reassuring. Of course he would know what to say – that was so him.

'I am now. I wasn't at first, obviously. That's why I was working at the restaurant. My family did all they could to keep me busy, and it meant they could keep an eye on me too, make sure I was okay.'

'You are lucky to have such a caring family.'

He was right, I was lucky.

'And now, how do you feel?'

I let out a sigh, and picked up my wine glass, took a sip.

'Do you know, I feel all right. I'm getting over it, like you are with the earrings. Being at Casa Stella has been good for me.'

'Yes, well, as I said at the beginning, Italy will revive you, recharge you back to one hundred per cent.'

I laughed. 'I'm not sure I am quite there yet, but certainly closer than I was when I arrived.'

'That is good to hear,' he said. 'But maybe you need to plug yourself in for a bit longer.'

I did like his analogy. Was he saying he wanted me to come back after the anniversary lunch?

'I keep meaning to ask if you've found the key for that cupboard yet?' I said.

He tipped his head to one side.

'I did search for the key the other night, but couldn't find it anywhere.'

'What a shame,' I said.

'I could break the lock perhaps?'

'If that's the only way of getting into it, I guess we'll have to do that.'

He thought for a moment, sipped his wine. Then his eyes lit up.

'Oh, aspetta... there was an envelope of miscellaneous things to go with Casa Stella when I was renting it out. Perhaps the key might be in there. Let me look as soon as we get back.'

'That would be great. I've been thinking... I need to find my great-grandmother's recipe book for Nonna, but also there might be a clue in there about why Nonna left Tuscany and what happened between her and Francesca,' I said.

'Yes, who knows what secrets you might find,' he said, lifting his eyebrows and throwing me a smile.

CHAPTER 26

JEN

We walked back to Matteo's car, parked round the corner. By now it was early evening, and people passed by all dressed up for aperitivi and dinners out, leaving wafts of perfume and cologne in their wake. The sun was sinking towards the horizon, the Tuscan hills glowing in the golden light. It couldn't be a more romantic setting. If Matteo wasn't driving, we could have stayed at the enoteca and polished off a whole bottle of wine, maybe ordered a board of antipasti. I could so easily have sat there with him for longer. But he did have an early start the next morning, and wouldn't want to drive to Milan after drinking a lot of wine. We reached the car, and Matteo pointed his key at the driver's door. The locks clicked, but he didn't get in. Instead, he just stood there, looking down at me, and opened his mouth to speak, but closed it again.

'What is it?' I said.

'Ginevra...' He paused. 'I've been thinking a great deal lately, and...'

He ran a hand through his hair. He seemed nervous. Did he want to tell me something?

'Yes?'

'And I... I would really like to kiss you.'

My heart leapt. Where had this come from, all of a sudden?

'But what about Natalia?'

'Natalia is my ex, we are just friends now. After the awards tomorrow night, I won't need to be seen in public with her anymore. We're only going together for the cameras. Just like the photo shoot yesterday.'

So he was going to the awards with her then.

'I just... I guess I'm not sure whether to believe you.'

'You don't trust me?'

He had no idea. After what Harvey had done, I wasn't sure if I'd ever trust a man again. But I did like Matteo. A lot. I knew deep down that he was a genuine, good person. And obviously I really fancied him. I'd so enjoyed our time together and would be sad when it came to saying goodbye. I wished he was going to be at Corte Paradiso on my last day, but there was nothing I could do about that.

I bit my lip. 'But she did stay over last night, didn't she?'

'She slept in the spare room. You have to believe me, Ginevra.'

He opened his car door, and I walked round to the passenger side. We both got in. He pressed a button and the windows whirred open, then he looked across at me. The radio came on and played some old romantic Italian song. He turned down the volume.

'I do really like you, Ginevra. Do you have to go back to England on Friday?'

'Yes, I have a big anniversary lunch to go to at Da Nonna.'

'Do you really have to be there?'

I nodded. 'Yes, absolutely, I have to support my family.'

'I understand. But after, will you be coming back to Tuscany?'

I shook my head. 'I don't know.' But maybe now he'd told me nothing was going on with Natalia, I should try to believe him. I would only come back though if she was completely out of the picture.

He started the car engine.

'Okay. Well, now I've told you how I feel at least, and you can think about it.'

'Thank you,' I said.

It wasn't the best thing to say, but he'd caught me off guard. I looked out of the window at the scenery, my thoughts and feelings all over the place. I was so glad that he wanted to kiss me. How I wanted to kiss him, too... And he'd told me that he liked me. But I just needed to be sure I was doing the right thing.

He laughed. 'You are welcome.'

Was I imagining the edge to his laugh, as if I'd offended him in some way? I hadn't meant to, but surely, he understood my position?

Neither of us said a word as he drove back the short journey to Corte Paradiso. When we arrived, we got out of the car. The mood was slightly tense, and I didn't know how to make it better.

'Why don't I see if I can find that key to the cupboard?' he said, matter-of-factly. Well, at least he'd given us something else to talk about.

I went inside Casa Stella, took a deep breath and leant against the door. Had he really said he wanted to kiss me? Butterflies fluttered in my stomach. I couldn't kiss him tonight, I just couldn't, however much I wanted to. No, it would have to wait, and if he really did like me he would understand. I went upstairs and changed into shorts and a T-shirt, and made a cup of tea in the kitchen. A knock came at the door, and Matteo walked in.

'Guess what, I found a key – so shall we see if it fits the mysterious cupboard?'

'Ooh yes, let's!' I said, all excited.

We went up the stairs, and Matteo slid the key into the hole.

It clicked, instantly – at last. He used the handle to open the door and we both stood there peering inside. All I could see were bags of clothes.

I scratched my head. 'Oh, so that's it then. Never mind.'

'Wait…' He bent down and rummaged around, behind the bags. Then he retrieved a box labelled LILIANA. Dear Nonna.

'How about this then?' he said.

He put the box on the floor, and I sat down cross-legged and lifted the flaps.

Inside were a variety of things – an A4 notebook labelled *Nonna Paola's Ricette* – ah, the recipe book Nonna had asked me to find. She would be so pleased. And then, what was this… a brown scrapbook with a giant love heart drawn on the cover. Inside the heart were the initials LM and underneath, the word ama, meaning love and then more initials – SR. There was also a pile of envelopes, held together with an elastic band. When I flipped through them, I saw they were made out to Liliana Maggini at various addresses in Cambridge. This was all very strange – how had these letters got here?

Curious to discover the identity of SR, I opened the scrapbook. On the first page, it said, in Italian: 'My Wedding Day to Salvatore Ricci'. I gasped.

'Matteo, look at this…' He sat down next to me and leant in so close I could smell his gorgeous scent. 'This must be her fiancé, the man who died during the war,' I said, shaking my head. 'It's so sad. Imagine loving someone so much, and then they're killed before you've had a chance to get married – and you'd pictured your whole future with them…' As I said these words, I realised that I'd had my future with Harvey mapped out in my head. He hadn't been killed during a war, but he'd chosen my best friend over me. And it had been devastating. But it would have been even more devastating for Nonna. I couldn't imagine how hard it must have been for her.

Matteo and I both sat there on the wooden floor at the top

of the stairs. We could have taken the box somewhere more comfortable, but there was a sense of urgency – I had to find out more right away. As I continued to flip through the scrapbook, a dried yellow flower fell out from in between the pages – the buds were all puffy like pompoms.

'Ah, mimosa, che bella,' Matteo said.

I held it to my nose, and it still had a scent – sweet, woody with a hint of almonds. What did this pretty flower signify? Knowing Nonna, she would have kept it for a reason, to hold on to a memory.

There were drawings of a bride and groom, labelled Liliana Maggini and Salvatore Ricci. And then as I turned the pages, there were sketches of wedding bouquets, all different flowers depending on the season. A double-page spread showed a menu of several courses with accompanying drawings. There were names of hymns, psalms, readings, and a lengthy guest list. Nonna had imagined a day she never got to have in so much detail. How tragic that he had died.

'Hold on... Salvatore Ricci. He used to own the olive farm, Oliviera Santa Chiara... up the road,' Matteo said, lifting his brows. 'Now it's run by his youngest brother, Pio, and his sons.'

'Oh yes, I've seen the sign about tours and tastings,' I said.

'But also, Salvatore Ricci was... your nonna's sister, Francesca's, husband.'

'What, are you serious?' I said, looking at him.

'Yes, he was definitely married to Francesca. Her surname was Ricci.'

'Could there be another Salvatore Ricci?'

'No, she used to talk about her time living at Oliviera Santa Chiara. And now when I think about it, I recall, when I was around fifteen, she moved back to Casa Stella, shortly before her mother died. My Great-Aunt Nicoletta came over that day, and we all had a special dinner out on the terrazza.'

This all seemed so strange. Nonna's fiancé wasn't dead, he'd gone and married her sister. But how could he do that to her? How could her own sister do that to her?

I looked inside the box again, hoping to find more clues. Something caught the light, and I reached inside and lifted out a silver case.

'What's this?' I said, opening it. Inside were cigarettes. Had this belonged to Nonna? Turning it over, I saw the initials SR. This must have belonged to Salvatore too, but then why was it here with Nonna's things?

And then the envelopes. I removed the elastic band and looked at them more closely. Yes, these letters had been sent to Cambridge from Italy, addressed to Nonna – one to an address on Parkside, and then a couple to a house on Milton Road. After that, my great-grandmother, Simonetta's address near Jesus Green. They were all unopened. Nonna must have been so upset she'd sent them back. What should I do with them? Take them to Nonna – would she want to read them now? Or perhaps that might be too upsetting for her.

My head was spinning, but everything started to become crystal clear. All this was obviously the reason why they'd fallen out.

Matteo leant back against the wall and rested his arms on his knees. I liked how he was here while I was making this discovery. If he hadn't been, I wouldn't have worked out that Francesca had been married to Salvatore so quickly, if at all. But also, it was as if we were in this together.

'It's all very strange.' He interlinked his fingers. 'Why would Francesca marry this man instead of your nonna?'

'It's so confusing.'

'Wait...' he said, scrunching up his forehead. 'I remember now that Francesca was born in October. I would buy her chocolates at the pasticceria every year, and they always had Halloween decorations in the window. Didn't you tell me about a superstition where an opal engagement ring should only be worn by women born in October?'

Oh yes, the ring! Of course. So, had he married her sister because of the ring? Surely it wasn't that simple? And how could he do that? Had Nonna's life been changed in such a big way all because of a superstition? I couldn't believe that. Why not get a different ring? There had to be more to it.

'Yes, because it has to be their birthstone, otherwise it supposedly brings bad luck,' I said.

He shook his head. 'It kind of makes sense, but there has to be something we don't know.'

'I'll just have to catch Nonna at the right moment and ask her outright. It's the only way I'll get any answers, I guess.'

Matteo stood up and dusted off his shorts with his hand. 'Well, I should go. It's getting late and I have to drive to Milan in the morning.'

He held out his hand and I took it, and he helped me off the floor.

'Yes, you must go,' I said, not meaning these words. 'Thanks for finding the key.'

'It's my pleasure,' he said, but with such a serious look on his face, he could have been anyone – rather than the man who'd asked me to kiss him only an hour or so earlier.

He placed his hand on the banister and went down the stairs. I followed him, not wanting him to leave just yet. Couldn't we sit on the terrace and have one last glass of Chianti? I could prepare a snack for us to share, perhaps a few crostini with my home-made pesto and cheese. Should I ask him to eat with me? No, asking him to sit with me would mean things might go back to how they'd been in the car. I couldn't bear for it to become any more awkward between us.

We found ourselves standing in the hall, by the door.

'So...' I said, sliding my hands into the back pockets of my shorts.

'I'll come and say goodbye in the morning,' he said.

'Goodnight, Matteo,' I said.

He opened the door, stepped outside, then turned around to face me, his eyes looking directly into mine. My stomach flipped, but no, not tonight. If anything was going to happen, the timing had to be right.

'Buonanotte, Ginevra. Dormi bene.'

I watched him go back to Casa Luna, heard him open and close the door behind him – perhaps a little more firmly than usual. And then I looked out at the twinkling lights coming from the houses scattered amongst the hills. The air was cooler now it was dark and almost September too. I took a long, deep breath. Casa Stella did feel like home to me. Before long, summer would be over. If I came back, I could squeeze in a few more days of Tuscan sun before autumn came. It was a play-it-by-ear situation, and I would see how I felt in the coming days.

The next morning, when I was preparing a pot of coffee in the kitchen, there was a knock at the door. In bed the night before, I'd drifted off to sleep thinking about what Matteo had said when we stood next to his car in San Gimignano, replaying the scene in my head. Imagining what it would have been like if we had kissed. Although nothing had happened yet, deep down I knew that it would when the moment was right. I switched off the hob and went to open the door.

Matteo stood there. This was it, he was leaving, and I had no idea when I would see him next. Outside, the sun was shining brightly already and the sky was a flawless blue. It was going to be a glorious hot day, but I would be spending it all alone.

He looked at me with those brown eyes, and, stupidly, I could feel mine welling up. No, I couldn't let him see me cry! I swiped my forefingers underneath my eyes.

'Ginevra. I've come to say arrivederci,' he said, softly.

The mood had turned from tense to melancholy. I sensed an ache in the pit of my stomach. I cleared my throat.

'Yes, you're going...' I attempted to say brightly, but the words came out all high-pitched.

He smiled the kind of smile when you don't show your teeth, the kind that you give when a situation isn't the best.

'I'm sad you won't be here on my last day.'

'Me, too. More than you know. I hope that you'll come back, maybe next week, after the lunch?'

I ran a hand through my hair, so aware that he'd told me he liked my curls the night before.

'I haven't decided yet.'

'I would really like to see you again soon.'

And how I would like to see him, as long as he was telling me the truth about Natalia.

'I'll have a think about it,' I said, tightening my grip on the doorknob. Why was this so hard? And then... unable to help myself, I added, quietly, 'I'll miss you.'

Matteo shook his head. 'Ah, Ginevra, I shall really miss you, so much.' He stepped towards me. 'If you do come back, I can show you more Tuscany. We can go back to Florence, and I would love to take you to Siena... there are so many beautiful places to visit. We could go to the coast...'

'I'd like all of that.'

'And don't forget, arrivederci doesn't just mean goodbye. It also means, "Until we meet again".'

He stepped over the threshold, aiming for my cheek, but as he leant slowly in our eyes locked and he pressed his lips to mine. And it was everything I'd imagined it to be as I became swept up in the tenderest of kisses – utterly perfect – and it went on and on. He placed his hands on my waist and pulled me to him, and I wrapped my arms around his neck. Breathing in the scent of him. And he held me so tightly, I didn't want him to let me go. But then he did, slowly, and I allowed him to, reluctantly. His handsome face was filled with a broad smile, this time genuine, showing his perfect white teeth.

'Come back to me, Ginevra,' he said, softly, and then he went out of the door. I watched him walk over to his car and get in.

He opened the window, and shouted, 'Arrivederci, Ginevra.'

I waved and then he started the engine and drove away. Closing the door behind me, I went over to the stove, poured myself an espresso, knocked it back and refilled the cup. My feelings were all mixed up. I couldn't help being overjoyed that we had finally kissed, and it had been *so* good, but now I had to get over us parting ways. Still I was determined to enjoy my last day and get down to that pool – feel the sun on my face. I would seriously consider flying back to Tuscany the following week, but needed to think about it some more. Matteo was going to the awards with Natalia tonight, and I wanted to see the photos before making any decisions. Surely then it would be easy to tell if there was actually anything going on between them.

CHAPTER 27

LILIANA

Time passed, and spring became summer. Some days were warm, but England was nowhere near as hot and humid as Tuscany in July. For this I was grateful because intense heat would only make carrying a baby even more cumbersome. Moving around became increasingly difficult as time went on, and at seven months pregnant I made the decision to stop going to Da Nonna. It would be blindingly obvious to Giulio that I was with child and there was no way he could find out the truth. So far, I'd managed to conceal my bump under old dresses given to me by Nancy, passed down from one of her sisters. I was grateful when Nancy kindly agreed to take over my daily visits to Da Nonna. The first time she went, I wrote Giulio a note, saying I had influenza, and she took it to him. Afterwards, she told me a sad look had crossed his face while he was reading it. He sent his best regards and hoped I would recover before too long.

We were sitting at the kitchen table with a pot of tea while she told me all of this. I counted myself lucky to know someone like Nancy, who had become a friend to me. She handed me a brown paper bag.

'What's this?'

'Giulio gave it to me for you.'

I opened the bag, and inside was a large amaretto biscuit with an almond in the centre, dusted with icing sugar – my favourite! He knew this too because I'd told him when he asked what I would like to see at Da Nonna. So, his mamma had baked them after all, and it had been my suggestion – larger than usual so he could charge customers more money. I took a bite, and the biscuit was soft, with a chewy texture. This small gesture had brightened my day.

'Mmm, this is delicious,' I said.

'Well, isn't that nice of him?' Nancy said.

'Indeed.' I broke off a piece and handed it to her.

She bit into it and closed her eyes as she chewed the biscuit. 'That tastes like heaven, that does,' she said.

I laughed. 'Well, you'll just have to buy more of them for us to share.'

Later, when I was sitting on my bed, I thought about Giulio and how thoughtful he'd been sending me that amaretto biscuit. How I hoped that I would get away with concealing the baby from him. There was no way in the world he could know as then he would certainly change his opinion of me. I would miss seeing him every day though.

There came a knock on my bedroom door, which made me jump out of my skin.

'Who is it?' I called.

'Nancy.'

I told her to come in, and she pushed the door open.

'Sorry to disturb you, Liliana, but the postman just brought this for you – from Italy.'

She handed me a letter, and I recognised Francesca's handwriting. Oh, how lovely to hear from my dear sister. Mamma had written a few times since I'd been in Cambridge, but I hadn't heard from Francesca at all. I had put this down to a letter going missing – why else would she not have been in touch? We'd always been so close, after all.

'Thank you, Nancy.'

'Is it from someone in your family?'

I nodded and smiled. 'Yes, I do believe it's from my sister.'

'Well, I'll leave you in peace.'

She left the room, closing the door behind her, and I ran my finger under the flap of the envelope. I carefully removed then unfolded the two sheets of airmail paper.

30 May 1945

Dear Liliana,

We all miss you terribly. I have something to tell you, and thought that I should write rather than wait for you to come back and find out for yourself. Nonna Paola asked me to take the opal ring back to Salvatore – and so I took the bus to Florence and did as she asked. I'm sorry to say that he still has no recollection of being engaged to you. He took back the ring, and we talked for an hour or so. And then he asked me to go and see him again the next day – he was so very lonely and sad in that hospital bed on his own, with scarcely any visitors.

Over the past few weeks, we have found ourselves falling in love – and the long and short of it is he has asked me to marry him. I understand how difficult this will be for you – and I am so sorry. We have set the date with Padre Luca at Chiesa Santa Maria with a reception to follow at the oliviera. His leg is better now, and he left the hospital yesterday, and came back to live with his family. If you write and say you don't want me to marry him, I won't do it.

So, dear Liliana, it is up to you what happens – it would be wonderful if you wrote back and gave us your blessing – for Mamma and Nonna Paola need this so much. We have no money. The pensione was left in such a terrible condition by the Tedeschi, and we can't afford to pay anyone to do the repairs. The housing market is in a state of crisis following the war so we cannot sell the pensione until the situation improves. If I marry Salvatore, I shall be secure, meaning they will be as well. And of course, you will be too when you return to Tuscany in the autumn. I do hope you understand, but if you can't bring yourself to give us your blessing, do write and tell me before our wedding day – 15 July.

All my love,

Francesca

I swallowed. This could not be real... She couldn't marry Salvatore, she just couldn't. And in the church where we'd planned to have our wedding ceremony too. This had all been Nonna Paola's doing. She would have sent Francesca to the hospital with the opal ring, hoping Salvatore would fall in love with her. How could he not? My sister was so beautiful and a lovely, sweet, kind person. What man wouldn't want her to be his wife? How dare Nonna Paola be so interfering – she had ruined everything. I would have to write to Francesca and say that I couldn't give my blessing. Could she find another man, any other man apart from my Salvatore? I couldn't return to Italy and live with seeing them together every day, in love.

But then it struck me, and my heart splintered even further: today was 15 July, the date of their wedding. It had taken over six weeks for the letter to reach me. I let out a cry as fury rose up inside of me. Although she'd intended to be respectful by asking for my blessing, there was absolutely nothing I could do now. They were probably already married. The ceremony would have been at noon so they could make the most of the day. Afterwards they'd spend the afternoon and evening celebrating the union of our families with a meal several courses long, followed by dancing under the stars.

How could I go back to Tuscany in the autumn now? There was just no way it could happen. The thought of seeing my amore with my sister as his wife, running the oliviera alongside him, didn't bear thinking about. That had been my future, not hers, and now she'd gone and stolen it from me.

Somehow, I'd fooled myself into thinking that, after having the baby, I'd return to Cintaldo as though nothing had happened. I'd even convinced myself that, one day, miraculously Salvatore's memory might return. Then we could have lived happily ever after, perhaps even seeking out our baby in the future. But this had all been a pipe dream, and now there was no chance whatsoever of a reunion with my amore. I burst into tears and scrunched up the letter and threw it on the floor. How could my own sister do this to me? Should I have sent that letter to Salvatore? Would this have happened if I'd confided in Francesca? If she'd known I was carrying his child, she wouldn't have agreed to marry Salvatore, would she? I could have prevented this catastrophe. Was it all my fault?

The baby kicked, producing a sharp pain in my stomach – ouch. It was as if he or she were saying, 'How could you allow this to happen, Mamma?' I took my handkerchief out of the pocket of my dress and dabbed my eyes. I was so upset, I could barely breathe. Would Francesca and I ever get past this? It didn't seem likely. I had lost my sister, and at the same time I had lost my whole family. There was no way I could go back to Tuscany in the autumn, as previously planned. And I'd have to move out of Bentley House after the baby was born. Time was short, I was completely alone and needed to come up with a new plan – and fast.

CHAPTER 28

JEN

The next morning, I took a taxi to Florence airport. As the car rumbled along the gravel drive, silent tears ran down my face. I really didn't want the driver to catch me sobbing. He glanced at me in the rear-view mirror, and then turned his attention to the radio, twisting the dial until some relaxing music came on. I found a tissue in my bag and discreetly dabbed my eyes. This house in the Tuscan hills, along with meeting Matteo, had impacted me so much in a matter of days. Together they'd woken me from a deep sleep. I couldn't help feeling sad, but at the same time I felt more alive than I had in a while. My emotions were all over the place, but I was actually living rather than merely existing, and somehow that kind of felt good.

After Matteo had driven away the previous morning, I'd finally got round to sunbathing by the pool. All I could do was lie there on the lounger with my eyes shut and think about *that kiss*. I was so glad that it had happened. How I wanted to kiss him again. When might that be? Would it happen? I still wasn't sure what to believe when it came to Natalia. For all I knew, he'd been spinning me a line, just so that he could kiss me. But why would he go to all that trouble? It wasn't as if we'd fallen into bed or anything. Thank goodness. And then I went for a swim, doing slow breaststroke laps up and down, feeling so relaxed and at peace. Apart from the thrumming of the cicadas, everything was so quiet. But then I had to wash my hair again. Matteo had complimented me on my curls, so I allowed them to dry naturally and, looking at myself in the mirror, I decided they were okay. I'd caught the sun on my face, and was looking better than I had in a while. All of the tension had dropped out of my face too and the bags had gone from underneath my eyes. I looked relaxed, and, dare I think it, happy? Yes, I was feeling rather content with life. Long may it continue.

Later, I filmed myself making focaccia. I pounded up garlic cloves and rosemary from the garden with olive oil in the old pestle and mortar. The act of doing this was really satisfying. When it was ready, I sat outside and watched the sunset with one last glass of Chianti and the focaccia I'd made, accompanied by sliced tomatoes and buffalo mozzarella from the deli in the village, drizzled with olive oil. It was all sublime. I left the rest of the focaccia in Matteo's kitchen with a note to say:

Here's a taste of the video recorded today, coming soon... thank you for getting me started with all this Gx

After I'd done that I packed my case and climbed into bed, tired out. When I got back to Cambridge, life would be non-stop for a few days, and so I needed to get plenty of sleep.

The flight was short and, after landing at Stansted airport in the early afternoon, I took the National Express coach to Cambridge. I could get a taxi to the flat, but now my parents were back in town I decided to go and see them first. The driver put my case in the boot and we set off. As we approached our street, I smiled at the sight of our old Victorian house, passed down through Dad's family from Nonno and Nonna. I loved my family home, and it was always filled with people passing through. All three of my brothers still lived there. As well as Alfonso and Giuseppe, there was Michele, who managed a shop that sold Italian designer clothes. I couldn't imagine any of them leaving in the near future. Mum looked after them so well, cooking their meals, and she did all their washing and ironing. They had no reason to go anywhere. Whenever they brought girlfriends back, Mum would be friendly towards them, but they'd soon realise that they were never going to replace her in their lives. I wouldn't want her as my mother-in-law, if it was me, and I didn't blame these girlfriends for running a mile. She loved having her sons at home, and I imagined she worried about it being just her and Dad, and the dogs and cats. Then the dreaded empty nest syndrome might set in.

But my parents did have many friends between them, all nurtured by Mum, who would invite them over to the house for parties, dinners, lunches and drinks. Not a week passed by without her hosting something. Most of their friends were from the Italian community, and they had friends from church too. Mum would dress up and go to the Catholic church on the corner of Hills Road every Sunday. If you were staying at her house at the time, you'd be obliged to go along. That was the price my brothers had to pay for living at home. Church on Sundays, unless they were working, and then she'd make everyone a delicious lunch.

The taxi driver pulled up outside the house, and I paid and got out. I pushed open the gate and wheeled my case down the passage at the side. The garden was thriving, it being the end of summer. The apple, fig and plum trees were heaving with fruit ready to be picked, and the vegetable patch was a sea of green, brimming with courgettes and broccoli and any other vegetable in season. Nonna had always encouraged Dad to grow his own food, and, when my parents took over the house from her and Nonno, they inherited a well-established vegetable patch and fruit trees. This was a hangover from living through the war –

that fear of not being able to get hold of food to feed your family. I couldn't wait to eat Mum's deep-fried courgette flowers stuffed with ricotta. And then I saw that Mum was waving at me through the kitchen window – she lived in the kitchen. I approached the back door, and she rushed to open it.

'Jen, bella! I'm so happy to see you.'

She wrapped her arms around me and squeezed me tightly. There was no getting away from Mum's hugs. Then she let go and ushered me inside.

'Come in, sit down. Let's have coffee, and I have some cantuccini biscotti that I made yesterday.'

I pulled out a chair and sat at the big oak table. Mum's father had been a carpenter, and he'd made it for my parents as a wedding present. The vast number of meals it had hosted over the years meant there were so many special memories to treasure.

Mum brought over a moka pot, and poured us both espressos. She put a bowl of sugar between us. I spooned some into my coffee and drank it. So good – Mum made the best coffee, always brought home from our deli.

'So, a lot has happened while Dad and I were in Italy, I hear?' she said.

I smiled. 'Yes, it has.'

'And so... this Casa Stella, how is it? When can I see it?'

I shrugged. 'Whenever you like. Next time I'm there.'

'When will that be?'

'I don't know ... maybe I'll go back before the end of the summer.'

'Nonna mentioned some young man called Matteo,' she said, with a wink.

'Oh did she? It's nothing, really.'

'Isn't it?'

'Matteo is just a friend. He helped me settle in, showed me around.'

'Nonna said he's a very nice young man.'

'He is.'

'Exceptionally handsome, she said.'

I rolled my eyes. I'd had enough of Mum interfering in my love life. If it hadn't been for her, I probably wouldn't have put pressure on Harvey for us to get married so soon when he asked me to move into his cottage in Grantchester. I'd had Mum's voice in my ear every time I saw her, saying when will you get married? You know you'll be living in sin. Don't let him lead you along for years and then it will be too late for you to meet anyone else and have babies. I've seen it happen with my friends' daughters. At first, I'd told her to stop it, but then somehow her voice had permeated my mind. I'd thought what if that's what he is doing, leading me on until he's tired of me, and then he'll upgrade to someone younger. Then it might be too late for me to have children. And so, one evening, I asked if he intended to marry me now that we were living together in his cottage. Not long after that he booked a night away in Paris, and took me there on the Eurostar, as a surprise – and there he proposed, on his knee outside the Louvre.

'I think I'll handle my next relationship all on my own, Mum,' I said.

'Okay, well I'd love to meet him if I ever get the chance.'

'So, what do I need to do for the lunch?'

She took a notebook and pen off the dresser and joined me at the table.

'Well, you can make your tiramisù cupcakes, and help out on the day, if you don't mind. You can eat with us, but if you oversee the food service, Dad will relax as he'll know you have everything under control. Giuseppe and Alfonso are working that day already.'

'Of course I can help out, and I'll make the cupcakes later.'

She clapped her hands together, and then put a tick next to my name on her big list.

'Perfetto. Giuseppe has dropped the ingredients and toppers at yours so you should have everything you need. If you bring the cupcakes to Da Nonna tomorrow, I'll put them in individual cellophane bags.'

'Okay, so you want me to come in tomorrow?'

'Yes, because there's something else too. A lady from the *Eastern Reporter* called the restaurant. She saw one of our ads about our celebratory prize draw, and seems to be very interested in the anniversary. Anyway, she's absolutely desperate to interview your nonna and write an article about the history of our family-run restaurant. She's coming to Da Nonna tomorrow with a photographer, and they'll print the article in their Sunday edition. It will be wonderful publicity for us.'

'Oh, that's a good idea. Will Nonna mind doing that though?'

'Dad has already cleared it with her. We'll have to be there for support, but she'll love the attention. Perhaps you can go over and help her work out what to wear in the morning.'

I'd planned to visit Nonna and talk about the things I'd found in the cupboard at Casa Stella.

'Sure, I'm going over there tomorrow morning anyway.' I stood up, pushing my chair under the table. 'I'd better get home. Do you mind dropping me back at the flat?'

Mum drove me back, and I wheeled my case inside and carried it up the flight of stairs. Inside, it was stuffy, and I went round opening all the windows. The garden looked even more overgrown than before I'd left and I breathed a deep sigh. After the lunch, I wouldn't need to be here. I could fly back to Tuscany on Monday if I wanted to, if there was a flight available. I undressed and stepped into the shower and changed into a T-shirt and baggy shorts. While I was sitting on the bed, I remembered the ring, and opened the drawer of my bedside table. I took out the cube-shaped box and opened it. There it was, the gold ring with milky-white stone, catching the light of my lamp. The ring that had possibly caused a lot of trouble back in the 1940s. Had Nonna's engagement to Salvatore really ended because of a superstition? There had to be more to it. When the moment was right, I would ask her.

The rest of the afternoon and evening would be spent vegging on the sofa watching television. I would make the cupcakes in the morning. The next couple of days were going to be full on and I needed to recharge. I smiled to myself when I remembered Matteo saying that I needed to plug myself in like a phone so that I could be one hundred per cent again. I'd only felt fifty per cent then, but now when I thought about it, I was more like eighty per cent. Maybe more than that, after only a few days. Casa Stella had certainly revived me. Perhaps if I went back, I could get myself up to one hundred per cent.

CHAPTER 29

JEN

The day before the anniversary lunch, I got up early to make the eighty tiramisù cupcakes. I needed to make a few batches, but it felt good helping my family give each guest something special to take home. I messaged Giuseppe, asking him to collect and take them to Da Nonna later. He did rounds in Cambridge every few days, dropping off deli items for some of our customers. Then I cycled over to see Nonna at her flat. I wanted to check she was okay, and that she'd have plenty of time to get ready before the journalist from the *Eastern Reporter* turned up. I really wanted to give her Nonna Paola's recipe book and the wedding scrapbook, and ask so many questions, but I'd realised when drifting off to sleep the night before that now wasn't the time. The last thing I wanted to do was upset her before she had her photo taken. This weekend would already be emotional for her as it was at times like this when she missed my nonno the most.

'Ciao, Nonna,' I said, as I walked through the front door.

'Jen, cara! Vieni,' she said.

I went into the living room where she was sitting on the sofa watching a shopping channel, muted. The lady was holding up a selection of silk scarves, one by one. Nonna loved shopping channels but never bought anything from them. She just liked to have them on in the background as company. She knew the names of all the presenters, and she would sometimes talk about them as if she knew them personally.

I leant down to kiss her on the cheek.

'Come va?' she said. 'How was Tuscany?'

'It was good,' I said.

'You like Casa Stella?'

I nodded.

'Yes, I do, it's really beautiful, Nonna.'

'Isn't it. Do you have any photos on that phone of yours?'

'Of course. And I sent you a postcard from San Gimignano, but who knows when it will arrive?'

I joined her on the sofa, and scrolled through the photos I'd saved as favourites.

'Ah,' she said as I swiped through them with a happy sigh. 'What memories...' Her eyes glazed over.

'I hope it doesn't make you sad to see them?' I said, gently.

'Oh no.' She shook her head vehemently. 'On the contrary, I am so pleased that the house has come back to my side of the family. Now you will have a chance to enjoy it, maybe pass it on to your children, if you choose to have them one day.'

I swallowed. 'Thanks, Nonna.'

'Did you take any pictures of Matteo?'

I rolled my eyes, and smiled. I remembered the photos from the booth, and took them out of my bag.

'Don't you look lovely together,' she said, throwing me a look.

I found a couple from the Ferragosto party too, and showed them to her.

'He took you to a party?' she said.

'Yes,' I said. 'It was his cousin, the solicitor's, flat. And that's his girlfriend standing behind him, Rosa.'

'Matteo's girlfriend?'

'No.' I shook my head. 'Rosa is the solicitor, Fabrizio's, girlfriend.'

'So Matteo doesn't have a girlfriend?'

I laughed. 'That's what he tells me...'

'What do you mean?'

'He's still in touch with his ex. But he says they're just friends now.'

'Mah.' She dismissed me with a wave of her hand. 'I doubt that he is interested in an ex, not with you in his life.'

I patted her on the arm. 'Who knows?' Nonna was being kind, but she hadn't seen Natalia. She always seemed to think that I was capable of more than I thought.

'So, what are you wearing for this photo shoot?' I said, realising this was the second photo shoot I was witnessing in the same week.

'Why don't you go and find something suitable, dear.'

I went into her bedroom, and opened the wardrobe, and skimmed the dresses and trousers and skirts and blouses. She had collected a number of lovely garments over the years. I found a navy-blue dress with a belt that tied at the waist, and then I went to her jewellery box and selected a pearl necklace.

I took the items back into the living room to show her.

'What do you think?'

'Perfetto.'

'If you get changed, I can help with your make-up, if you like.'

I helped her out of the chair, and she pootled off to her bedroom. I sank into the sofa and took a breath. Talking to Nonna had reminded me of Matteo again when I'd been trying not to think about him. I needed to decide whether to go back to Tuscany before the end of the summer.

. . .

When Nonna was ready, we went down the stairs with her arm threaded through mine. She seemed very chirpy, and it was lovely to see her getting the attention she deserved. She had played a huge part in the growth of Da Nonna during the post-war years. It had been her idea to lease the property next door when it came up for renewal, and to create our now award-winning restaurant.

Dad was standing over by the coffee machine, and I went and gave him a hug.

'It's good to have you back, Jen,' he said. 'I can't wait to see the house.'

'You and Mum will have to come out and see it.'

'Tutto bene, Mamma?' he said to Nonna. They tended to speak to each other in Italian, which she liked – he was fluent in spoken Italian, but could barely write a word.

'Si, caro.'

He leant down and kissed her on the cheek, and led her to the Mimosa room, where we hosted private events. It was all set up for the journalist and photographer, with tea and coffee and a plate of our signature Da Nonna amaretti biscuits. Mum had put a vase of pastel-pink roses from our garden in the centre of the table.

The door opened and a journalist, a woman in her forties, came in, and shook hands with all of us. She was accompanied by a photographer who wore jeans and a shirt with a bright funky pattern on it. His hair was long, and he had a moustache. He was carrying a screen, a light and a camera, so his hands were full. He grinned at us all.

'I'm Helen Wright,' the journalist said. 'And this is my photographer, John Jones.'

'Thank you for coming to see us,' Nonna said.

'It's a pleasure. So... I'm going to ask you a few questions about the history of Da Nonna, and then John will take a few photos of you, and maybe one of you and your son, and any grandchildren, if they're around?'

Dad explained that two of his sons were working at the restaurant, and then he introduced me as his daughter. He said he'd go and call Michele to get him to come down too. It wouldn't take him long to get here as he worked down the road. Dad left the three of us alone, and suddenly I felt responsible for Nonna. This woman was a journalist, and I needed to make sure that she didn't make Nonna feel uncomfortable with questions that probed too much.

Helen looked at her notepad, and then she asked Nonna when she'd first come to Cambridge, what brought her here, and how did she meet my grandfather.

Nonna explained how she had come over from Italy with an expat English couple at the end of the war. He had been a university lecturer at St Catherine's College, only a few hundred yards away, and his wife was a poet. They had enjoyed her cooking so much that they invited her to come over from Tuscany with them.

'That must have been hard for you, leaving your family in Italy?' Helen said.

Helen was asking the questions that I wanted to ask. Nonna's hand started to shake, and this worried me. Perhaps she was thinking about her falling-out with Francesca. Nonna was a private person, and she wouldn't want Helen to write about that in her newspaper.

'I think my grandmother happened to like this couple – they were offering her a well-paid job when it was hard to find work in Italy after the war. Is that right, Nonna?'

'Yes, cara, that's about right,' she said, throwing me an appreciative look.

'But still, I can't quite understand...' Helen said.

She really needed to stop this line of questioning. I clenched my jaw.

'Can we just move on to how she met my grandfather?' I said. 'Isn't this article supposed to be about the restaurant?'

Helen shrugged. 'Well, okay, how did you meet your husband then?'

Nonna's face broke into a smile. 'Well, the English couple, Professor and Lady Enid Beaumont, liked Italian food. Their maid, Nancy, gave me the name of an Italian deli, saying I needed to buy some items there. And so I walked here from their house, across Parker's Piece, to what was just a delicatessen then with a handful of tables for coffee. Let me explain... I didn't know anyone in Cambridge, apart from the professor and Lady Enid, and Nancy. And I was feeling lost, all alone in a foreign country, until I walked through the door out there. And...' Her eyes lit up. 'There he was – my Giulio, standing at the counter. He was so warm and kind. He sat me down at table six, facing King's College Chapel – still our best table – and presented me with an espresso and a biscuit, freshly baked that morning.'

'Ah, what a lovely story,' Helen said, smiling. Do you have any photos of you and Giulio that I can print? Perhaps one from your wedding day, and one of his family?'

'Well, yes, I do have photos somewhere upstairs in my flat. But how would I get them to you?'

'I can scan them and email them over, Nonna,' I said.

'That's great. Thanks, Jen,' Helen said. 'If you could send them today, that would be great. I would like to write this up and get it published tomorrow.'

She went on to ask a few more questions about Da Nonna. When did it become a restaurant too? Who was in charge? Were we thrilled with our Authentic and Tasty Award?

Dad came back into the room, and I was glad when he got more involved with the questions, taking the pressure off Nonna. I refilled her cup of coffee and put a plate with a biscuit in front of her.

'Right then,' Helen eventually said, much to my relief. 'I think we're all done here. Now we just need to take the photos.'

Dad glanced at his phone.

'My middle son, Michele, has just arrived at the restaurant. Shall we take the photos out there?'

Helen looked at John, and he nodded.

'Yes, that would work well, as long as we can get the lighting right.'

John picked up all of his stuff, and we went into the restaurant. There were a few people sitting in the coffee shop next door, but the restaurant would be empty until noon.

Alfonso came out of the kitchen wearing his chef's whites and tall hat, and Giuseppe appeared in his Da Nonna polo shirt and jeans. Michele wore a Giorgio Armani suit. I had chosen a cheery yellow dress, and Dad wore his trademark black shirt and jeans. Mum had been to the hair salon for a blow-dry, and she was sporting an orange maxi dress that enhanced her suntan and gold sandals.

'Right, let's gather you all together in a group.' John looked around and arranged his screen. 'The light is best over here, in this corner.'

We all stood in front of the dresser, which was the perfect background as the shelves were filled with bottles of Italian olive oil and wine and balsamic vinegar. On the wall above, Da Nonna was written in maroon swirly writing.

John snapped several photos of us as a group. Then, as directed by Helen, he took one of just Nonna and Dad, the heir to the business.

'Okay, we're all done,' Helen said. 'Thanks very much, all.' Then she turned to me and Dad. 'It's a shame that Liliana can't tell us more about her reasons for leaving Italy, but never mind. It does seem that there's a story there she doesn't want to tell.'

'You are quite mistaken,' Dad said, bluntly. 'This article is supposed to be about the restaurant, isn't it?'

'Yes, of course it is,' Helen said, plastering a smile across her face. Something about the way she was talking and looking at us made me feel uneasy.

Mum came over from the coffee shop and handed Helen a Da Nonna paper bag with handles.

'Here are a few of our goodies for you to try: extra-virgin olive oil from Tuscany, aged balsamic vinegar, home-made breadsticks, a bag of freshly baked large amaretti biscuits. And then you have half a salami, our handmade orecchiette, and a jar of passata made using a secret family recipe.' Mum said all of this so proudly, and really, it made me realise how fabulous our business was. 'And you'll also find there's a Da Nonna voucher for dinner for two.'

Helen took the bag. 'Thank you very much. That all sounds lovely. Well, I'd better get to work so I can send this to my editor. And I shall see you all tomorrow at the anniversary lunch.'

Dad saw her and John out. I wasn't sure whether we could trust Helen now she'd picked up on the mystery even I wondered about. She didn't know anything concrete, but I hoped she wouldn't write anything in the article we didn't want to see. For Nonna's sake.

CHAPTER 30

LILIANA

A few weeks passed and, before I knew it, the end of summer came. There was a chill in the air and it began to get darker earlier. Nancy started to spend more of her time going round the house building fires and keeping them all going. When I opened the curtains in the mornings, I noticed the leaves turning on the trees outside. Each day became more of a struggle. I was now so heavy that I moved around at a snail's pace, and it took forever to get up and down the stairs. But also, I'd had to deal with the upsetting letter received from Francesca. What a blow that news had been. Sleepless nights had followed. If I did manage to drift off, I would wake up to find I'd been grinding my teeth while asleep. And then my jaw ached all day long. I still couldn't fathom how she could do that to me. Salvatore had amnesia, and I would no doubt find a way to forgive him in time. The poor man had no recollection of who I was. Although when I thought about it, surely he would have known I was Francesca's sister, considering she'd returned the engagement ring to him on my behalf. After almost losing his life during those final days of the war, perhaps he'd chosen to embrace every opportunity with both hands. When Francesca had turned up at the hospital to see him, she would have brightened his days with her angelic face and gentle demeanour. How could he not have fallen in love with her? Mamma had informed me in one of her letters that his papa, Giorgio, had been suffering from problems with his heart and so he'd be retiring sooner than originally planned. Salvatore would be under pressure to take over as soon as he had recovered. And he'd need a wife by his side at the oliviera. I would find it much harder to forgive my sister for what she'd done and I wasn't sure if I ever could.

One Sunday morning, there came a knock at the door. Nancy had the day off, and so I went to open it. The air was damp as it had been raining. There stood Giulio, wearing his Sunday best, all ready for church, looking rather handsome. I was glad to see him. Being extra cautious, I hadn't fully opened the door, and I stood there, half-facing him, doing my best to conceal the bump that stuck out of me like a football. He removed his hat and studied me with earnest eyes.

'Buongiorno, Liliana,' he said, softly.

I cleared my throat.

'Oh, hello, Giulio,. Are you on your way to church?'

'Yes, I was just wondering how you are. I haven't seen you for such a long time. Are you feeling well enough to accompany my family and me to Mass this morning?'

Faking a cough, I covered my mouth with a hand, and shook my head. More recently, I'd been attending Mass on Monday evenings, as I hadn't wanted to bump into Giulio and his family. I also went to the church every week to sit in the confession box and speak to the resident priest – Father John, who was Irish. I found him to be a good listener. He didn't often say very much, but I'd been able to get my worries off my chest. The one thing he had told me was that I must find a way to forgive Francesca when I was ready. I'd told him that this was impossible, but deep down I knew I ought to try, one day perhaps. I was still so furious with her, and the dust needed to settle before I could find a way forward. After confession, I would always light a candle for Papa before returning to Bentley House, my eyes welling with tears.

'I am still not fully recovered, and I have this dreadful cough.' I coughed again, for emphasis. 'I wouldn't want the congregation to have to endure it, or to pass on this dreadful influenza that has knocked me for six.' Knocked for six was an expression I'd picked up from Nancy, along with many others.

He nodded, lifting his eyebrows in understanding.

'Well, I do hope to see you again soon,' he said.

'Yes, of course. I shall come to Da Nonna as soon as I am completely better.'

He placed his hat back on his head and started to turn to walk back down the steps. Piles of leaves had collected between them, and they were all wet from the rain. I worried he might slip.

'Mind how you go,' I said.

He stopped, inhaled and said, 'I do miss you, Liliana.'

My cheeks warmed. I was flattered, but couldn't help wondering if he viewed me in a romantic way, just by how he looked at me and the things he said. I liked him, but could I love him? I touched my finger where the ring from Salvatore had been. Could I give myself to another man? I wasn't sure if I could love any man like I'd loved Salvatore. But he no longer wanted me in his life. And Giulio was here, standing outside my front door, and he was making it very clear that he wanted to know me more. But I was due to have Salvatore's baby in a matter of days.

'Thank you for stopping by,' I said.

He gripped the handrail with a gloved hand.

'Perhaps when you are better, we could go to the pictures and see a film together?'

I nodded. 'Yes, I would like that very much. Arrivederci, Giulio.'

He gave me a nod, and went down the steps and through the gate, his polished shoes tapping on the pavement as he headed towards Parker's Piece. I so wished that I could walk by his side, and catch up on all his news, then attend Mass with him. But for now it was not to be.

One afternoon, a few days later, I couldn't bring myself to make supper. My head ached and my ankles were so swollen that it was a struggle to be on my feet. I went to the drawing room and told Lady Enid that I needed to lie down.

'You go and rest dear. Nancy can make supper today, and I'll ask her to come and check on you.'

'Thank you, signora.'

I went upstairs, and climbed onto the bed and lay down, on my side, for the baby was too heavy for me to lie on my back or front. I tried to get comfortable, but it wasn't easy. The window was open, and a light breeze came through. I studied the view of the rooftops of the houses opposite, Victorian like this one – tall and grand, and built from red brick. I counted the chimneys, so many of them in a row, and then I looked up at the sky, a brilliant blue with clusters of cloud. And then it came – my first contraction, and it was immensely painful. I placed a hand on my stomach and groaned. The baby was coming.

The baby was a girl, and the professor and Lady Enid named her Deborah. I had no influence over this decision as she belonged to them now. When Nancy had come to check on me, she'd called a doctor, who came within the hour. Many, many hours later, the baby arrived, and she was so beautiful. I held her to my breast and she drank my milk, her eyes closed as she suckled, seemingly content. As I looked down at her tiny head, covered with dark hair like her father's, I tried not to think about what was to come. I had carried this child, the product of my and Salvatore's love, conceived on Christmas Eve in Tuscany, for nine whole months. Her father had no idea who I was, despite the night of passion we'd shared. And now I was living in a foreign country and my only option was to give our child away. Lady Enid wasn't exactly going to throw me out onto the street, but I needed to find somewhere else to live and work as soon as I could. I was so privileged to have brought this beautiful girl into the world, but, at the same time, devastated because I would have to part with her. Society simply wouldn't allow me to be her mother. This didn't make any sense to me, because I could be a better mother to my daughter than anyone else. But I had no home, no husband, no money. I couldn't give her anything apart from my love, and my cooking. And sadly, those two things weren't enough on their own.

Deborah settled into a routine relatively quickly. After the first few days, I handed her over to a wet nurse employed by Lady Enid. She had acted swiftly and I was grateful. Because I knew that the more time I spent with my daughter, the harder it would be to let her go. After giving birth, my stomach was still larger than before my pregnancy, and I had put on weight in my face, and on my arms and legs. But after I stopped breastfeeding, my energy levels began to increase.

After a week, I decided to go and see Giulio at Da Nonna. I had missed him and perhaps he might be able to advise me how to find another job as well as somewhere to live. One morning, after breakfast, I left Bentley House and walked across Parker's Piece. By now, autumn was properly setting in. The leaves on the trees were turning yellow, with a carpet of them collecting underneath. Acorns crunched underfoot as I walked and there were shiny horse chestnuts scattered on the ground, amongst their spiky green shells. The light breeze brushed my face, and I was glad to be outside again, to be venturing into the centre of the city.

When I arrived at Da Nonna, I pushed open the door, and the bell jangled. When Giulio laid eyes on me, he couldn't have come out from behind the counter any faster.

'Liliana, you're back!' He gestured for me to follow him to the table facing King's Chapel. 'Your usual table, signorina?'

Uplifted by his enthusiastic welcome, I found myself beaming. It was nice to have someone who cared about seeing me as I'd been feeling so alone lately.

He pulled out the chair, and I sat down. 'So, are you feeling better now?' he asked.

'Yes, I am, thank you.'

'Well, I'm glad to hear it. Can I get you an espresso?'

Still beaming, I nodded.

Giulio went over to the machine and it hissed and gurgled while he prepared my coffee. After a minute or two, he brought over an espresso, and an amaretto biscuit on a small plate.

'Oh, I do adore these biscuits. Thank you for the one you sent to the house that day with Nancy.'

'It was your idea to make them bigger and place an almond in the centre so we could charge more. They are selling very well, like hot cakes as the English say.'

I laughed. He sat down opposite me.

'So, does this mean you're coming to church on Sunday?'

'Indeed it does.'

'Oh good... and one day soon, we can go to the pictures maybe?'

'Yes, I would like that very much.'

'All right, I'll find out what's showing.'

I smiled. 'Giulio... I need your advice.'

Leaning forward, he rested his elbows on the table. 'Tell me.'

'How would I go about finding another job?'

He sat up in his chair. 'So, you're not going back to Tuscany like you said?'

I shook my head. 'Not at the moment, no. My circumstances have changed.'

He paused, looked out of the window, the corners of his lips upturned.

'Well, if you want another job, you can always work here.'

'That's very kind, but I need to live in. I can't afford to pay rent as well.'

He pressed the palms of his hands together and thought for a moment.

'My aunt, Zia Maria, has a big house on Milton Road, near Jesus Green. She's been talking about renting out a room since her youngest son got married. You would be the perfect lodger for her.'

'But how much would she charge?'

He shrugged. 'For you, not much. She will give you a special price because we are friends.'

My heart warmed. I knew we were friends, but when he said this out loud, it meant something to me.

'I know she'd appreciate the company, especially if you cook for her sometimes,' he went on. 'I can take care of it – and if you want to work here at Da Nonna, I'll pay you enough to cover the rent. In fact, why don't I just pay her the rent on your behalf?'

This was a generous and thoughtful offer, and I appreciated it very much. Working at Da Nonna, surrounded by other Italians and our food, would feel like home to me.

'Thank you, Giulio, but really, are you absolutely sure?'

'Certo, of course I am. Why don't I go and see Zia Maria

later today, and tomorrow when you come here, I will confirm everything.'

'I am speechless, you are too kind.'

He blushed, and ran a hand through his hair.

'It is nothing, really. Anything for you, Liliana. Okay…' He stood up. 'So what do you need to buy, the usual?'

I nodded.

'I'll go and put everything in a bag for you.'

I watched him walk away, and sat there, sipping my espresso, looking out of the window at passers-by on King's Parade. Somehow, Giulio might just save me by giving me a job and finding me somewhere to live. This would buy me time while I decided whether I could bring myself to return to Tuscany. But how could I, if my sister was married to the love of my life? I couldn't bear the thought of the two of them together – the vision of them even holding hands made me feel physically sick. Salvatore wouldn't know about our child, and neither would she. What would either of them think if they were aware of her existence? Francesca wouldn't have any idea that Salvatore had made love to me on Christmas Eve, only months before proposing to her. And she wouldn't have any idea that I had given birth to her husband's daughter only days before, her niece. Would she care if she knew the truth? I would have liked to think so. If I told her, what would that do? They were married now, and there was no going back.

CHAPTER 31

JEN

On Sunday morning, I cycled over to the restaurant early to help set up for our special eightieth-anniversary celebration. We'd invited eighty guests from the local community – mostly Italians, but also people who had been there for our family over the years, as well as the mayor. And we'd invited a few local journalists and food influencers, along with Helen from the *Eastern Reporter*. Dad and Alfonso, with Nonna's approval, had created a four-course exquisite menu as a celebration of our family business. Guests would sit down to a board of antipasti and individual plates of burrata with fresh tomatoes and basil leaves. To follow, pumpkin ravioli with a butter and sage sauce, and then osso bucco, braised veal shanks. Dessert would be pistachio semifreddo. And they'd be given one of my tiramisù cupcakes to take home with the number '80' in gold as a topper.

The tables were set up for groups, and I'd folded our maroon napkins into fan shapes. Each setting had a bombiniera, a maroon tulle bag of five ivory-coloured sugared almonds to take home. There were five almonds for a reason – they symbolised health, wealth, fertility, happiness and long life and it was traditional for us to give them out at special celebrations.

When the guests arrived, they were served bellinis, cocktails made with white peach purée and prosecco, in our private room upstairs, with its view of King's College and the iconic chapel. We served crostini topped with olive tapenade and mushroom paste as canapés. Then the guests were ushered downstairs and seated according to our table plan. There was a head table for my family – with Nonna, my parents and Michele. Alfonso, Giuseppe and I were all working. Dad had invited us to sit with them, but we'd wanted to make the lunch a memorable occasion for Nonna. We could drink wine and eat leftovers afterwards. Dad had shrugged and made a show of reluctantly agreeing, but I could tell he was secretly pleased. He knew we'd give guests the best possible experience. Besides, there was no way any of us could relax if we weren't contributing to the day – we'd just be monitoring what the staff were doing the whole time.

After serving the pumpkin ravioli, I went upstairs to Nonna's flat for a break, and sank into her sofa. I was so tired, but glad to be able to make it a special day for Nonna and my parents. My shoulders were all tense from being run off my feet, and I stretched out my arms to loosen them up. As I did so, I spotted today's edition of the *Eastern Reporter* on the coffee table, hot off the press, and in mint condition as it would only have been delivered that morning. Nonna usually read this newspaper from cover to cover. I picked it up, curious to read Helen's article and to see the photos that John had taken.

I flicked through the pages until I reached the double-page spread – KING'S PARADE RESTAURANT, DA NONNA AT 80 YEARS. Helen had used both of the old photos I'd emailed to her after the shoot. They were at the centre of the page: one of Nonno Giulio and his brothers and parents standing outside Da Nonna. And a wedding photo of Nonna and Nonno, standing outside the Catholic church on Hills Road. Nonna looked glamorous, her curls piled on top of her head in a bun. They were both smiling as if they couldn't be any happier. I knew that they'd been truly made for each other. Yesterday's photos were underneath: Nonna and Papa, and then one of our whole family. They were fantastic photos and John had captured us all looking our best.

I skimmed the article. It was complimentary about Da Nonna, referencing the Authentic and Tasty Award. It went on to say that celebrities were often spotted dining with us, and how influencers visited and posted photos on Instagram. I nodded along, glad that she'd written a flattering piece. Helen described us as one of Cambridge's top spots, *the* perfect venue for a special occasion. Dad would be so pleased. But then: in the last column, she started to talk about Nonna coming over from Italy in 1945, and I didn't like what I read after that.

> Liliana Farina, née Maggini, is in her nineties, and I was grateful for the opportunity to speak to her. But I remain curious about her real reason for coming to Cambridge. She claimed that an English couple living in Tuscany liked her cooking so much that they asked her to come and work for them here. Did she really leave her whole family at the age of nineteen for that reason – never to return? Apparently, it was difficult to find paid work in Italy while the country was recovering from the war, but still I sensed that there was something she wasn't telling me. However, I would like to thank the Farina family for hosting me at Da Nonna, and for providing me with a delectable bag of goodies from their delicatessen. If the restaurant is out of your price range, you must at least treat yourself to a bag of giant home-made amaretti biscuits from the delicatessen – you won't regret it!

A sick feeling engulfed me. I leant forward, resting my elbows on my knees, and put my head in my hands. 'How could she?' I groaned. Helen from the *Eastern Reporter* had seemed *so* nice on the surface. But I'd had an inkling that she would let us down in some way. Now here she was downstairs, being treated to our special celebratory lunch. I had a good mind to go down there and throw her drink over her. How dare she take advantage of our hospitality and write something like this about my dear nonna? I rolled up the newspaper and tucked it under my arm. There was no way my grandmother would be reading that. I would do my best to keep it away from her. Perhaps, if she remembered to ask, I could tell her the article hadn't been printed. I wasn't sure whether she'd believe me, but I could try. I returned to the restaurant, hid the newspaper in the top drawer of the dresser, and carried on serving the rest of the meal. Helen was sitting next to John, and they were laughing together while chatting with someone else at their table. It took all my strength to not go over and have a word. But creating a scene on Da Nonna's special day would not be the best idea. My parents and Nonna would never forgive me, even though Helen would be to blame.

When everyone had been served their pistachio semifreddo, we handed out the cupcakes in their cellophane bags, tied with maroon ribbon to match the Da Nonna logo. We then served tea and coffee, and glasses of vin santo with cantucci biscuits for dunking. When everything was done, I was at last able to pull up a chair at the head table, in between Nonna and Dad.

He put his hand on my shoulder and gave it a squeeze. 'Well done, cara.'

'Thanks, Dad.' I turned to Nonna. 'Have you had a lovely day?' I asked.

She looked at me, her eyes shining. 'It's been really wonderful, Jen. Thank you for all your hard work.'

We exchanged a smile. I picked up my glass of vin santo and took a sip. I was so glad my brothers and I had managed to pull off such a successful event between us. It meant so much to do this for my family. Now I could relax and enjoy myself.

Dad stood up and took a piece of paper out of his trouser

pocket. Oh yes, time for his speech. He tapped his glass with a fork.

'Buonasera, tutti!'

Everyone stopped talking and the room went quiet. Dad cleared his throat as he unfolded the piece of paper.

'I just wanted to say a few words... Eighty years ago, my grandfather, Vittorio Farina, founded a delicatessen here on King's Parade and he called it Da Nonna after his grandmother, Stefania. Sadly, he tragically died during the war, but his son, Giulio senior, my father, continued his legacy with his wife, Liliana, my dear mother, by his side – and now here she sits beside me. It was she who helped him build the family business into something truly magnificent. It was she who shared her vast knowledge of Italian cuisine from Tuscany. And it was she who suggested we lease the building next door to the deli – the restaurant where you are all sitting now. I would like to propose a toast, and ask you to stand and raise your glasses of vin santo – you should all have one in front of you – to Liliana Farina.'

He started to clap, and then the guests stood up and gave my nonna such a huge round of applause. I was so proud of everything that she had achieved in her lifetime – my grandmother. When I turned to look at her, her eyes were welling with tears as she sat there quietly, her wrinkled hand resting on the table. This was such an emotional moment, and I found that I had a lump in my throat. Nonna had played her part in continuing a legacy that had started back in the 1930s. Dad gestured for everyone to sit back down and turned his piece of paper over.

'I would also like to thank my children, who are all here today. Alfonso, who runs our kitchen, Jen, who is our acting manager, and Giuseppe, who runs the floor...'

He raised his glass again, and everyone stood up and applauded us before sitting back down.

'And so, it just remains for me to say thanks to you, our guests for making this a—'

It was then that the door opened, the bell jangling, and two women walked in. Hadn't they read the sign saying there was a private event today? Perhaps I should have locked it. I could have kicked myself for allowing anyone to interrupt Dad's speech. He glanced over at the women and paused for a moment. Some of the guests turned to look at them.

So much for getting to relax. I drew in my breath, got up and went over to speak to them. Dad started talking again, and I was glad to see the guests fix their eyes back on him.

'Hi there,' I said to the women, quietly. 'We're closed, I'm afraid, for a special anniversary lunch.'

One of the women, who had grey-white hair, lifted something out of her coat pocket. I saw it was today's copy of the *Eastern Reporter*, open at the page of the article about Da Nonna. Oh, it was creating publicity already. She must want to book a table and that was great, but how was she not getting that we were closed?

'I'm not here for a table,' she said. 'I have something to say about this article. Is Liliana Farina here?'

What did she want with Nonna?

'It's not a good time, I'm afraid. We're having a special celebration today. My father is actually making a speech, as you can see.'

'Yes, I can and I'm sorry to interrupt, but it's imperative that I speak with her right away, well, when he's finished speaking, if that's possible.'

I really couldn't understand the urgency. Couldn't this woman wait? Why was she so desperate to see Nonna?

'Tomorrow would be much better. I can let her know you're coming, and arrange a time to meet in our coffee shop.'

'I don't think I can wait until then... you see, I've just—'

A big round of applause interrupted us, and we all stood there, waiting for it to end.

When it was quiet again, I raised my eyebrows, encouraging the woman to carry on.

She pressed her lips together. 'Today, in this newspaper, I've discovered something rather shocking.'

What was this all about? The woman just wasn't getting the hint that it would be better to come back another time, at all. My patience was wearing thin. Remaining polite was a struggle after a long old day and the interruption of Dad's special speech.

'Something shocking?' I said, through gritted teeth. 'In relation to Liliana, my grandmother? Are you sure? You do know she's in her nineties?'

'Yes, well, she would be… I've been searching for her but had no luck until I happened to read this article today. It reveals her maiden name is Maggini. You see, I wasn't aware that her married name was Farina. I am quite certain that she is my mother. Please tell her my name is Deborah Beaumont.'

I blinked, beyond confused. 'What on earth are you talking about?'

'And this is her granddaughter, Victoria,' Deborah went on.

I turned my attention to Victoria, who was in her forties. She had the same distinctive curls as Nonna and me. I didn't understand any of this. So this Victoria was supposedly my cousin?

When I glanced over my shoulder, I could see that some of the guests were looking over at us, clearly sensing that something was going on. With this information, Deborah and Victoria had the potential to create some kind of scene, and I needed to remove them from our special event.

'You'd better come with me,' I said, leading them through a door to the coffee shop and deli. It was closed for the day. I gestured for them to sit down. 'Please wait here for a moment.'

I returned to the restaurant and approached the family table.

'Nonna,' I said, quietly.

'What is it, dear?'

'Something really strange is going on. One of those women who just came in is claiming to be your daughter. She is called Deborah Beaumont, and she says the woman with her is your granddaughter.'

'What...?' Her hand started to shake. 'Deborah, are you sure? Wh... where are they now?' she stuttered.

'I put them in the coffee shop.'

'Please keep them there. I need to speak to your father.'

I nodded. 'Okay.'

I went back into the coffee shop, and busied myself behind the counter. A few minutes later, Nonna and Dad appeared. Dad had a face of thunder. There was something going on, and I didn't know what it was. How could this Deborah be Nonna's daughter?

Dad introduced himself, and then Nonna, and we all joined them at the table.

'So, may I ask why you are here today?' Dad said.

'This woman is my mother,' Deborah said, once again, pointing at the wedding photo of Nonna in the article. She put the newspaper on the table in front of him.

'What's that, the article about our restaurant?'

'Yes, it gives Liliana's maiden name, and says she came here from Italy the year I was born – 1945. When I read it, I realised she is the mother I've been looking for.'

Dad shook his head. But he didn't seem that surprised, just irritated that she was telling us this. I wondered if Nonna had told him something I wasn't aware of. Did this all relate to the things I'd found at Casa Stella, in the locked cupboard with Matteo? I sensed it did, but wasn't sure how.

'Your mother, Lady Enid, agreed not to tell you,' Nonna

said to Deborah, her face pale. 'I thought that would be best for you, and me. For both of us,' she added, her voice cracking.

'Yes, well, Lady Enid sadly passed away a few months ago. We've been clearing out her house and I found a shoebox with my birth certificate, which says you are my mother and a man called Salvatore Ricci is my father. Also, there's this photo of you holding me, I think?'

Deborah took a small black-and-white photo out of her handbag, and put it on the table for us all to see. I'd seen photos of Nonna when she was younger, and I knew this was her. How had she kept this quiet for all these years?

Dad and Nonna exchanged a glance. And then it all became clear. I thought back to the cupboard where I'd found the wedding scrapbook with Matteo. Nonna had been engaged to Salvatore Ricci and then he'd married her sister, Francesca. Had she come to England because she was pregnant with Deborah? But then, why hadn't she just married Salvatore if she was already engaged to him? None of it made any sense. And how cruel of him to move on to her sister after rejecting her. But why would he do that? How could he do that to my dear nonna? Fury rose up inside of me. Poor Nonna. She'd been through so much and I still didn't know all of the details. Had Francesca known about the baby? If she had, how could she possibly go on and marry the father? First Matteo bringing the opal ring and news about the house in Tuscany, and now this – some woman claiming to be Nonna's daughter. When he'd brought the ring to us, all of these memories would have come flooding back. No wonder Nonna had been so sad that day, after he left. She must have been through such an ordeal, and having to live with her sister letting her down like that too.

'Why are you here, do you want money?' Dad said, brusquely. He was always so protective of Nonna. Deborah sat back in her chair. I felt bad for her. No one would want to get on the wrong side of Dad. He didn't take any prisoners when it came to standing up for his family.

'Not at all! I recently found out that Lady Enid, the woman who I always called Mother, wasn't actually my mother after all. I was in the process of hiring a genealogist but this article has saved me the trouble. That's a...' Her voice trailed off.

'I should never have agreed to that newspaper interview,' Dad said.

'At first, I thought no, how could it be, but then that paragraph saying there was a story that wasn't being told, well it all added up – didn't it, Victoria?'

Victoria nodded and put her hand on Deborah's. 'Yes, it did, Mum.'

And then Nonna spoke. 'I'm sorry... This has all come as quite a surprise, and I might need some time to come to terms with it. Could I ask you to come back another day and we can have coffee?'

Deborah looked down at the table and wrung her hands.

'All right, that's a good idea. I understand that this must be a bit of a shock.'

'It certainly is,' Dad said.

I didn't know what to think.

'Well,' Deborah continued. 'It will have to be before Victoria goes to see Salvatore next week – I can't travel at the moment, but—'

'What, hold on. Did you say she's going to see Salvatore?' Nonna said.

'Yes.'

'But isn't he dead?'

'No, he's very much alive, and living with his nephew in Florence,' Deborah said. 'It didn't take Victoria long to track him down, with a little help from Facebook.'

Nonna turned to Dad. 'When Matteo said Francesca lived on her own, I assumed Salvatore had died.'

'Perhaps they were divorced or something,' he said. Then he spoke to Deborah. 'Come back tomorrow, at ten o'clock. We can have coffee and talk more then.'

'Okay, thank you,' Deborah said.

He stood up and ushered them both out of the front door – thankfully the coffee shop had its own door, so they didn't need to pass through the restaurant again.

Nonna and I looked at each other.

'What a shock, Nonna,' I said.

She let out a sigh. 'It was bound to come out eventually, dear.'

I wanted to ask more questions, but Dad came back over, and placed a hand on Nonna's shoulder. 'Are you all right, Mamma?'

'I am feeling rather tired. Perhaps you can help me upstairs, dear?'

'Of course. Let's go now... thanks, Jen for bringing those two in here while I was speaking.'

I shrugged. 'Sure, of course. And that was a wonderful speech, Dad.'

Dad threw me an appreciative nod, but his face was understandably filled with concern for Nonna. He helped her out of the chair. She threaded her arm through his and they went off towards the back of the deli, through the door to the stairs for her flat.

What a bolt out of the blue. If Dad hadn't agreed to the interview with the *Eastern Reporter*, none of this would have happened. But I supposed that, when Victoria visited Salvatore, he might have told her everything. And maybe if she'd hired a genealogist, it wouldn't have taken long to find out Nonna's married name, and then that she lived on King's Parade.

CHAPTER 32

LILIANA

The following week, I moved in with Giulio's aunt, Zia Maria, on Milton Road. She lived in a grand old Victorian house, and it would just be the two of us. Her husband had died many years ago, and her children were all married. Giulio had told me that, since her youngest son had flown the nest, she'd been lonely, and the extra income would be welcome. She was a petite, buxom woman with snow-white hair that she always wore in a bun. She lived in house dresses and red velvet slippers. I found her to be warm and kind. On the day Giulio dropped me off with my suitcase, she held out her arms and pulled me into a warm embrace. This was the closest I'd had to maternal affection since leaving Tuscany. My eyes welled with tears – it was comforting after all I'd been through. Zia Maria led me up the stairs to a vast bedroom on the first floor with its own fireplace and a few lumps of coal in a basket on the hearth. I had my own bathroom next door and her house instantly felt like home to me.

When I moved in, I had just left my baby and my heart was in tatters, but I was lucky to have many distractions. After working all day at Da Nonna, apart from on Sundays, I would cycle back to Milton Road, across Jesus Green, and then set about helping Zia Maria to make supper. She taught me new recipes from her part of Italy, Calabria, and I taught her some of mine from Tuscany. We enjoyed cooking together, and she would sit at the table and peel vegetables while I stood at the stove, looking out through the window onto a pretty garden. We would tell each other stories. I talked about my family, and she told me that she and her husband had moved to Cambridge from Calabria in the early 1900s, shortly after Giulio's parents.

I was quite content living in that house on Milton Road and the weeks flew by. Giulio took me to the pictures every Tuesday, after work. We laughed together at Noël Coward's witty comedy, *Blithe Spirit*. When I burst into tears towards the end of *Brief Encounter*, he took my hand, gave it a squeeze and held it in his right until THE END appeared on the screen. I liked the way he seemed to want to take care of me – he was indeed a true friend. After our cinema trips, he would always walk me home, right up to the door. I would put the key in the lock and turn round to say goodbye to find him standing there, shuffling his feet, looking at me intently, as if he wanted to say something. He never did. Instead, he'd lift his hat and bid me buonanotte.

On Christmas Eve, his mamma invited Zia Maria and me to their house on the edge of Jesus Green. I was delighted to have a place to go on an evening that was celebrated in Italy, and I offered to help with the preparation of our traditional fish supper. I bought cod fillets from the fishmonger and made baccalà with Zia Maria the day before. His mamma and brothers made me feel very welcome. The Farina family was grieving for a husband and father who had lost his life during the war too, and his mamma mentioned Vittorio when saying grace. Giulio had told me his father had been on the SS *Arandora Star*, which was torpedoed by a German submarine in the summer of 1940. He'd been on this ship, bound for Canada, because he was viewed as an enemy alien when Italy joined the war.

I thought back to the previous Christmas Eve, when I'd cooked for Salvatore's family. Then how I'd spent the night with Salvatore in the frantoio, the night Deborah was conceived. Now she was living at the other side of Cambridge with the professor and Lady Enid. I'd told them that it would be better for all concerned if she thought they were her real parents. One day maybe, when she was old enough, if she asked, they could show her the birth certificate with me as her mother and Salvatore Ricci as her father. In the meantime, Lady Enid had promised to keep that certificate in a safe place, along with a photograph of me holding dear little Deborah shortly after she was born. It did seem strange that my child with Salvatore should have such an English name. I considered what we might have called her. Lucia, Isabella, Clara? It was too late to be thinking about that now. I wouldn't get to name my daughter, but, one day, I might have more children with someone else. I liked to think that I would have the opportunity to be a mother again. Next time, I would ensure I was married so I wouldn't end up in the same situation. I could not bear to go through all that again.

I sent my new address to Mamma, but I didn't reply to Francesca's letter delivering the news about her marriage to Salvatore. I couldn't bring myself to give my blessing or to send my congratulations. Instead, I acted as though I had never received her letter in the first place, which was rather childish. But I couldn't see any alternative. Father John kept telling me at confession that I needed to come to terms with what she'd done and find a way to forgive her, in time. Deep down, I knew he was right, but didn't know how long it would take. Mamma wrote to me at Milton Road, urging me to return to Tuscany as promised. She also tried to tell me that I should be happy for

Francesca. There was no point in being married to a man who didn't know who I was, she'd written. Although her words rang true, they only brought me down further and I cast the letter into the fire. I couldn't see myself ever going back to Italy. How could I face the sight of my sister and my amore together? Perhaps with the passing of time, I might change my mind, but that wasn't likely. Francesca sent me a second letter, this time to Milton Road. Once again, I couldn't bring myself to read her words. Instead, I put the letter in a drawer unopened. A third one arrived. That letter went in the drawer too. The situation was far too raw. Maybe one day I would find the strength to open and read them, but not quite yet.

Spring came and then summer, and before we knew it autumn arrived once again. Deborah's first birthday passed, and I spent the day thinking about her, feeling sad, but there was no going back. Apart from having to give her up and live with the knowledge that Salvatore had married my sister, I was fairly content living with Zia Maria and working at Da Nonna, and I didn't feel as alone as I'd feared. I was satisfied with my lot, and I didn't feel a need for anything more. I even accepted that I might not actually get married. The pool of eligible men was small because of the war, and I could end up as a spinster. People had lived through and endured terrible things during the war. I was grateful to be alive as well as to have a job, a home, and food on the table.

One Friday afternoon, when I'd finished my work for the day, I was untying the strings of my apron when Giulio called me over to the counter.

He handed me my wages for the week. This was always my favourite day and I loved to open that envelope and peer at the notes and coins inside.

'Thank you, Giulio,' I said, putting the envelope into my handbag.

He pinched the bridge of his nose.

'Liliana, I've been thinking.'

'Yes?' I said, folding up my apron.

'Well, I err... I have this bottle of Chianti, sent to me by my uncle who owns a restaurant in Soho in London. I was wondering whether you might like to try it with me, seeing as it's come all the way from Tuscany?'

I hadn't tasted Chianti for over a year. What a kind gesture. I rubbed my hands together.

'Well, yes, I would really like that.'

Giulio came out from behind the counter and tapped me on the shoulder.

'Come on then, let's go and sit down.'

He led me over to the special table in the corner – where I'd sat the first time I came into Da Nonna, and a few times since. But today, it was covered with a white cloth and set for two, complete with cutlery, wine glasses and napkins. There was even a candle flickering away.

This table was meant for someone else, surely?

'Who is all this for?' I asked.

He looked down at me and blinked.

'It's all for you, Liliana.'

'Oh, but...?'

Pulling out a chair, and gesturing for me to sit down, he said, 'I thought we could celebrate one year since you started working here.'

When noting that Deborah's first birthday had recently passed, it hadn't occurred to me that I'd been working for Giulio for that long too.

'Mamma mia, has it been a year already?'

He nodded. 'I only know this because I was updating the

books today with your wages. This is your twelfth month at Da Nonna.'

He took out a corkscrew and opened the bottle of Chianti on the table and poured a little into the glasses.

We said, 'Cin cin,' and clinked glasses.

'Aspetta,' he said, getting up. He disappeared into the kitchen and came back with a board of antipasti. There was ham, salami, cheeses, slices of tomato and a basket of bread.

'Well, isn't this just lovely,' I said, unfolding the napkin and placing it on my lap.

'Liliana, I have something to ask you. I was going to wait until we'd finished eating, and drinking this wine. But I am so impatient, I have to ask you now.'

He knelt down on the floor, and took something out of his pocket.

I gasped. What was he doing, proposing to me? Was I ready to move on from Salvatore?

He looked up at me with his large chocolate-brown eyes.

'Liliana Maggini, I have loved you since the moment you first walked through that door. Please will you marry me and run Da Nonna by my side, as my wife?'

I put a hand over my mouth. Giulio had completely caught me by surprise and my tongue was tied. He held out a ring with a blue stone.

'This sapphire ring belonged to my grandmother,' he said.

Oh no, not again... I hoped sapphires weren't unlucky in any way. I really did want to marry him. I needed to move on from Salvatore, as he had from me more than a year ago. I could envisage a good life in Cambridge. As Giulio's wife, I could help him make Da Nonna even better than it already was. He wanted to open a restaurant one day. And now transport links were improving, he planned to bring over more produce from Italy. I liked his mamma and brothers, and Farina as my surname had a nice ring to it.

Yes, Giulio and I were meant to be together. Most importantly of all, I realised... I loved him. Differently from how I'd loved Salvatore. In hindsight, I hadn't known Salvatore as well as I knew Giulio. My love for Salvatore had been based on infatuation, and my family had encouraged our union because he was heir to the oliviera. Giulio and I had found our own way to each other, with no external pressure from anyone. We genuinely cared for each other deeply. Over the past year, Giulio had shown me the true meaning of love. He'd given me a job, found me a home, welcomed me into his family, and so much more. Giulio had been there for me.

While all these thoughts were running through my head, he remained on his knee, eyebrows raised as he held out the ring.

'Dai, Liliana, what is your answer?' he said.

I burst out laughing. 'Yes, I will marry you,' I said.

He put a hand on his chest and let out a big sigh.

'Ah, I am the luckiest man in England!'

He slid the ring onto my finger and took my hands, pulling me up from the chair. Then he lifted me up and spun me around. Our eyes locked and we both laughed. What a moment – one that I would never forget. Then he put me back down and pressed his lips to mine. It was the most glorious kiss – one to cherish – and butterflies fluttered inside of me.

'Let's get married as soon as we can,' he said. 'At Our Lady of the Assumption and the English Martyrs. We can speak to Father John on Sunday. I want you to be my wife, and for us to have many children. And together we shall make Da Nonna a special place for us to pass down to future generations. Che pensi?'

'I think that all sounds wonderful,' I said.

He leant forwards and kissed me again.

'We have to tell Mamma and Zia Maria and my brothers. Everyone will be so happy to hear our news. They all adore you. Let's go back to my house. Aspetta, I'll get my car.'

'What about the Chianti, and all this food?' I said.

'Why don't you put everything in a bag and we'll take it with us. We have to go and celebrate with my famiglia – there is no time to waste.'

CHAPTER 33

JEN

When I got back to the flat, I made myself a much-needed vodka and tonic, and went into the living room. I wanted to sink into the sofa and chill out for a bit, maybe watch some television. But the tenants on the ground floor were playing heavy metal complete with drums and the volume seemed to be getting louder. I took a couple of sips of my vodka, opened Spotify on my phone and pulled up a smooth playlist. Sade played on the speaker and I turned the volume up high. I put my feet on the coffee table, let out a long sigh and allowed my shoulders to relax. What a day it had been.

How did Nonna have a daughter and granddaughter none of us had known about? She'd lived with that secret for all those years... had she not told anyone at all? Had Nonno Giulio known the truth? Dad hadn't seemed that surprised, although she might have only made him aware in the restaurant, moments before they came into the coffee shop. No doubt she'd taken comfort at confession when attending church – I knew this was how she dealt with difficult matters. How else would she have got through such a trying time all on her own? Had she known Nonno when she was pregnant with Deborah? If she had, presumably she'd found a way to conceal her pregnancy from him. Otherwise, in the 1940s, he couldn't have married her, however much he wanted to. She might have told him the father of her child had died during the war. But if that had been the case, she would have kept the baby. There were so many thoughts to process, and I was worn out from all the excitement of the day. I would speak to Nonna in the morning and try to find out more. I had planned to take her the scrapbook and ask a few questions after the anniversary lunch was over anyway. I had to get to the bottom of all this – it had started with Matteo coming to our restaurant that evening with the ring and telling me I'd inherited the house. And now, since discovering the box in the locked cupboard at Casa Stella, more had come to light. Then Deborah turning up today out of nowhere... all of these things were connected, I just needed to work out how.

I went to put on my pyjamas, and climbed into bed with my phone and laptop. Matteo and that kiss had interrupted my thoughts on and off over the past few days, and I wondered how he was getting on at Casa Luna. Did he miss me? How had the awards ceremony gone? Was he back with Natalia? Could I trust him when he told me it was over between them? I needed to see pictures from the other night. I did a Google search on my laptop and there they were. I clicked on a video of Matteo with Natalia, standing together on the red carpet. She wore a tight-fitting red dress with push-up bra, creating an enviable cleavage. He wore a suit with a white shirt, open at the collar. He put an arm around her shoulder as they posed for photos, cameras flashing. They were both beaming and being all touchy-feely with each other. They couldn't have looked any more like a dream couple. Anyone who didn't know better would assume they were madly in love. Did I know better though? Or had I been taken in by Matteo's parting words? I scrolled through all the content online, and there she was again making a speech while holding an award. So she'd won. As producer of the show,

Matteo was standing by her side. My gut churned. I couldn't bear the thought of him having lied to me. Were they just acting for the cameras? It was impossible to tell. What if he'd been using me to make her jealous? Men did this kind of thing all the time, and women did too. I hadn't heard from him since that kiss the morning he departed for Milan. And I hadn't messaged him because I'd been run off my feet with the lunch. But also, the ball was in his court to get in touch, surely?

My phone vibrated all of a sudden next to me, making me start. Someone was trying to call. Who could it be at this time of night? The number for Da Nonna flashed up on the screen. Had I left something at the restaurant? I answered, putting the phone on speaker.

'Jen?' came Dad's voice.

'Yes, is everything okay? Why are you calling so late?'

'Sorry, cara, it's just that there's someone here to see you.'

'What do you mean? Who is it?'

'He tells me his name is Matteo Bianchi.'

No way, just when I'd been thinking about him too. What was going on?

'Are you serious? What is he doing there?'

'Hold on.'

There came the sound of muffled voices. Presumably, Dad was putting his hand over the receiver. He would have no idea where the mute button was.

'He says he'd planned to be at our lunch today, but his flight was delayed.'

I'd mentioned the lunch, but I hadn't invited him. Why would he just turn up like that?

I leant back on the headboard. 'But I don't understand,' I said, clutching my forehead. 'What—'

Dad interrupted me. 'Your nonna invited him.' I could almost hear him suppressing a fatherly smile. What had she been thinking? And how had she got in touch with him? As if reading my mind, Dad added, 'I believe Giuseppe helped her find him on that thing called the internet.'

'You knew about this?'

'Yes, I'd forgotten all about it, actually. She asked if I minded him being added to the guest list when I told her someone had dropped out.'

How savvy of Nonna.

'Oh, okay.'

'So what do you want to do?'

Suddenly I was aware that Matteo was standing there, listening to our conversation. I found myself craving him, and pictured those dark-brown eyes looking into mine. But it was nine o'clock at night, and I'd just got into bed, exhausted from the day.

I heard Matteo's voice in the background and my stomach flipped. Had he really flown here to see me?

Dad coughed down the line. 'He just said to tell you he's staying at the same hotel as before, round the corner from here.' And then more muffled voices. 'I've asked him to come to the coffee shop tomorrow at eleven. You can come and meet him then.'

'All right, thanks, Dad.'

'Buonanotte, cara,' Dad said before hanging up.

Now what? Instantly I found myself thinking about what I would wear. I so wanted to look my best for him. If he was here in Cambridge, he must be telling the truth about Natalia, despite all the photos and videos online from the awards that made them seem like a happy couple. I would see what he had to say when I asked him.

The next morning I went to Da Nonna at ten thirty, so I'd have a chance to catch up with Nonna before meeting Matteo. I'd chosen my pale-blue summer dress with spaghetti straps that enhanced the suntan picked up in Tuscany. When I arrived, Nonna and Dad were having what appeared to be a serious conversation at one of the tables in the coffee shop. Dad's face was all scrunched up, and he had his hand on her arm. He spotted me and waved me over. I approached and double-kissed them both.

Dad pushed back his chair and stood up.

'I need to get on with some work. I'll leave you both to it.' He put a hand on my shoulder. 'Can I bring you a coffee, cara?'

'Don't worry, Dad. I'll wait for Matteo to get here.'

'Ah yes, Matteo...' he said, rolling his eyes.

Nonna looked down at the floor.

'What were you doing inviting him along, yesterday, Nonna?' I said, with a laugh. How could I be cross with her?

She took hold of my hand. 'I'm sorry, Jen, but I just know it's for the best – that you see him again.'

I pressed my lips together. 'Well, we'll see how it goes when he gets here.' I wasn't going to tell her about the whole Natalia scenario – that would be too much information. I decided to change the subject.

'How did it go with Deborah this morning?'

She shrugged. 'It went okay. Everything was going to come out sooner or later.'

'I'm sorry if it was upsetting for you,' I said. I took Nonna Paola's recipe book out of my tote bag. 'I brought something that might cheer you up.'

Her hand started to shake. 'Oh, you found it. Dear Jen, I can't believe it.' She gulped. I passed her the recipe book and she opened it on the table. There in beautiful handwriting were recipes for meatballs, gnocchi, ravioli, ragù – oh so many things that Nonna had taught me how to make over the years. And she had learnt those recipes from her nonna Paola. I swallowed. This was pure nostalgia. Here was a special part of our family history, our heritage.

'Thank you so very much for bringing this to me, Jen,' Nonna said. A tear ran down her face, and I passed her a tissue from my bag. She closed the book and slid it across the table to me.

'It's yours now. I wanted you to have it all along because you love cooking so much.'

This was such an honour. I would treasure it.

'I don't know what to say... thank you.'

'Promise me you'll do good things with it. Keep on trying to get that cookery book of your own published. You'll get there, I know you will in the end.'

'I'm grateful that you have so much faith in me.' I reached into my tote bag and took out the wedding scrapbook. This was only going to make her more emotional, but would there ever be a right time?

I put it on the table. 'I also found this.'

Nonna placed her hand on the cover. 'Oh my, I'd forgotten all about this.'

When she opened the scrapbook, the sprig of dried mimosa fell out.

She gasped and picked it up, 'Mamma mia.'

'Does that hold a special memory for you, Nonna?' I said.

Glancing at me, she said, 'It does indeed, cara.' She held it to her nose and closed her eyes, then put it down. She then flipped through the pages of the scrapbook, before closing it again.

'I don't think I can bring myself to look at it anymore. Maybe I'll save this for another day.'

'I can't imagine it's easy.'

'No, it isn't. I loved him so much, Jen. But I ended up loving your nonno Giulio even more. He was the right man for me, not Salvatore. It all worked out for the best in the end.'

'But why did he marry Francesca instead of you when you were carrying his child and already engaged?'

She looked at me, her eyes filled with sadness. 'When he came back at the end of the war, he was injured quite badly. He'd broken his leg, but also banged his head – he had amnesia.'

'He couldn't remember you?'

'When I went to see him in the hospital, he had no idea who I was.'

'And you were already pregnant?'

'Yes, so when the nice English couple asked me to come to Cambridge as their cook, it was the only way for me to have the baby without anyone knowing. They adopted Deborah because they couldn't have children of their own. When Francesca wrote to say she and Salvatore were getting married, well, I couldn't believe the words I was reading.'

'How could she do that to you?'

'Firstly, she didn't know about the baby. But also, our nonna Paola encouraged their union because Francesca was born in October. It was she who made a big thing about the opal ring. When Salvatore first proposed to me with it, she said it would be unlucky for us, that he needed to find another ring. Neither of us saw it as a problem, and the ring was a family heirloom, from his nonna.'

'Oh, so this all happened because of the ring?'

'Well partly, and because of his amnesia.'

Poor Nonna, it must have been a terrible time for her, all alone.

'But then, one morning, I walked into this place, and there standing behind the counter was your nonno Giulio...'

'And you fell in love?'

She nodded. 'Don't forget, you wouldn't be here if I hadn't come to Cambridge in the first place.'

This was an astonishing thought. I actually existed because of everything that had happened.

'And now I've discovered he is still alive. Victoria has been in touch with Salvatore. His nephew set up a video call with her and Deborah apparently and they all talked for some time. He has a heart condition and has been given weeks to live, and so Deborah told him there and then that he is her father. She can't travel, but would like Victoria to meet him in person before he declines any further. So Victoria will visit him in Florence next week. Can I ask you to go with her as she doesn't speak Italian? And report back? Could you do that for me, Jen – let me know what he has to say?'

This would force me to make up my mind about returning to Tuscany before the end of the summer, but I would do anything for Nonna.

'Of course I can do that.'

'And there's something else. I've been talking to your father about this... I hope you don't mind, Jen, but I think it's only right that Victoria should get to have the opal ring, seeing as you have the house.'

'Yes, of course.'

'It belonged to her grandfather originally, and his nonna before that. She told me that her son plans to propose to his girlfriend this year.'

'Is his girlfriend born in October?' I said, smiling.

'It's funny you should say that,' she replied with a laugh. 'That's what gave me the idea in the first place. I asked when her birthday was. Victoria must have thought it an odd question.'

'And...?'

'She was actually born in October. I thought, "Well, this is just meant to be!" Perhaps it will give the ring the happy ending it deserves.'

This didn't matter to me at all. I was so grateful to have the house – the house that had brought me back to life.

'Nonna, I have no use for the ring. Everything you're saying makes sense to me. Besides, I'm so lucky to have Casa Stella, aren't I?'

'Yes, you must hold on to that house. I would really like you to pass it down to your children, if and when you might have them.'

We looked at each other. 'Thank you, Nonna.'

Dad came over.

'You must be tired after all that's happened this morning. Why don't I help you upstairs, Mamma?'

She nodded. Dad helped her out of the chair, and they crossed the coffee shop towards the stairs leading to her flat. Glancing at my watch, I saw that Matteo was due to arrive soon. I couldn't help feeling excited by the thought of seeing him again. So I would need to go back to Tuscany next week, after all. I'd be more than happy to go and see this Salvatore on Nonna's behalf and report back. Hopefully it would bring her the closure she'd probably needed for all these years.

CHAPTER 34

LILIANA

We got married at the church on Hills Road in November. Giulio's brother, Marco, was his best man, and Nancy was my bridesmaid. On our wedding night, Giulio told me that he couldn't wait to have a big family. While I could never replace the daughter I'd given up, my only option was to move on and create a new life. Like so many people who had been affected by the war in some way. We moved into his family home near Jesus Green. They had a large house, and the top floor was all ours. This was temporary until we could afford to buy a home of our own. My days were spent working at Da Nonna and helping Giulio's mamma, Simonetta, in the kitchen. We all ate together at the kitchen table every night, and often his brothers would join us as well. I didn't mind spending my time in the kitchen both at work and at home, as cooking was what I loved doing the most for the people I cared about. I did miss Nonna, Mamma and Francesca. I wrote to Mamma to tell her about my marriage to Giulio. She sent her congratulations, but I knew that she would be sad to lose me to another country. I considered visiting my family in Tuscany, but couldn't bear the thought of seeing Salvatore and Francesca together. My sister continued to send me letters. One day, when adding another to the pile that had collected in my drawer, I decided that I was never going to read them. And so I put them all in a big envelope and posted them back to her, unopened. Nothing she had to say would change the way I felt about what she'd done. I hoped to find a way to forgive her somehow, as suggested by Father John. But I could never forget how she'd hurt me.

Time passed, and I had four sons – Giulio junior, Luciano, Mauro and Pietro. How I wanted a daughter, to make up for losing Deborah – but it was not meant to be. After I'd given birth to Pietro, the doctor at Addenbrookes Hospital in Cambridge told me that it wouldn't be a good idea to get pregnant again. My body wouldn't be able to cope. My last two pregnancies had been more difficult, and I was tired. But how I longed for a girl. Perhaps one of my boys would one day give me a granddaughter.

I loved my boys, and when I cooked for them I felt as though my life had a purpose. I had been put on this earth to create a beautiful family and to cook for them and to love them. I went to evening classes to learn how to read and write English, and Giulio helped me with my reading too. I was determined to be able to communicate properly with the people around me. My ignorance of the language became apparent when my sons started to bring homework back from school. They needed my help with learning how to read and I was embarrassed at how illiterate I was. Giulio's father, Vittorio, had apparently struggled with the paperwork at Da Nonna. His mamma, Simonetta, could not read a word in Italian or English. She would sometimes tell me how it made her sad that she couldn't read books or write diaries. If she'd had the opportunity to study, she might have enjoyed doing these things. The 1950s brought television to her home, and at last she had some form of entertainment – she was completely addicted to television, and she would watch it whenever she wasn't in the kitchen.

We bought a house in the same street as Giulio's mamma and brothers – it was a beautiful Victorian three-storey house, and I felt so lucky to be living there. We had five bedrooms, and so each of our sons had their own room, and Giulio and I shared the master bedroom. The kitchen overlooked a pretty back garden and there I started a vegetable patch, and planted fruit trees – apple and pear and plum and fig. We bought a few chickens, and became quite self-sufficient. I enjoyed gardening, as I had done at Casa Stella in my youth and during the war. When we went for walks in the Cambridgeshire countryside with our boys, I would still find myself foraging – for it was in my blood – and we would bring back wild mushrooms, and wild garlic, and wild asparagus. At the end of the summer, we would go to the fields and pick wild blackberries. As supermarkets began to spring up, replacing the greengrocer and butcher and fishmonger and baker – combining them all – I was saddened by this development. For I found much joy in going between all of the different shops to select the very best produce for the meals I wanted to make for my family. But I didn't need to rely on shops too much for our food, because we produced so much in our garden.

Da Nonna grew and grew, as Giulio and I put our hearts into the place. When the shop next door came up for a new lease, I encouraged Giulio to take it on. We then expanded to create the restaurant we'd always dreamt of. And we brought over more and more products from Italy, including our favourite Italian wines, too. Our boys worked for the family business from the age of fourteen, helping out in the deli, waiting on tables, working in the kitchen. I was delighted to see them help out, and Giulio junior was a worthy successor for his father. I just knew that one day he would take over the reins and make us proud. When the flat above Da Nonna came up for sale, we took that on too. Giulio junior moved in there, so he was on site all of the time. A few months later, he met Clara, whose parents were Italian. They had moved to England in the 1960s – her father had come over to work in a factory in Bedford, where there was a large Italian community. Clara worked as a waitress at an Italian restaurant down the road. Giulio junior met her at church – and they were soon dating. He proposed within months and they had a beautiful wedding with the reception at Da Nonna. She moved into the flat upstairs, and they had a baby the following year – in 1992 – a girl who they named Ginevra. She was a real beauty, and when I looked at her all I could see was Deborah. At last, I had a granddaughter to dote on – and I would spoil her rotten and treat her as if she were my own. I was determined for us to become firm friends. Ginevra was followed by three boys – Alfonso, Michele and Giuseppe. They all worked at Da Nonna, apart from Michele, who was interested in fashion – so he got a job at a shop that sold Italian designer clothes. It pleased me a great deal that Ginevra was particularly interested in cooking from an early age, and I taught her everything I knew.

When my dear Giulio died of stomach cancer in 1995, I moved into the flat above Da Nonna. How they all looked after me – my sons and their wives, and my grandchildren. I was utterly heartbroken, but the luckiest nonna in the world. I would never be lonely with such a wonderful family. Still, I often thought about Deborah – I was aware that she lived only a fifteen-minute walk away, at the other side of Parker's Piece. Sometimes, I wondered if I might have passed her in the street, without her knowing, without either of us knowing. What if she'd come into Da Nonna – how would I know it was her? I guessed if she booked a table at the restaurant, I would see her name, but I didn't look at the reservations. I knew that the professor and Lady Enid would have looked after her well, and that was all I could ask for. Perhaps one day, she'd come looking for me – maybe she would come across that birth certificate and photo of us. She was bound to find those things when Lady Enid died, unless Lady Enid had thrown them away.

Ginevra decided to call herself Jen, because everyone at school kept getting her name wrong. And so Jen she became – and the name suited her. How I loved my dear granddaughter. As my other sons got married and had children, she remained the only girl – the only continuation of the female line, as I'd heard through Mamma – as we still corresponded – that Salvatore and Francesca were unable to have children. Although I'd had to give up Deborah, and lost my amore to my sister, I counted myself so lucky to have met Giulio that day when I walked into Da Nonna. Meeting him changed everything for me.

Sadness always had a place in my heart, but I would shut those melancholy thoughts away, only bringing them out every now and again when I was feeling strong enough. Then I would allow myself to have a good cry, when no one else could see. I would think about dear Papa, Salvatore forgetting me, my own sister marrying my amore, giving up my daughter, and moving away from my family. How I missed cooking together and sitting on the terrazza, talking and laughing together. I had so much to be grateful for, and suppressing the sadness was my only way to survive.

CHAPTER 35

JEN

After Nonna had gone upstairs with Dad, I went over to the coffee machine and was about to make myself a cappuccino when there he was, Matteo coming through the door. Butterflies gathered in my gut. Even though it had only been a few days, I'd missed him. How I wanted to carry on where we'd left off that morning when he'd driven away to Milan.

He set eyes on me, and his face broke out into a broad smile.

'Ciao, Ginevra.'

We walked towards each other, and he leant in to kiss me on each cheek. I breathed in that now-familiar citrus scent of him.

'So, how have you been?' he said.

'Busy! There has been a lot going on here lately.'

'Oh, really?'

I nodded. 'Yes, more information has come out relating to the locked cupboard at Casa Stella.'

'Oh? You must tell me all about it. Also, I really need to talk to you about something else, Ginevra,' he said.

Was this why he'd flown all the way here? The sun was shining, and it struck me that we should go outside – I wanted to show him Cambridge.

'How do you feel about going for a walk?' I said.

'Certo, why not.'

I approached the coffee machine. 'Why don't I make us coffees to take?'

'Okay, for me an Americano, no milk.'

I made the coffees in paper cups with lids, and used a pair of tongs to put a couple of amaretti biscuits in a paper bag. He held the door open, and we stepped outside onto King's Parade. The sky was a flawless blue, the air warm, one of the last days of summer before autumn came. There were still clusters of tourists ambling along, and a few groups of students who had returned to Cambridge early.

I handed Matteo his Americano, and we sipped as we walked. I couldn't wait to show him the Cambridge Backs. I led him to Trinity Street, where we turned left. Five minutes or so later, we came to a bridge that ran over the River Cam. It was so pretty with willow trees and people punting below. We crossed the bridge and I took him to sit on a favourite bench, with a view of King's College.

'So, what do you have to tell me?' he said.

'Oh... well, you won't believe what happened at the lunch, towards the end when my dad was giving a speech.' I went on to tell him about Deborah and Victoria coming in and demanding they see Nonna. '... and to cut a long story short, Deborah revealed that Nonna is her mother!'

'What?' he said, lifting his eyebrows.

'She even had her birth certificate with her – Nonna is her mother, and Salvatore is her father.'

'Oh, so all those things from the cupboard are now beginning to add up. She left because she was pregnant and they weren't married. Perhaps it was before Salvatore had come back from the war and she couldn't wait any longer?'

I shook my head. 'I went back and spoke to Nonna this morning. Apparently, when he came back at the end of the war, she was thinking they'd get married right away. But he'd lost his memory. He had no idea who she was.'

'Oh, well, that explains why she came to England. Francesca always seemed like such a lovely lady – I can't believe she went and married him instead.'

'Nonna explained that her nonna Paola encouraged it all because Francesca was born in October, and her family needed the security. Their pensione in Florence was badly damaged during the war and they had no money. Salvatore's family was wealthy – he was heir to the olive farm.'

He nodded, understanding. 'How times have changed.'

'There is one more thing that you won't believe.'

'What's that?'

'Salvatore is actually still alive, living in Florence with his nephew. Deborah's daughter, Victoria, is going to see him next week. Nonna wants me to go with her.'

'Oh well, that will be interesting. And it's good for me because it means you'll be coming back to Casa Stella.'

'Yes, I will.'

'Will you fly back with me? I can drive you to Florence to see Salvatore, if you like?'

'I would like that, thank you.'

He cleared his throat.

'So, I wanted to talk to you about Natalia,' he said. I waited for him to go on, hoping this was good news for me. 'I wanted to reassure you that we really were pretending to be a couple for PR reasons. Our relationship brought so much good publicity for the show, and they've commissioned another series. But we don't need to pretend to be together anymore, now the awards are over and done.'

'But how do I know I can believe you, that I can trust you? How do I know she won't turn up at Corte Paradiso again, asking for another photo shoot?'

'She won't. I told her not to do that again. I don't love her and she doesn't love me. It's over, and besides... I love someone else.'

He put down his coffee and reached out to cup my chin, gently turning my face towards him.

'I love *you*, Ginevra.'

My gut leapt. 'How can you know that, so soon?'

'I just do. I loved you from the moment I came into Da Nonna and saw you standing there in that maroon polo shirt. My eyes were glued to you all evening, when you weren't looking. I enjoyed every single second that we spent together when you came to Corte Paradiso.'

Then he leant in and pressed his lips to mine, and it really was the most mind-blowing kiss, which went on and on. He pushed his tongue into my mouth, and there we were, carrying on like a pair of teenagers. But I didn't care. My head was spinning and I didn't want it to stop. I put my arms around his neck, and he placed his hands on my waist, bringing me in closer.

After a minute or two, we pulled slowly away from each other.

He looked at me, his eyes all lit up. 'I couldn't wait to do that again after the other morning.'

'Me too.'

He wrapped an arm around me and squeezed me to him tightly. And it was all so perfect – just being there with him in that moment.

'Allora, what do you think about those words I said before we kissed?' he said.

I wasn't ready to tell him that I loved him. But I did find him so attractive and really liked his company. I was curious to know where this would go if we spent more time together. But could I really trust what he was saying about Natalia? Harvey had destroyed my ability to trust fully. But Matteo had flown all the way here, for the lunch, which he had missed. He had come to see me, to ask me to go back to

Tuscany and spend more time with him. He must really like me to do that.

'Are you sure Natalia doesn't still love you? Rosa seemed so sure she was missing you at the Ferragosto party.'

He shook his head. 'Natalia is madly in love with someone else, and she has been for some time.'

'But Rosa said—'

'Natalia doesn't trust Rosa because she likes to gossip.'

'Okay, so who is Natalia in love with then?'

'She has a girlfriend in Milan, called Flora.'

'A girlfriend?'

'Yes, she prefers women. She decided to try being with a man, well me, for a while, but really it's not who she is.'

He took out his phone and ran his fingers over the screen.

'Look, this is the two of them together.'

He showed me an Instagram account with a photo of Natalia and a pretty woman with short blonde hair. Their faces were pressed together and they were both smiling. The caption just said, 'La mia ragazza', meaning 'my girlfriend', followed by two red love hearts.

'This is her private Instagram account, and she posted this a couple of nights ago, as you can see. Please, Jen, you have to believe me now.'

I smiled. 'Okay, I guess this is strong evidence. But...' I scratched my head. 'I hope you understand that I can't say those words to you just yet. I'd really like to spend more time with you and see how it goes. If that's okay?'

I met his gaze and he looked at me intently. I didn't want to lose him, lose this. But also, I didn't want to say those words before I was ready.

Matteo took my hand and squeezed it. 'Of course I understand. Let's enjoy each other's company for now, there is no rush.'

I breathed a sigh of relief, 'Oh good. I would like that very much.'

He leant forward and brushed a hair out of my face. 'So when we get back to Corte Paradiso, we need to make more cooking videos,' he said, softly. 'I noticed the meatball one is still performing well.'

I hadn't checked my social media for a couple of days. 'Oh, is it?'

'Yes, if you post more, you might have a video really take off. Imagine!'

I smiled to myself. There was so much to be excited about. I couldn't wait to go back to Casa Stella and spend more time with Matteo. And I was curious to meet Salvatore and find out what he had to say too.

The next morning, we flew back to Florence together. Matteo had left his car at the airport, and he drove us back to Corte Paradiso. It felt good to be in Tuscany again, as we drove along the country roads. But also, there was no denying the tension in the air. Something was going to happen between us, at last. I could feel it in my bones. We kept stealing glances at each other as he drove. When Matteo stopped at a traffic light, he put his hand on my knee and gave it a squeeze, sending a thrill right down my spine. Our eyes met and I bit my lip. When the light went green, he kept his hand there and I looked out of the window, smiling to myself. The journey seemed to be taking forever and I couldn't wait to arrive.

When he pulled up in the drive, we got out of the car. He took my hand and walked over to his door, unlocked it, opened it and pulled me inside. There in his hall, he brushed my face with his hand and leant in to kiss me. I wrapped my arms around his neck and he picked me up and carried me up the stairs, into his bedroom, and laid me gently down on the bed.

'You are so beautiful, Jen,' he said, softly.

The words every woman wanted to hear. But these words weren't empty and meaningless as they sometimes could be when uttered by a man. He wasn't just talking about how I looked to him. The way in which he said them, the way in which we'd got to know each other meant that he liked who I was too. I inhaled, my heart racing. He gently peeled my top over my head and then he took off his T-shirt to reveal the incredible torso I'd been so impressed to see in the garden that day. We carried on until we'd removed all our clothes, and then we lay there naked, studying each other with smiles on our faces. He ran his hand lightly over my breasts and I shuddered in delight. Then he kissed me, his hand slowly moving further down my body. All I could think was how lucky I was, to be here now with him about to make love to me. I would savour every single second.

A couple of days later, Matteo drove me to Florence to meet Victoria and visit Salvatore. He parked outside his flat and I walked to meet her from there. We'd spent two perfect days at Corte Paradiso together, mostly in bed, but also we sunbathed by the pool and swam. We cooked together and ate on the terrace with wine. After dinner, we went for walks in the surrounding fields, holding hands. And we talked, a lot, about everything. Our lives, our plans. I was really excited about my future for the first time in a while.

I met Victoria outside Salvatore's nephew, Luca's, flat in Florence. She'd already spoken to Luca on the phone, and they were expecting us. I couldn't help feeling nervous. How would he react when I turned up – Liliana's granddaughter? But then he didn't know who she was anymore, so I supposed it wouldn't be much of a problem. I would act as Victoria's interpreter and, if the opportunity arose, I would explain who I was.

We pressed the button on the intercom for Luca Ricci, the door buzzed and we went inside. The flat was on the ground floor.

A male voice said, 'Buongiorno, Ginevra?' and I could see that there was a man in his fifties standing at the door.

'Sì, piacere,' I said.

We all shook hands and introduced ourselves.

'Come in. Salvatore is looking forward to meeting his granddaughter. I am Luca, take a seat in the living room – Salvatore is in there. Would you like coffee?'

'Sì, grazie,' I said. Victoria said the same.

We went into the living room, where a very old and frail man sat in an armchair by the window. The patio doors were open, bringing in a light breeze – now we were in September, and the temperature had dropped – and he was looking out at a pretty garden with beds of red roses and terracotta pots filled with bright flowers. Even though I wasn't related to this man, I still felt some kind of connection to him. I was here on this earth because of him, after all. Nonna had come to Cambridge after he lost his memory, pregnant with a child he hadn't known about. If he hadn't had amnesia, she would have married him and stayed in Italy. And then she wouldn't have met my grandfather. So, I owed my whole existence to the superstition about the ring, which was a bizarre thought.

Seeing as I spoke Italian, it was up to me to communicate on Victoria's behalf. I introduced her to him, and he nodded and smiled slightly, and said, 'Piacere'. She leant down and shook his hand. Victoria and I sat on a sofa and Luca brought in a tray of coffee and left it on a trestle table.

'I'll leave you all to it,' he said.

I picked up my coffee and took a sip. Salvatore turned to face us. The whole situation was a little awkward. Here I was turning up with his long-lost granddaughter after all these years

– the daughter of a woman he hadn't known existed until recently.

'Well, it is good to finally meet you,' Victoria said. I translated.

'What happened with Liliana was very sad,' he said. 'I did love her.'

'But how – I thought you lost your memory. Are you saying you now remember who she was?' I said.

Salvatore shuffled in his chair, and wrung his hands. He coughed, and Victoria and I exchanged a glance.

'When I woke up in that hospital – just down the road from here – all those years ago, I couldn't remember a thing, but then everything came back to me quite quickly. I remembered that I was engaged to a woman called Liliana and that there was a problem with the opal engagement ring, given to me by my nonna Claudia. Her nonna kept on saying that we'd have a life of bad luck because of the ring as she wasn't born in October. I didn't feel unlucky though. I felt that I'd been lucky indeed to have survived being shot in the woods and the blow to my head.'

I frowned, taking in what he was saying. So Salvatore had actually known who Nonna was when she went to see him in hospital? And what... he faked not getting back his memory? But why would he do that? And then go on to marry her sister?

'So hold on... you did know who Liliana was when she came to visit you at the hospital?' I said.

He coughed again, then sighed, and shook his head. 'I am truly ashamed to say I was fully aware of who she was. I was only a young man, foolish and immature, and I'd had a bang to the head. That's no excuse, obviously.'

'I don't believe it,' Victoria said.

He looked at her, then at me. 'I'm sorry. For some reason, while lying in that bed, I found myself thinking about what had happened in the woods. I nearly died. I felt lucky to be alive.

There had been so much fuss made about that ring by both our families.'

'So let me get this clear – you pretended to have amnesia because of the opal ring?' I said.

He nodded. 'Somehow, I got it into my head that here was my chance to let her down gently without her thinking I was an ogre. No man likes to tell a woman he doesn't want to be with her anymore – to see the look on her face, the disappointment, the hatred. I couldn't bear for her to hate me. It was a cowardly way out.'

'It certainly was,' Victoria said, curtly, her face reddening.

Salvatore went on, 'You both have to believe, I thought that I was doing the right thing – that damned ring wasn't good for either of us. At least, that's what both of our families kept on telling us.'

'Well, I just don't know what to say,' Victoria said.

I could understand her reaction, of course. He was her actual grandfather, and her mother had been given up for adoption instead of raised by Nonna. But I could also see his side too. He'd thought he was doing the right thing and he hadn't known she was pregnant.

A question came to mind that I just had to ask.

'Salvatore, would you have done the same thing if you'd known she was carrying your child?'

He looked at me, his eyes welling with tears. 'Of course not. If only I'd known.'

'But then what would you have done?'

'I would have had to find a way to make it work. Perhaps then we would have given the ring away to someone else, and replaced it.'

Although he was speaking in hindsight, I wondered if he would actually have done this. But it was at least reassuring to know he was thinking this now.

'You have to understand – at the time, I was trying not to

bring her a life of bad luck. I'd been lucky enough to survive in that moment, but I felt certain my luck was about to run out. That I'd used up all the good luck we could have together. If I'd known she was expecting, that would have changed everything.'

'So, if you'd known about Deborah, you would have acted differently?' Victoria said. I translated.

'Yes, of course. I wouldn't have allowed her to go to a foreign country, carrying my child like that.'

I sighed. But it seemed he really had believed he was doing the right thing, and he hadn't known about Deborah.

'But then how did you end up being engaged to Francesca?' I asked.

'Liliana and Francesca's nonna had always said that, because Francesca was born in October, I had chosen the wrong sister. And why hadn't I thought to marry her instead? I hadn't given it much thought, but when Liliana's nonna sent Francesca to the hospital to return the ring to me I was so grateful for her company. She came every day for weeks and we just... fell in love. And then I asked her to marry me.'

'How manipulative of Liliana's nonna,' Victoria said. I translated as, 'That wasn't very fair of Liliana's nonna.'

'Yes, I think she did it intentionally. Here was a chance for at least one of her granddaughters to be taken care of financially. You mustn't forget, we'd just lived through a long, horrific war. Anyone who'd made it through alive couldn't help feeling very fortunate indeed. Many of us did things we wouldn't necessarily do in peacetime, in order to survive.'

Had Nonna Paola believed she was doing the best thing for her family? My nonna had told me how poor Italy was at the end of the war, that they were almost starving. It had been my great-great-grandmother's way of saving her family. It would be easy to think that she had been a cold and heartless woman, but what Salvatore was saying made some sense. And I was here now because of all her meddling.

'So, when you married Francesca, you knew what you were doing – that you had let Liliana go?' Victoria asked. I translated.

He nodded. 'Sadly, yes I did. But now I discover that she was carrying my child when she went to Cambridge. Why didn't she tell me this? Francesca and I couldn't have children – I had no idea that I was a father.'

'I believe that she wrote you a letter to tell you, and she kept it for a few days as she was afraid to send it, and then she received a letter from Francesca to say the two of you were getting married. It was too late. She had missed her chance,' I said.

'If she'd sent the letter, and it had reached me in time, I would not have married Francesca.'

'But as soon as she knew you were both married, there was no way she could tell you.'

'Yes, there would have been nothing I could do if she had told me then. Perhaps it was better that I didn't know.'

'And then you separated from Francesca later, is that right?'

'Yes, I fell in love with another woman and I left her. Francesca and I remained separated and never got round to getting divorced. It wasn't legal to get divorced in this country until the 1970s, and after that it was complicated, with a lot of paperwork and then the division of all the assets. When Francesca's nonna died, she went back to live with her mamma at Casa Stella. I managed the olive farm until I retired. Then my younger brother, Pio, and his sons took it over from me.'

I couldn't help finding it ironic that he hadn't even stayed with Francesca in the end. Salvatore faking not getting back his memory was such surprising news to me – but now I had the difficult task of telling Nonna. Should I tell her that he remembered her all along? Could any good come of it? I felt she deserved to know the truth, but I didn't want to upset her too much. But then I would tell her my spin on the whole story – that I thought it was all a good thing because otherwise she wouldn't have met and married Nonno Giulio, and my brothers and I wouldn't be here now. Deborah would have had a different kind of life, but what was done was done – and it seemed that the professor and Lady Enid had done a good job of bringing her up. Nothing could be changed now. The opal ring had played such a huge part in the lives of all of us sitting there at that moment, and I reflected on this. All of us in this room were impacted by a superstition that had influenced Nonna's grandmother – and that was a very strange thought indeed. And now the ring was rightfully Victoria's to do with what she wished, and she wanted to give it to her son for his fiancée, who was born in October. I had no use for it, and I counted myself lucky to have Casa Stella – the beautiful house in the Tuscan hills that had been a refuge for Nonna's family during the war, and now me. It was the house that had brought me back to life.

CHAPTER 36

JEN

After visiting Salvatore, Victoria and I parted ways. She was going to spend a few days in Florence doing touristy things – a friend was flying out to meet her and they were going to rent an Airbnb near the Ponte Vecchio. We agreed to stay in touch, as we were actually related, and I quite liked her – she wanted to introduce me to her children and said she would invite me over for a Sunday roast next time I was in Cambridge.

On a whim, I decided to walk to the Ponte Vecchio and call Nonna from there. I went to stand on the bridge, and couldn't help thinking back to when I'd been there with Matteo. So much had happened since then. I looked out at the River Arno and pressed Nonna's number in my phone.

'Ciao, Jen. How did it go?'

I started by saying that Salvatore had been separated from Francesca, as I hoped this information would please her in some way.

'He had an affair?'

'I think so.'

'Poor Francesca. She did write to me, but I sent back her letters.'

'Ah yes, I did find a pile of them in a cupboard at Casa Stella – that explains how they got there then.'

Nonna cleared her throat.

'I couldn't bear to read her words after what she'd done. Nothing she wrote could have changed how I felt.'

I was curious to read them – but doubted they'd now tell me anything I didn't know already.

'You hold on to them,' Nonna said. 'Maybe I'll be ready to read them one day. We can look at them together, perhaps.'

And now was the time to tell her that Salvatore had been faking the amnesia when she visited him in hospital that day. I could wait until I was back in Cambridge, but I wasn't sure when that would be yet. This wasn't information I could keep from her.

'Nonna, I have something to tell you... Salvatore said he had amnesia when he first woke up in hospital, but by the time he saw you, his memory had returned.'

'What?'

'Yes, I know. I'm so sorry.'

'Go on. Tell me more, cara.'

'He'd almost died in those woods, and he lay there in that bed thinking long and hard about the superstition relating to the opal ring. He made up his mind that faking amnesia would resolve the whole problem without hurting your feelings quite as much.'

'Ah, I see,' Nonna said.

And then she went very quiet.

'Are you still there?'

'Yes, I am here, cara.'

I could hear that she was sniffing.

'But if it's any consolation, it wasn't his intention to then marry Francesca.'

'What do you mean?'

'It was Nonna Paola who sent Francesca to return the ring

to him, hoping Salvatore would fall in love with her and propose marriage.'

'Francesca mentioned Nonna Paola had sent her to return the ring in her letter telling me of her engagement. So I thought as much.'

'If it helps in any way, he did say that if he'd known about the baby he would have acted differently.'

'Differently how?'

'I don't know. He is talking in hindsight. Who knows if he would have changed anything? I would like to think so though, Nonna.'

'Thank you for going to see him for me, Jen. I am glad that you did. I've found a way to forgive Francesca over the years and now I shall need to forgive him as well.'

'You were so brave, Nonna, going to England all on your own at such a young age, carrying a child, not having any idea what the future held.'

'I was very fortunate to meet your nonno Giulio. He changed everything for me. Marrying him meant I lived a good life, surrounded by food and family, and so much love. What more could anyone ask for?'

'In some strange way, perhaps it all worked out for the best then. Besides, I wouldn't be here if you hadn't met him.'

'Exactly, Jen. It all worked out in the end. Although I would like to know Deborah, and Victoria.'

'Well, now you can get to know them both. We can arrange a lunch or something when I come back.'

'That would be really lovely, cara. And now, there you are, staying at Casa Stella. We have swapped places!'

'I'm actually standing on the Ponte Vecchio right now. Matteo will be driving me back to the house later.'

'Oh really?' She paused. 'Do you know that's where I stood when making my decision to come here?'

I drew in my breath. We really had swapped places. 'I don't know what to say... that's kind of sad, but also rather poignant.'

'It is, my dear. You make the most of every single minute in Tuscany. Get to know that Matteo – and don't let him go. He looks at you like your nonno Giulio used to look at me.'

We said our goodbyes, and I hung up. Poor Nonna. She'd lived through so much, and she had been so courageous. And now I was getting to live the life that I wanted to live – I was thankful for that.

As I walked to Matteo's flat, I felt somehow that a huge weight was lifted off my mind. I had at last found out the truth, and discovered that everything had happened as it should, otherwise I wouldn't exist. And Nonna had really loved my grandfather, Giulio – they had probably been a better match than she and Salvatore. They'd had so much in common, and she had enjoyed helping him develop Da Nonna into the successful business it had become. Food was her whole world, and my grandfather had given her the chance to do something she loved. And food was my whole world too. I needed to make the most of my opportunities and keep making the cooking videos – and then try to get that cookbook deal I'd always wanted. When Matteo had brought the ring to me, it had brought him to me too. I hoped we had a future together.

Matteo drove me back to the house and I updated him on everything. But when he pulled up at Corte Paradiso, he said, 'Who is that man?'

I couldn't believe my eyes when I saw Harvey was sitting at the table on the terrace. Liking my Instagram stories was one thing, but actually turning up at my house was something else altogether. I didn't want any exchange we had playing out in front of Matteo. Now I'd finally got my life together, I couldn't let Harvey come along and ruin it all.

Shaking my head, I groaned. 'Oh no, what is he thinking?'

'What, do you know him?'

'It's Harvey, my ex-fiancé, who I told you about.'

'Oh Dio... what do you want me to do? Stay or leave you to talk to him?

'I'd better talk to him on my own.'

'Okay.'

Matteo got out of the car, and gave Harvey a nod as he unlocked his door and went inside.

I approached the table and inhaled. He looked up at me with pleading eyes.

'Harvey, what are you doing here?' I said.

He stood up so we were facing each other. I flinched as he leant forwards, almost as if he wanted to give me a hug. I took a couple of steps back. We were no longer on hugging terms.

Running a hand through his hair, he said, 'Jen, I've come to talk.'

'How did you find me?'

'I saw your cooking videos with this pink house – you posted the location.'

Of course I had, to show I was in Tuscany, hoping to get more views. And I'd included some shots of Casa Stella from the outside too. How foolish of me.

'But how did you actually find the house?'

'Well, I did some googling, found it on Airbnb... and so I asked around in the village shops – showed them a photo. They suggested I try this house at Corte Paradiso.'

'That was industrious of you.'

He shrugged. 'I was desperate to find you, Jen, and speak face to face.'

'What did you want to tell me?'

'That I'm sorry.'

Where had this apology been when I actually needed it?

'You're sorry?'

He nodded. 'Could we sit down and talk – do you have a glass of water? I'm so thirsty.'

I rolled my eyes. 'Sure.'

I unlocked the door and went into the kitchen. He followed, and I poured him a glass of water from a bottle kept in the fridge. We went back outside and sat down at the table on the terrace.

'So, why are you really here?' I asked.

'I want you back, Jen.'

'You want me back?' I laughed. This was the moment all rejected women dreamt of – just so they could then have the satisfaction of doing the dumping. 'Are you serious?'

'Yes, I'm ready to get married now. I made a huge mistake. I've been doing a lot of thinking. You are the one, and I was wrong. I just got distracted.'

'Have you forgotten that you completely humiliated me a week before our wedding day?' My voice was wavering and I had to stop to take a breath. No, I couldn't allow him to make me lose my cool. I interlaced my fingers together, determined to speak more calmly. 'And that you put me in the position of having to contact guests and tell them the wedding was off?'

He shook his head, ruefully.

'I can't turn back time, Jen. But you know I'm the best man for you. You love my cottage in Grantchester. Come back and move in with me, please, Jen.'

'You're really asking me to come back after what you did?'

He nodded. 'Yes, I am.'

I couldn't believe his arrogance. Who did he think he was?

'What happened with Amanda?'

'It's over.'

'Who decided that?'

'It was a mutual decision.'

I doubted this very much.

'Was it?'

'Yeah, we realised that when you took away the sex there wasn't really anything there. We had nothing to talk about. She doesn't listen like you did. I miss our chats where you always gave me such great advice about work stuff. Amanda just never knew the right thing to say – it was as if she wasn't really interested in my problems. Not like you were, Jen.'

I suppressed another laugh. After the humiliation of what they'd both done to me – I couldn't help feeling rather smug. Here he was more or less begging me to go back, telling me that I was a better match for him than Amanda. That I was the one he should have chosen in the first place. But the moment had passed.

Matteo came out of his door. 'Is everything okay here?'

'Who are you?' Harvey said, in such a rude tone of voice that I was embarrassed to be associated with him.

'I am Matteo, and also, I would like to say, if Ginevra agrees, her boyfriend.'

I looked at him and smiled. 'Yes, Matteo, you are my boyfriend.' He smiled back, and my heart warmed. And then I turned to Harvey. 'You should fly back home.'

'You're calling yourself Ginevra now?'

I nodded. 'Yes, Harvey. I am.'

He pinched the bridge of his nose. 'All right, clearly you're happy, Jen. I thought coming here was worth a try. I'm so broken without you,' he said, his voice cracking.

A small part of me wanted to feel sorry for him, but no I couldn't allow myself to. He only had himself to blame, after all.

Nobody said anything. It was all so awkward, the buzzing of cicadas the only sound.

'But,' he went on, 'the next flight isn't until tomorrow – early in the morning.'

Matteo and I exchanged a glance.

'Okay, you can sleep at my house. I'll stay with Matteo. We'll drive you to the airport in the morning, okay?'

He nodded.

'All right, thanks, Jen.'

It was a crushing situation for him, but what had he been thinking turning up like this? Had he really thought I would take him back?

'Well, you'd better come inside and I'll get you set up for the night.'

The journey was a silent one, and it was still pitch black. Lights twinkled from San Gimignano, and the village, and the houses in the hills. As we approached Florence airport, lights twinkled from the magnificent city too. I sat in the passenger seat, and Harvey was in the back of the car. When Matteo pulled up at the drop-off point, Harvey got out of the car and lifted his holdall out of the boot – it had been presumptuous of him to bring that. I opened the passenger window, and he leant down to say 'Thanks, mate,' to Matteo, who nodded and said, 'Prego.' Then Harvey leant forwards and kissed me gently on the cheek.

'I'm sorry for everything, Jen. I've been such an idiot.'

He certainly had been, and I was glad at least that he was admitting to this.

'Have a good flight, Harv,' I said.

He threw me a nod, and turned round, pulled the holdall onto his shoulder, and walked away, towards departures. And that was it, Harvey was leaving, departing from my life. For ever. For it was all totally over and done. I would never see him or have contact with him again – I was absolutely sure about that.

Matteo started the engine. 'Are you okay?'

I nodded and said, 'Yes, yes, I am. Thank you. I'm glad that he came out here – now I have the closure that I needed. Before that, I was so confused by all that had happened with him and Amanda the week before our wedding, blaming myself.

Thinking it was all my fault for not being a better fiancée, and future prospective wife. When it was he who made the mistake, not me. And I'm so glad he did, because if he hadn't I wouldn't be here now – with you.'

'I would still have brought you the opal ring though and you would have inherited Casa Stella.'

'That's true, but I wouldn't have been at Da Nonna that night. So, we wouldn't have met then. If I'd been married, I would perhaps have rented the house out. Or I would have visited with Harvey – imagine that.'

'Oh Dio, having the two of you next door – that would have been awful,' he said.

I laughed at the thought. It was funny how these sliding-doors moments had happened for both Nonna and me. For her with Salvatore. And now for me with Harvey. What would our lives have been like if Salvatore and Harvey hadn't made those decisions? I expected that I would have worked out that Harvey wasn't right for me in the end. Thank goodness it hadn't been after we were already married.

Then it was just the two of us, driving back to Corte Paradiso, and through the windscreen was the most glorious sunrise – patches of purple and pink graduating to orange crossed the sky. We drove back along the country roads – which were delightfully empty – but we didn't talk. The sunrise accompanied us for the whole journey, and it almost marked the end of one era and the beginning of a new one – a new dawn. All kinds of thoughts were running through my mind. What had Harvey been thinking turning up like that? I took out my phone and went into Instagram and blocked him – something I should have done much sooner. I didn't want to see his name popping up anymore, reminding me of how badly he'd behaved. Yes, he could follow me from a fake account, but at least I wouldn't know it was him. Every time I'd seen his name in my notifications, it had stirred something inside of me. What had it been – hope? But surely deep down I'd known that, even if he did come back to me, as he just had, we couldn't be together again. That I couldn't just take him back. What kind of fool would I have been to do that? What kind of message was that sending – that he could cheat while we were married and I'd always forgive him. Amanda's Instagram had gone very quiet lately. She hadn't posted for over a week, which was unlike her. Perhaps she was upset about their break-up. Had it been her decision? When I thought about it, I realised that I didn't actually care. They had both betrayed me for each other, and now they were both alone. I doubted it would be for long, but I smiled at the thought that it hadn't worked out between them.

Really, Harvey and Amanda had done me a favour, saving me from a marriage that was never supposed to happen. A little like Nonna and Salvatore's marriage that was never supposed to happen. It was far too early to know if I'd want to marry Matteo one day, but I wanted to be with him now. I liked his company, and found him so attractive, and I knew that he loved me. I looked over at him as he focused on the road. It was time to admit to myself that I really did love this man. I would tell him when the time was right.

We approached Cintaldo, and he put a hand on my thigh. 'Why don't we stop at the pasticceria – they always have the side door open at this time – we can get some of those pistachio brioches?' he suggested.

'Ooh yes please, I would love that,' I said.

'And then we get back, make a pot of coffee and take them upstairs... to my bed.'

'That all sounds pretty perfetto to me.'

'Okay.' He pulled up outside the pasticceria on Via del Bacio. 'And what recipe shall we film tomorrow?'

'I'm thinking, spaghetti cacio e pepe, then we can eat it for dinner – what do you think?'

'Ah, Ginevra, you know I've been waiting for you to make

that – my favourite, our favourite. We shall film it together, and you can save it to post on Saturday night. It'll be a smash hit, I know it.'

I smiled to myself. Life was pretty good. We had a couple of days before Matteo went back to work and we'd make the most of every moment. Tonight, we'd eat the spaghetti cacio e pepe and drink Chianti on the terrace by candlelight. Later, he'd lead me into his house, and we'd go upstairs, back to his bed. Because we were like that couple I'd envied the night Matteo had come into Da Nonna – immersed in that first few weeks of glorious intense longing for each other.

EPILOGUE

A BOOKSHOP IN FLORENCE, AUGUST 2021

Matteo filled the flutes with prosecco and took the limoncello cupcakes out of their boxes and put them on a plate. I looked at him, my boyfriend of almost two years and the man who I loved. I thought back to when he'd turned up at Da Nonna on that busy Saturday night. At the time, I'd been so lost, keeping myself busy in every way I could to forget what had happened with Harvey and Amanda. But then I went to Casa Stella and everything changed for me – the house in the Tuscan hills lifted me out of the slump I'd been in. And I was grateful – to Nonna, to Francesca, to Matteo for how between them they'd made it all happen.

I went over to the table where my books had been laid out beautifully. I wore a lemon-yellow dress with cap sleeves, bought especially to match the cover, and my nails were painted yellow too. I was wearing my hair down, and au naturel, complete with curls – this was how I wore it these days. The bookshop had set up a banner with my photo on and then the book cover with Jen Farina in capital letters and the title,

Authentic Italian Bites, and subtitle: Bring Italy into your home with family recipes passed down generations. There was another pile of the Italian edition. The bookshop had bought both, because Florence attracted a lot of English-speaking expats and tourists who knew me from social media. I swallowed. I had actually achieved my dream, in the end. The videos had certainly been a huge part of making it happen. I'd continued to film them at Casa Stella, and then one went viral – it was the cacio e pepe recipe that had done it, during that first lockdown the previous year when so many people were glued to TikTok. After that the offers from literary agents had flooded in. I'd signed with someone I could only have dreamt of being interested in my books months earlier. She'd sold my book in twenty territories, so far – and now here I was at a very special launch in Florence, Nonna's birthplace.

I went round the room, taking a few photos for Instagram – of the pile of books, the room as people began to arrive, the flutes of prosecco, the limoncello cupcakes. I'd made a couple of batches with toppers of my book cover, for old times' sake. I smiled to myself – at last I'd accomplished my actual real dream.

People streamed through the doors after that, and I sat down at the table to sign copies of my book. Matteo took some photos and made a video for me to post later.

Afterwards, when it was over, it was just Matteo and me and a couple of booksellers clearing up. I found Nonna's number in my phone and pressed FaceTime. These days, she was living in a care home in Cambridge, and she was happier than ever. Being as gregarious as she was, she'd made many friends and her social life was fuller than mine. When I'd moved to Italy, I'd bought her an iPad and shown her how to use it – and now we FaceTimed every few days.

She answered.

'Ciao, bella,' she said.

'Ciao, Nonna. Well, it's done. I had my launch at the bookshop in Florence tonight.'

She shook her head. 'Brava. I can't believe it. All those recipes that my nonna and mamma, and you and I, made together over the years. Now other people can enjoy them, too. And you have launched your book where my life began all those years ago, in Florence, just round the corner from our pensione. The bookshop I used to visit with my papa when I was a little girl. I am so proud of you, Jen.'

We said goodbye, and I swallowed, my eyes welling with happy tears. It felt so good to make my nonna proud, and to keep our recipes going. I would make sure that future generations got to see them, too. It was our family legacy, after all.

Matteo came over. 'Are you ready to go, carina?'

We'd planned to go to Pensione Firenze nearby for a limoncello spritz in the pretty garden to celebrate – like on that first night in Florence together, after the Ferragosto party. Afterwards we'd pick up a takeaway pizza and, as it was a balmy August evening, we'd eat it on the balcony at his flat with a bottle of Chianti. Tomorrow we'd drive back to Corte Paradiso and spend those last few days of August together before Matteo went back to work.

He held out his hand and I took it. 'Yes, I am,' I said as we walked out of the doors onto the street. He stopped, leaning down to kiss me on the lips, and he lingered there for a moment before eventually breaking away.

He squeezed my hand. 'You have done so well, Ginevra. And now we go to celebrate your big success.'

I looked up at him, unable to wipe the big smile from my face. I couldn't help feeling like the luckiest woman in the world.

A LETTER FROM ANITA

Dear reader,

Thank you for choosing to read *The House in the Tuscan Hills*. If you enjoyed my latest novel, and would like to be notified about my upcoming books, do follow me on Amazon. You can subscribe to my personal newsletter via my website – link below.

It would be so lovely if you have a minute or two to write an Amazon review – even if it's just a few words. A rating is much appreciated too.

If you'd like to follow me on social media, you will find me mostly on Instagram these days @neetschapman. More links below.

Thanks, and best wishes,

Anita Chapman

www.anitachapman.com

facebook.com/anitachapmanauthor
instagram.com/neetschapman
x.com/neetschapman
tiktok.com/@neetschapman

ACKNOWLEDGEMENTS

Thank you so much to the following people for helping to make this book happen:

My editor, Lucy Frederick; cover designer, Debbie Clement for yet another phenomenal cover; copy-editor Jacqui Lewis and proofreader Anne O'Brien.

To the rest of the Bookouture team. To see who has worked on this book, you can find the information in the following pages.

To readers who read advance copies via NetGalley and for the virtual book tour. I really appreciate you taking the time to read *The House in the Tuscan Hills* and write reviews before publication day. It always gives me such a warm feeling to see your social media posts and reviews go up during launch week. I would like to give a special mention to Barbara Wilkie, Liz Lloyd and Linda McFall, who have reviewed my novels from the beginning.

To my university friend Julia Di Cicco, who talked to me about her family history in Italy during the Second World War and about Italian food. It was Julia who taught me how to cook many Italian dishes when we shared a flat in Siena in 1994.

I always read a few research books when writing my novels, but there is usually one in particular that inspires me the most. If you found the part of this novel about the Second World War in Tuscany interesting, you might enjoy Franco Zeffirelli's autobiography that partly inspired his film *Tea with Mussolini*. It covers his childhood in Florence and teenage years in the

Tuscan countryside and around Italy during the Second World War.

And I often go on a research trip when writing my novels too. This time, I stayed in a hotel called Relais Santa Chiara just outside San Gimignano (a town I first visited as a child with my parents). Thank you to the staff for making it such a wonderful stay – the panoramic views from my balcony were just breath-taking. If you ever stay there, look out for a signed copy of *The Italian Vineyard* in the hotel library.

To my social media followers, especially all those who continue to cheer me on and share news about my books. For any readers who'd like to follow my writing journey and research trips to Italy, you will mostly find me on Instagram these days @neetschapman. There are photos and videos from my research trip to the Tuscan Hills on my grid.

To my family and friends.

To everyone who bought, read, spread the word about and wrote reviews for my other novels, *The Venice Secret*, *The Florence Letter*, *The Tuscan Diary* and *The Italian Vineyard*. Thank you for encouraging me to write more books with your lovely words.

PUBLISHING TEAM

Turning a manuscript into a book requires the efforts of many people. The publishing team at Bookouture would like to acknowledge everyone who contributed to this publication.

Commercial
Lauren Morrissette
Hannah Richmond
Imogen Allport

Cover design
Debbie Clement

Data and analysis
Mark Alder
Mohamed Bussuri

Editorial
Lucy Frederick
Kathy Callesen

Copyeditor
Jacqui Lewis

Proofreader
Anne O'Brien

Marketing
Alex Crow
Melanie Price
Cíara Rosney
Martyna Młynarska

Operations and distribution
Joe Morris
Kiah Tooke

Production
Hannah Snetsinger
Mandy Kullar
Nadia Michael
Charlotte Hegley

Publicity
Noelle Holten
Jess Readett
Sarah Hardy

Rights and contracts
Peta Nightingale
Richard King
Saidah Graham

RAISING READERS
Books Build Bright Futures

Dear Reader,

We'd love your attention for one more page to tell you about the crisis in children's reading, and what we can all do.

Studies have shown that reading for fun is the **single biggest predictor of a child's future life chances** – more than family circumstance, parents' educational background or income. It improves academic results, mental health, wealth, communication skills, ambition and happiness.

The number of children reading for fun is in rapid decline. Young people have a lot of competition for their time, and a worryingly high number do not have a single book at home.

Hachette works extensively with schools, libraries and literacy charities, but here are some ways we can all raise more readers:

- Reading to children for just 10 minutes a day makes a difference
- Don't give up if children aren't regular readers – there will be books for them!

- Visit bookshops and libraries to get recommendations
- Encourage them to listen to audiobooks
- Support school libraries
- Give books as gifts

There's a lot more information about how to encourage children to read on our websites: **www.RaisingReaders.co.uk** and **www.JoinRaisingReaders.com**.

Thank you for reading.

Made in the USA
Las Vegas, NV
27 April 2026

45992965R00187